Tales of Fishes by Zane Grey

Pearl Zane Grey was born January 31st, 1872, in Zanesville, Ohio. From an early age, he was intrigued by history, fishing, baseball, and writing, all of which would stimulate his later success.

Grey was an avid reader of adventure stories, consuming dime store novels by the dozen. By age fifteen he had written his first story; Jim of the Cave. His father, a difficult man, tore it to shreds and then beat him.

He and his brother were keen fisherman and baseball players with aspirations of playing in the major leagues. Eventually, Grey was spotted by a baseball scout and received offers from colleges.

Grey took up an offer from the University of Pennsylvania to studied dentistry. Naturally arriving on a scholarship really meant you had to be able to play. He rose to the occasion by playing against the Riverton club, pitching five scoreless innings and a double in the tenth which tied down the win.

Sports scholarship kids can be average scholars. Grey certainly was. He preferred to spend his time outside class not trying to raise his grades but playing baseball, swimming, and writing.

At university he was shy and teetotal, more of a loner than a party animal. Grey struggled with the idea of becoming a writer or baseball player for his career, but unhappily resolved that dentistry was the practical choice.

Grey set up his dental practice in New York as Dr. Zane Grey after graduating in 1896. Though a dentist his real ambition now was to be a writer and New York had lots of publishers. Evenings were set aside for writing to offset the tedium of his dental practice.

His first magazine article, "A Day on the Delaware," a human-interest story about a Grey brothers' fishing expedition, was published in the May 1902 issue of Recreation magazine.

After some rejections he wrote his first Western, The Heritage of the Desert in 1910. It was the breakthrough. It quickly became a bestseller. Here was Grey's over arching themes; Manifest Destiny, the conquest of the Old West, and men wrestling with elemental conditions.

Two years later Grey produced his best-known book, Riders of the Purple Sage (1912), his all-time best-seller. With its publication Zane Grey became a household name.

Grey started his association with Hollywood when William Fox bought the rights to Riders of the Purple Sage for $2,500 in 1916. His writing career would now rise in sync with that of the movie industry.

During the crash and subsequent depression of the 1930s, the publishing industry was hard work. Sales fell off. Serializations were harder to sell. Grey was lucky. He had avoided investing in the Stock Market, he was still writing and very popular and continued to earn royalty income. This also coincided with the time that nearly half of the film adaptations of his novels were made.

Zane Grey died of heart failure on October 23rd, 1939, at his home in Altadena, California. He was interred at the Lackawaxen and Union Cemetery, Lackawaxen, Pennsylvania.

Index of Contents

ZANE GREY by W. Livingston Larned
CHAPTER I - BYME-BY-TARPON
CHAPTER II - THE ISLAND OF THE DEAD
CHAPTER III - THE ROYAL PURPLE GAME OF THE SEA
CHAPTER IV - TWO FIGHTS WITH SWORDFISH
CHAPTER V - SAILFISH
CHAPTER VI - GULF STREAM FISHING
CHAPTER VII - BONEFISH
CHAPTER VIII - SOME RARE FISH
CHAPTER IX - SWORDFISH
CHAPTER X - THE GLADIATOR OF THE SEA
CHAPTER XI - SEVEN MARLIN SWORDFISH IN ONE DAY
CHAPTER XII - RANDOM NOTES
CHAPTER XIII - BIG TUNA
CHAPTER XIV - AVALON, THE BEAUTIFUL
ZANE GREY - A SHORT BIOGRAPHY
ZANE GREY - A CONCISE BIBLIOGRAPHY

ZANE GREY by W. Livingston Larned

Been to Avalon with Grey ... been most everywhere;
Chummed with him and fished with him in every Sportsman's lair.
Helped him with the white Sea-bass and Barracuda haul,
Shared the Tuna's sprayful sport and heard his Hunter-call,
Me an' Grey are fishin' friends.... Pals of rod and reel,
Whether it's the sort that fights ... or th' humble eel,
On and on, through Wonderland ... winds a-blowin' free,
Catching all th' fins that grow ... Sportsman Grey an' Me.

Been to Florida with Zane ... scouting down th' coast;
Whipped the deep for Tarpon, too, that natives love th' most.
Seen the smiling, Tropic isles that pass, in green review,
Gathered cocoanut and moss where Southern skies were blue.
Seen him laugh that boyish laugh, when things were goin' right;
Helped him beach our little boat and kindle fires at night.
Comrades of the Open Way, the Treasure-Trove of Sea,
Port Ahoy and who cares where, with Mister Grey an' Me!

Been to Western lands with Grey ... hunted fox and deer.
Seen the Grizzly's ugly face with danger lurkin' near.

Slept on needles, near th' sky, and marked th' round moon rise
Over purpling peaks of snow that hurt a fellow's eyes.
Gone, like Indians, under brush and to some mystic place—
Home of red men, long since gone, to join their dying race.
Yes ... we've chummed it, onward—outward ... mountain, wood, and Key,
At the quiet readin'-table ... Sportsman Grey an' Me.

CHAPTER I

BYME-BY-TARPON

To capture the fish is not all of the fishing. Yet there are circumstances which make this philosophy hard to accept. I have in mind an incident of angling tribulation which rivals the most poignant instant of my boyhood, when a great trout flopped for one sharp moment on a mossy stone and then was gone like a golden flash into the depths of the pool.

Some years ago I followed Attalano, my guide, down the narrow Mexican street of Tampico to the bank of the broad Panuco. Under the rosy dawn the river quivered like a restless opal. The air, sweet with the song of blackbird and meadowlark, was full of cheer; the rising sun shone in splendor on the water and the long line of graceful palms lining the opposite bank, and the tropical forest beyond, with its luxuriant foliage festooned by gray moss. Here was a day to warm the heart of any fisherman; here was the beautiful river, celebrated in many a story; here was the famous guide, skilled with oar and gaff, rich in experience. What sport I would have; what treasure of keen sensation would I store; what flavor of life would I taste this day! Hope burns always in the heart of a fisherman.

Attalano was in harmony with the day and the scene. He had a cheering figure, lithe and erect, with a springy stride, bespeaking the Montezuma blood said to flow in his Indian veins. Clad in a colored cotton shirt, blue jeans, and Spanish girdle, and treading the path with brown feet never deformed by shoes, he would have stopped an artist. Soon he bent his muscular shoulders to the oars, and the ripples circling from each stroke hardly disturbed the calm Panuco. Down the stream glided long Indian canoes, hewn from trees and laden with oranges and bananas. In the stern stood a dark native wielding an enormous paddle with ease. Wild-fowl dotted the glassy expanse; white cranes and pink flamingoes graced the reedy bars; red-breasted kingfishers flew over with friendly screech. The salt breeze kissed my cheek; the sun shone with the comfortable warmth Northerners welcome in spring; from over the white sand-dunes far below came the faint boom of the ever-restless Gulf.

We trolled up the river and down, across from one rush-lined lily-padded shore to the other, for miles and miles with never a strike. But I was content, for over me had been cast the dreamy, care-dispelling languor of the South.

When the first long, low swell of the changing tide rolled in, a stronger breeze raised little dimpling waves and chased along the water in dark, quick-moving frowns. All at once the tarpon began to show, to splash, to play, to roll. It was as though they had been awakened by the stir and murmur of the miniature breakers. Broad bars of silver flashed in the sunlight, green backs cleft the little billows, wide tails slapped lazily on the water. Every yard of river seemed to hold a rolling fish. This sport increased until the long stretch of water, which had been as calm as St. Regis Lake at twilight, resembled the quick current of a Canadian stream. It was a fascinating, wonderful sight. But it was also peculiarly exasperating, because when the fish roll in this sportive, lazy way they will not bite. For an hour I trolled through this whirlpool of flying spray and twisting tarpon, with many a salty drop on my face, hearing all around me the whipping crash of breaking water.

"Byme-by-tarpon," presently remarked Attalano, favoring me with the first specimen of his English.

The rolling of the tarpon diminished, and finally ceased as noon advanced.

No more did I cast longing eyes upon those huge bars of silver. They were buried treasure. The breeze quickened as the flowing tide gathered strength, and together they drove the waves higher. Attalano rowed across the river into the outlet of one of the lagoons. This narrow stream was unruffled by wind; its current was sluggish and its muddy waters were clarifying under the influence of the now fast-rising tide.

By a sunken log near shore we rested for lunch. I found the shade of the trees on the bank rather pleasant, and became interested in a blue heron, a russet-colored duck, and a brown-and-black snipe, all sitting on the sunken log. Near by stood a tall crane watching us solemnly, and above in the tree-top a parrot vociferously proclaimed his knowledge of our presence. I was wondering if he objected to our invasion, at the same time taking a most welcome bite for lunch, when directly in front of me the water flew up as if propelled by some submarine power. Framed in a shower of spray I saw an immense tarpon, with mouth agape and fins stiff, close in pursuit of frantically leaping little fish.

The fact that Attalano dropped his sandwich attested to the large size and close proximity of the tarpon. He uttered a grunt of satisfaction and pushed out the boat. A school of feeding tarpon closed the mouth of the lagoon. Thousands of mullet had been cut off from their river haunts and were now leaping, flying, darting in wild haste to elude the great white monsters. In the foamy swirls I saw streaks of blood.

"Byme-by-tarpon!" called Attalano, warningly.

Shrewd guide! I had forgotten that I held a rod. When the realization dawned on me that sooner or later I would feel the strike of one of these silver tigers a keen, tingling thrill of excitement quivered over me. The primitive man asserted himself; the instinctive lust to conquer and to kill seized me, and I leaned forward, tense and strained with suspended breath and swelling throat.

Suddenly the strike came, so tremendous in its energy that it almost pulled me from my seat; so quick, fierce, bewildering that I could think of nothing but to hold on. Then the water split with a hissing sound to let out a great tarpon, long as a door, seemingly as wide, who shot up and up into the air. He wagged his head and shook it like a struggling wolf. When he fell back with a heavy splash, a rainbow, exquisitely beautiful and delicate, stood out of the spray, glowed, paled, and faded.

Five times he sprang toward the blue sky, and as many he plunged down with a thunderous crash. The reel screamed. The line sang. The rod, which I had thought stiff as a tree, bent like a willow wand. The silver king came up far astern and sheered to the right in a long, wide curve, leaving behind a white wake. Then he sounded, while I watched the line with troubled eyes. But not long did he sulk. He began a series of magnificent tactics new in my experience. He stood on his tail, then on his head; he sailed like a bird; he shook himself so violently as to make a convulsive, shuffling sound; he dove, to come up covered with mud, marring his bright sides; he closed his huge gills with a slap and, most remarkable of all, he rose in the shape of a crescent, to straighten out with such marvelous power that he seemed to actually crack like a whip.

After this performance, which left me in a condition of mental aberration, he sounded again, to begin a persistent, dragging pull which was the most disheartening of all his maneuvers; for he took yard after yard of line until he was far away from me, out in the Panuco. We followed him, and for an hour crossed to and fro, up and down, humoring him, responding to his every caprice, as if he verily were a king. At last, with a strange inconsistency more human than fishlike, he returned to the scene of his fatal error, and here in the mouth of the smaller stream he leaped once more. But it was only a ghost of his former efforts—a slow, weary rise, showing he was tired. I could see it in the weakening wag of his head. He no longer made the line whistle.

I began to recover the long line. I pumped and reeled him closer. Reluctantly he came, not yet broken in spirit, though his strength had sped. He rolled at times with a shade of the old vigor, with a pathetic manifestation of the temper that became a hero. I could see the long, slender tip of his dorsal fin, then his broad tail and finally the gleam of his silver side. Closer he came and slowly circled around the boat, eying me with great, accusing eyes. I measured him with a fisherman's glance. What a great fish! Seven feet, I calculated, at the very least.

At this triumphant moment I made a horrible discovery. About six feet from the leader the strands of the line had frayed, leaving only one thread intact. My blood ran cold and the clammy sweat broke out on my brow. My empire was not won; my first tarpon was as if he had never been. But true to my fishing instincts, I held on morosely; tenderly I handled him; with brooding care I riveted my eye on the frail place in my line, and gently, ever so gently, I began to lead the silver king shoreward. Every smallest move of his tail meant disaster to me, so when he moved it I let go of the reel. Then I would have to coax him to swim back again.

The boat touched the bank. I stood up and carefully headed my fish toward the shore, and slid his head and shoulders out on the lily-pads. One moment he lay there, glowing like mother-of-pearl, a rare fish, fresh from the sea. Then, as Attalano warily reached for the leader, he gave a gasp, a flop that deluged us with muddy water, and a lunge that spelled freedom.

I watched him swim slowly away with my bright leader dragging beside him. Is it not the loss of things which makes life bitter? What we have gained is ours; what is lost is gone, whether fish, or use, or love, or name, or fame.

I tried to put on a cheerful aspect for my guide. But it was too soon. Attalano, wise old fellow, understood my case. A smile, warm and living, flashed across his dark face as he spoke:

"Byme-by-tarpon."

Which defined his optimism and revived the failing spark within my breast. It was, too, in the nature of a prophecy.

CHAPTER II

THE ISLAND OF THE DEAD

Strange wild adventures fall to the lot of a fisherman as well as to that of a hunter. On board the Monterey, from Havana to Progreso, Yucatan, I happened to fall into conversation with an English globe-trotter who had just come from the Mont Pelée eruption. Like all those wandering Englishmen, this one was exceedingly interesting. We exchanged experiences, and I felt that I had indeed much to see and learn of the romantic Old World.

In Merida, that wonderful tropic city of white towers and white streets and white-gowned women, I ran into this Englishman again. I wanted to see the magnificent ruins of Uxmal and Ake and Labna. So did he. I knew it would be a hard trip from Muna to the ruins, and so I explained. He smiled in a way to make me half ashamed of my doubts. We went together, and I found him to be a splendid fellow. We parted without knowing each other's names. I had no idea what he thought of me, but I thought he must have been somebody.

While traveling around the coast of Yucatan I had heard of the wild and lonely Alacranes Reef where lighthouse-keepers went insane from solitude, and where wonderful fishes inhabited the lagoons. That was enough for me. Forthwith I meant to go to Alacranes.

Further inquiry brought me meager but fascinating news of an island on that lonely coral reef, called Isla de la Muerte (the Island of the Dead). Here was the haunt of a strange bird, called by Indians rabihorcado, and it was said to live off the booby, another strange sea-bird. The natives of the coast solemnly averred that when the rabihorcado could not steal fish from the booby he killed himself by hanging in the brush. I did not believe such talk. The Spanish appeared to be rabi, meaning rabies, and horcar, to hang.

I set about to charter a boat, and found the great difficulty in procuring one to be with the Yucatecan government. No traveler had ever before done such a thing. It excited suspicion. The officials thought the United States was looking for a coaling-station. Finally, through the help of the Ward line agent and the consul I prevailed upon them to give me such papers as appeared necessary. Then my Indian boatmen interested a crew of six, and I chartered a two-masted canoe-shaped bark called the Xpit.

The crew of the Hispaniola, with the never-to-be-forgotten John Silver and the rest of the pirates of Treasure Island, could not have been a more villainous and piratical gang than this of the bark Xpit. I was advised not to take the trip alone. But it appeared impossible to find any one to accompany me. I grew worried, yet determined not to miss the opportunity.

Strange to relate, as I was conversing on the dock with a ship captain and the agent of the Ward line, lamenting the necessity of sailing for Alacranes alone, some one near by spoke up, "Take me!"

In surprise I wheeled to see my English acquaintance who had visited the interior of Yucatan with me. I greeted him, thanked him, but of course did not take him seriously, and I proceeded to expound the nature of my venture. To my further surprise, he not only wanted to go, but he was enthusiastic.

"But it's a hard, wild trip," I protested. "Why, that crew of barefooted, red-shirted Canary-Islanders have got me scared! Besides, you don't know me!"

"Well, you don't know me, either," he replied, with his winning smile.

Then I awoke to my own obtuseness and to the fact that here was a real man, in spite of the significance of a crest upon his linen.

"If you'll take a chance on me I'll certainly take one on you," I replied, and told him who I was, and that the Ward-line agent and American consul would vouch for me.

He offered his hand with the simple reply, "My name is C—."

If before I had imagined he was somebody, I now knew it. And that was how I met the kindest man, the finest philosopher, the most unselfish comrade, the greatest example and influence that it has ever been my good fortune to know upon my trips by land or sea. I learned this during our wonderful trip to the Island of the Dead. He never thought of himself. Hardship to him was nothing. He had no fear of the sea, nor of men, nor of death. It seemed he never rested, never slept, never let anybody do what he could do instead.

That night we sailed for Alacranes. It was a white night of the tropics, with a million stars blinking in the blue dome overhead, and the Caribbean Sea like a shadowed opal, calm and rippling and shimmering. The Xpit was not a bark of comfort. It had a bare deck and an empty hold. I could not stay below in that gloomy, ill-smelling pit, so I tried to sleep on deck. I lay on a hatch under the great boom, and what with its creaking, and the hollow roar of the sail, and the wash of the waves, and the dazzling starlight, I could not sleep. C. sat on a coil of rope, smoked, and watched in silence. I wondered about him then.

Sunrise on the Caribbean was glorious to behold—a vast burst of silver and gold over a level and wrinkling blue sea. By day we sailed, tacking here and there, like lost mariners standing for some far-off unknown shore. That night a haze of clouds obscured the stars, and it developed that our red-shirted skipper steered by the stars. We indeed became lost mariners. They sounded with a greased lead and determined our latitude by the color and character of the coral or sand that came up on the lead. Sometimes they knew where we were and at others they did not have any more idea than had I.

On the second morning out we reached Alacranes lighthouse; and when I saw the flat strip of sand, without a tree or bush to lend it grace and color, the bleak lighthouse, and the long, lonely reaches of barren reefs from which there came incessant moaning, I did not wonder that two former lighthouse-keepers had gone insane. The present keeper received me with the welcome always accorded a visitor to out-of-the-world places. He corroborated all that my Indian sailors had claimed for the rabihorcado, and added the interesting information that lighthouse-keepers desired the extinction of the birds because the guano, deposited by them on the roofs of the keepers' houses, poisoned the rain water—all they had to drink.

I climbed the narrow, spiral stair to the lighthouse tower, and there, apparently lifted into the cloud-navigated sky, I awakened to the real wonder of coral reefs. Ridges of white and brown showed their teeth against the crawling, tireless, insatiate sea. Islets of dead coral gleamed like bleached bone, and beds of live coral, amber as wine, lay wreathed in restless surf. From near to far extended the rollers, the curving channels, and the shoals, all colorful, all quivering with the light of jewels. Golden sand sloped into the gray-green of shallow water, and this shaded again into darker green, which in turn merged into purple, reaching away to the far barrier reef, a white wall against the blue, heaving ocean.

The crew had rowed us ashore with my boatmen Manuel and Augustine. And then the red-shirted captain stated he would like to go back to Progreso and return for us at our convenience. Hesitating over this, I finally gave permission, on the promise that he would bring back the Xpit in one week.

So they sailed away, and left us soon to find out that we were marooned on a desert island. When I saw how C. took it I was glad of our enforced stay. Solitude and loneliness pervaded Alacranes. Of all the places I had visited, this island was the most hauntingly lonely.

It must have struck C. the same way, and even more powerfully than it had me. He was a much older man, and, though so unfailingly cheerful and helpful, he seemed to me to desire loneliness. He did not fish or shoot. His pleasure appeared to be walking the strand, around and around the little island, gathering bits of coral and shells and seaweeds and strange things cast up by the tides. For hours he would sit high on the lighthouse stairway and gaze out over the variegated mosaic of colored reefs. My bed was a hammock in the loft of the keeper's house and it hung close to an open door. At night I woke often, and I would look out upon the lonely beach and sea. When the light flashed its long wheeling gleam out into the pale obscurity of the night it always showed C.'s dark figure on the lonely beach. I got into the habit of watching for him, and never, at any time I happened to awake, did I fail to see him out there. How strange he looms to me now! But I thought it was natural then. The loneliness of that coral reef haunted me. The sound of the sea, eternally slow and sad and moaning, haunted me like a passion. Men are the better for solitude.

Our bark, the Xpit, did not come back for us. Day by day we scanned the heaving sea, far out beyond the barrier reef, until I began to feel like Crusoe upon his lonely isle. We had no way to know then that our crew had sailed twice from Progreso, getting lost the first time, and getting drunk the second, eventually returning to the home port. Some misfortunes turn out to be blessings.

What adventures I had at Alacranes! But, alas! I cannot relate a single story about really catching a fish. There were many and ferocious fish that would rush any bait I tried, only I could not hold them. My tackle was not equal to what it is now. Perhaps, however, if it had been it would have been smashed just the same.

In front of the lighthouse there had been built a little plank dock, running out twenty yards or so. The water was about six feet deep, and a channel of varying width meandered between the coral reefs out to the deep blue sea. This must have been a lane for big fish to come inside the barrier. Almost always there were great shadows drifting around in the water. First I tried artificial baits. Some one, hoping to convert me, had given me a whole box of those ugly, murderous plug-baits made famous by Robert H. Davis. Whenever I made a cast with one of these a big fish would hit it and either strip the hooks off or break my tackle. Some of these fish leaped clear. They looked like barracuda to me, only they were almost as silvery as a tarpon. One looked ten feet long and as big around as a telegraph pole. When this one smashed the water white and leaped, Manuel yelled, "Pecuda!" I tried hard to catch a specimen, and had a good many hooked, but they always broke away. I did not know then, as I know now, that barracuda grow to twelve feet in the Caribbean. That fact is mentioned in records and natural histories.

Out in the deeper lagoons I hooked huge fish that swam off ponderously, dragging the skiff until my line parted. Once I was fortunate enough to see one, which fact dispelled any possibility of its being a shark. Manuel called it "Cherna!" It looked like a giant sea-bass and would have weighed at least eight hundred pounds. The color was lighter than any sea-bass I ever studied. My Indian boatmen claimed this fish was a man-eater and that he and his crew had once fought one all day and then it broke away. The fish I saw was huge enough to swallow a man, that was certain. I think this species must have been the great June-fish of the Gulf. I hooked one once at the mouth of the Panuco River in Mexico and it nearly swamped the boat.

Soon my tackle was all used up, and, for want of better, I had to use tiny hooks and thread lines—because I was going to fish, by hook or crook! This method, however, which I learned first of all, is not to be despised. Whenever I get my hand on a thin, light, stiff reed pole and a long, light line of thread with a little hook, then I revert to boyhood days and sunfish and chubs and shiners and bullheads. Could any fisherman desire more joy? Those days are the best.

The child is father of the man
And I could wish my days to be
Bound each to each by natural piety.

In the shallow water near the dock there always floated a dense school of little fish like sardines. They drifted, floated, hovered beside the dock, and when one of the big fish would rush near they would make a breaking roar on the surface. Of me they evinced no fear whatever. But no bait, natural or artificial, that I could discover, tempted them to bite. This roused my cantankerous spirit to catch some of those little fish or else fall inestimably in my own regard. I noted that whenever I cast over the school it disintegrated. A circle widened from the center, and where had been a black mass of fish was only sand. But as my hook settled to the bottom the dark circle narrowed and closed until the school was densely packed as before. Whereupon I tied several of the tiny hooks together with a bit of lead, and, casting that out, I waited till all was black around my line, then I jerked. I snagged one of the little fish and found him to be a beautiful, silvery, flat-sided shiner of unknown species to me. Every cast I made thereafter caught one of them. And they were as good to eat as a sardine and better than a mullet.

My English comrade, C., sometimes went with me, and when he did go, the interest and kindly curiosity and pleasure upon his face were a constant source of delight to me. I knew that I was as new a species to him as the little fish were to me. But C. had become so nearly a perfectly educated man that nothing surprised him, nothing made him wonder. He sympathized, he understood, he could put himself in the place of another. What worried me, however, was the simple fact that he did not care to fish or shoot for the so-called sport of either. I think my education on a higher plane began at Alacranes, in the society of that lonely Englishman. Somehow I have gravitated toward the men who have been good for me.

But C. enjoyed action as well as contemplation. Once out on the shoals when Manuel harpooned a huge hawk-bill turtle—the valuable species from which the amber shell is derived—we had a thrilling and dangerous ride. For the turtle hauled us at a terrific rate through the water. Then C. joined in with the yells of the Indians. He was glad, however, when the turtle left us stranded high upon a coral bed.

On moonlight nights when the tide was low C. especially enjoyed wading on the shoals and hunting for the langustas, or giant lobsters. This was exciting sport. We used barrel-hoops with nets, and when we saw a lobster shining in the shallow water we waded noiselessly close to swoop down upon him with a great splash. I was always afraid of these huge crayfish, but C. was not. His courage might have been predatory, for he certainly liked to eat lobster. But he had a scare one night when a devilfish or tremendous ray got between him and the shore and made the water fly aloft in a geyser. It was certainly fun for me to see that dignified Englishman make tracks across the shoal.

To conclude about C., when I went on to Mexico City with him I met friends of his there, a lord and a duke traveling incognito. C. himself was a peer of England and a major in the English army. But I never learned this till we got to Tampico, where they went with me for the tarpon-fishing. They were rare fine fellows. L., the little Englishman, could do anything under the sun, and it was from him I got my type for Castleton, the Englishman, in The Light of Western Stars. I have been told that never was there an Englishman on earth like the one I portrayed in my novel. But my critics never fished with Lord L.!

These English friends went with me to the station to bid me good-by and good luck. We were to part there, they to take ship for London, and I to take train for the headwaters of the Panuco River, down which unknown streams I was to find my way through jungle to the Gulf. Here I was told that C. had lost his only son in the Boer War, and since then had never been able to rest or sleep or remain in one place. That stunned me, for I remembered that he had seemed to live only to forget himself, to think of others. It was a great lesson to me. And now, since I have not heard from him during the four years of the world war, I seem to divine that he has "gone west"; he has taken his last restless, helpful journey, along with the best and noblest of England's blood.

Because this fish-story has so little of fish in it does not prove that a man cannot fish for other game than fish. I remember when I was a boy that I went with my brother—the R. C. and the Reddy of the accompanying pages—to fish for bass at Dillon's Falls in Ohio. Alas for Bill Dilg and Bob Davis, who never saw this blue-blooded home of bronze-back black-bass! In the heat of the day my brother and I jabbed our poles into the bank, and set off to amuse ourselves some other way for a while. When we returned my pole was pulled down and wabbling so as to make a commotion in the water. Quickly I grasped it and pulled, while Reddy stared wide-eyed and open-mouthed. Surely a big bass had taken my bait and hooked himself. Never had I felt so heavy and strong a bass! The line swished back and forth; my pole bent more and more as I lifted. The water boiled and burst in a strange splash. Then! a big duck flew, as if by magic, right out from before us. So amazed was I that he nearly pulled the pole out of my hands. Reddy yelled wildly. The duck broke the line and sped away.... That moment will never be forgotten. It took us so long to realize that the duck had swallowed my minnow, hooked himself, and happened to be under the surface when we returned.

So the point of my main story, like that of the above, is about how I set out to catch fish, and, failing, found for such loss abundant recompense.

Manuel and Augustine, my Indian sailors, embarked with me in a boat for the Island of the Dead. Millions of marine creatures swarmed in the labyrinthine waterways. Then, as we neared the land, "Rabihorcado!" exclaimed Manuel, pointing to a black cloud hovering over the island.

As we approached the sandy strip I made it out to be about half a mile long, lying only a few feet above the level of the sea. Hundreds of great, black birds flew out to meet us and sailed over the boat, a sable-winged, hoarse-voiced crowd. When we beached I sprang ashore and ran up the sand to the edge of green. The whole end of the island was white with birds—large, beautiful, snowy birds with shiny black bars across their wings.

"Boobies," said Manuel and motioned me to go forward.

They greeted our approach with the most discordant din it had ever been my fortune to hear. A mingling of honk and cackle, it manifested not excitement so much as curiosity. I walked among the boobies, and they never moved except to pick at me with long, sharp bills. Many were sitting on nests, and all around in the sand were nests with eggs, and little boobies just hatched, and others in every stage of growth, up to big babies of birds like huge balls of pure white wool. I wondered where the thousands of mothers were. The young ones showed no concern when I picked them up, save to dig into me with curious bills.

I saw an old booby, close by, raise his black-barred wings, and, flapping them, start to run across the sand. In this way he launched himself into the air and started out to sea. Presently I noticed several more flying away, one at a time, while others came sailing back again. How they could sail! They had the swift, graceful flight of a falcon.

For a while I puzzled over the significance of this outgoing and incoming. Shortly a bird soared overhead, circled with powerful sweep, and alighted within ten feet of me. The bird watched me with gray, unintelligent eyes. They were stupid, uncanny eyes, yet somehow so fixed and staring as to seem accusing. One of the little white balls of wool waddled up and, rubbing its fuzzy head against the booby, proclaimed the filial relation. After a few rubs and wabbles the young bird opened wide its bill and let out shrill cries. The mother bobbed up and down in evident consternation, walked away, came back, and with an eye on me plainly sought to pacify her fledgling. Suddenly she put her bill far down into the wide-open bill, effectually stifling the cries. Then the two boobies stood locked in amazing convulsions. The throat of the mother swelled, and a lump passed into and down the throat of the young bird. The puzzle of the flying boobies was solved in the startling realization that the mother had returned from the sea with a fish in her stomach and had disgorged it into the gullet of her offspring.

I watched this feat performed dozens of times, and at length scared a mother booby into withdrawing her bill and dropping a fish on the sand. It was a flying-fish fully ten inches long. I interrupted several little dinner-parties, and in each case found the disgorged fish to be of the flying species. The boobies flew ten, twenty miles out to the open sea for fish, while the innumerable shoals that lay around their island were alive with sardine and herring!

I had raised a tremendous row; so, leaving the boobies to quiet down, I made my way toward the flocks of rabihorcados. Here and there in the thick growth of green weed were boobies squatting on isolated nests. No sooner had I gotten close to the rabihorcados than I made sure they were the far-famed frigate pelicans, or man-of-war birds. They were as tame as the boobies; as I walked among them many did not fly at all. Others rose with soft, swishing sound of great wings and floated in a circle, uttering deep-throated cries, not unlike the dismal croak of ravens. Perfectly built for the air, they were like feathers blown by a breeze. Light, thin, long, sharp, with enormous spread of wings, beautiful with the beauty of dead, blue-black sheen, and yet hideous, too, with their grisly necks and cruel, crooked beaks and vulture eyes, they were surely magnificent specimens of winged creation.

Nests of dried weeds littered the ground, and eggs and young were everywhere. The little ones were covered with white down, and the developing feathers on their wings were turning black. They squalled unremittingly, which squalling I decided was not so much on my account as because of a swarm of black flies that attacked them when the mothers flew away. I was hard put to it myself to keep these flies, large as pennies and as flat, from eating me alive. They slipped up my sleeves and trousers and their bite made a wasp-sting pleasure by comparison.

By rushing into a flock of rabihorcados I succeeded several times in catching one in my hands. And spreading it out, I made guesses as to width from tip to tip of wings. None were under seven feet; one measured all of eight. They made no strenuous resistance and regarded me with cold eyes. Every flock that I put to flight left several dozen little ones squalling in the nests; and at one place an old booby waddled to the nests and began to maltreat the young rabihorcados. Instincts of humanity bade me scare the old brute away until I happened to remember the relation existing between the two species. Then I watched. With my own eyes I saw that grizzled booby pick and bite and wring those poor little birds with a grim and deadly deliberation. When the mothers, soon returning, fluttered down, they did not attack the booby, but protected their little ones by covering them with body and wings. Conviction came upon me that it was instinctive for the booby to kill the parasitical rabihorcado; and likewise instinctive for the rabihorcado to preserve the life of the booby.

A shout from Manuel directed me toward the extreme eastern end of the island. On the way I discovered many little dead birds, and the farther I went the more I found. Among the low bushes were also many old rabihorcados, dead and dry. Some were twisted among the network of branches, and several were hanging in limp, grotesque, horribly suggestive attitudes of death. Manuel had all of the Indian's leaning toward the mystical, and he believed the rabihorcados had destroyed themselves. Starved they may very well have been, but to me the gales of that wind-swept, ocean desert accounted for the hanging rabihorcados. Still, when face to face with the island, with its strife, and its illustration of the survival of the fittest, all that Manuel had claimed and more, I had to acknowledge the disquieting force of the thing and its stunning blow to an imagined knowledge of life and its secrets.

Suddenly Manuel shouted and pointed westward. I saw long white streams of sea-birds coming toward the island. My glass showed them to be boobies. An instant later thousands of rabihorcados took wing as if impelled by a common motive. Manuel ran ahead in his excitement, turning to shout to me, and then to point toward the wavering, swelling, white streams. I hurried after him, to that end of the island where we had landed, and I found the colony of boobies in a state of great perturbation. All were squawking, flapping wings, and waddling frantically about. Here was fear such as had not appeared on my advent.

Thousands of boobies were returning from deep-sea fishing, and as they neared the island they were met and set upon by a swarming army of rabihorcados. Darting white and black streaks crossed the blue of sky like a changeful web. The air was full of plaintive cries and hoarse croaks and the windy rush of wings. So marvelous was this scene of incredibly swift action, of kaleidoscopic change, of streaking lines and curves, that the tragedy at first was lost upon me. Then the shrieking of a booby told me that the robber birds were after their prey. Manuel lay flat on the ground to avoid being struck by low-flying birds, but I remained standing in order to see the better. Faster and faster circled the pursued and pursuers and louder grew the cries and croaks. My gaze was bewildered by the endless, eddying stream of birds.

Then I turned my back on sea and beach where this bee-swarm confused my vision, and looked to see single boobies whirling here and there with two or three black demons in pursuit. I picked out one group and turned my glass upon it. Many battles had I seen by field and stream and mountain, but this unequal battle by sea eclipsed all. The booby's mother instinct was to get to her young with the precious fish that meant life. And she would have been more than a match for any one thief. But she could not cope successfully with two fierce rabihorcados; for one soared above her, resting, watching, while the other darted and whirled to the attack. They changed, now one black demon swooping down, and then the other, in calculating, pitiless pursuit. How glorious she was in poise and swerve and sweep! For what seemed a long time neither rabihorcado touched her. What distance she could have placed between them but for that faithful mother instinct! She kept circling, ever returning, drawn back toward the sand by the magnet of love; and the powerful wings seemed slowly to lose strength. Closer the rabihorcados swooped and rose and swooped again, till one of them, shooting down like a black flash, struck her in the back. The white feathers flew away on the wind. She swept up, appeared to pause wearily and quiver, then disgorged her fish. It glinted in the sunlight. The rabihorcado dropped in easy, downward curve and caught it as it fell.

So the struggle for existence continued till I seemed to see all the world before me with its myriads of wild creatures preying upon one another; the spirit of nature, unquenchable as the fires of the sun, continuing ceaseless and imperturbable in its inscrutable design.

As we rowed away I looked back. Sky of a dull purple, like smoke with fire behind it, framed the birds of power and prey in colors suitable to their spirit. My ears were filled with the haunting sound of the sea, the sad wash of the surf, the harmonious and mournful music of the Island of the Dead.

CHAPTER III

THE ROYAL PURPLE GAME OF THE SEA

To the great majority of anglers it may seem unreasonable to place swordfishing in a class by itself—by far the most magnificent sport in the world with rod and reel. Yet I do not hesitate to make this statement and believe I can prove it.

The sport is young at this writing—very little has been written by men who have caught swordfish. It was this that attracted me. Quite a number of fishermen have caught a swordfish. But every one of them will have something different to tell you and the information thus gleaned is apt to leave you at sea, both metaphorically and actually. Quite a number of fishermen, out after yellowtail, have sighted a swordfish, and with the assistance of heavy tackle and their boatmen have caught that swordfish. Some few men have caught a small swordfish so quickly and easily that they cannot appreciate what happened. On the other hand, one very large swordfish, a record, was caught in an hour, after a loggy rolling about, like a shark, without leaping. But these are not fighting swordfish. Of course, under any circumstances, it is an event to catch a swordfish. But the accidents, the flukes, the lucky stabs of the game, do not in any sense prove what swordfishing is or what it is not.

In August, 1914, I arrived at Avalon with tuna experience behind me, with tarpon experience, and all the other kinds of fishing experience, even to the hooking of a swordfish in Mexico. I am inclined to confess that all this experience made me—well, somewhat too assured. Any one will excuse my enthusiasm. The day of my arrival I met Parker, the genial taxidermist of Avalon, and I started to tell him how I wanted my swordfish mounted. He interrupted me: "Say, young fellow, you want to catch a swordfish first!" One of the tuna boatmen gave me a harder jolt. He said: "Well, if you fish steadily for a couple of weeks, maybe you'll get a strike. And one swordfish caught out of ten strikes is good work!" But Danielson was optimistic and encouraging, as any good boatman ought to be. If I had not been fortunate enough to secure Captain Dan as my boatman, it is certain that one of the most wonderful fishing experiences on record would have fallen to some other fisherman, instead of to me.

We went over to Clemente Island, which is thirty-six miles from Catalina Island. Clemente is a mountain rising out of the sea, uninhabited, lonely, wild, and beautiful. But I will tell about the island later.

The weather was perfect, the conditions were apparently ideal. I shall never forget the sight of the first swordfish, with his great sickle-shaped tail and his purple fin. Nor am I likely to forget my disappointment when he totally ignored the flying-fish bait we trolled before him.

That experience was but a forerunner to others just like it. Every day we sighted one or more swordfish. But we could not get one to take hold. Captain Dan said there was more chance of getting a strike from a swordfish that was not visible rolling on the surface. Now a flying-fish bait makes a rather heavy bait to troll; and as it is imperative to have the reel free running and held lightly with the thumb, after a few hours such trolling becomes hard work. Hard as it was, it did not wear on me like the strain of being always ready for a strike. I doubt if any fisherman could stand this strain.

In twenty-one days I had seen nineteen swordfish, several of which had leaped playfully, or to shake off the remoras—parasite, blood-sucking little fish—and the sight of every one had only served to increase my fascination. By this time I had realized something of the difficult nature of the game, and I had begun to have an inkling of what sport it might be. During those twenty-one days we had trolled fifteen hundred miles, altogether, up and down that twenty-five-mile coast of rugged Clemente. And we had trolled round these fish in every conceivable way. I cannot begin to describe my sensations when we circled round a swordfish, and they grew more intense and acute as the strain and suspense dragged. Captain Dan, of course, was mostly dominated by my feeling. All the same, I think the strain affected him on his own account.

Then one day Boschen came over to Clemente with Farnsworth—and let me explain, by the way, that Boschen is probably the greatest heavy tackle fisherman living. Boschen would not fish for anything except tuna or swordfish, and up to this visit to Clemente he had caught many tuna, but only one swordfish, a Xiphias. This is the broadbill, or true, swordfish; and he is even rarer, and certainly larger and fiercer, than the Marlin, or roundbill, swordfish. This time at Clemente, Boschen caught his first Marlin and it weighed over three hundred pounds, leaped clear into the air sixty-three times, and gave a spectacular and magnificent surface fight that simply beggared description.

It made me wild to catch one, of like weight and ferocity. I spent several more endless days in vain. Then on the twenty-fifth day, way off the east end of Clemente, we sighted a swordfish with a tail almost pink. He had just come to those waters and had not yet gotten sunburnt. We did not have to circle round him! At long distance he saw my bait, and as he went under I saw he had headed for it. I remember that I shook all over. And when I felt him take that bait, thrill on thrill electrified me. Steadily the line ran off the reel. Then Captain Dan leaned over and whispered, hoarsely:

"When you think he's had enough throw on your drag and strike. Then wind quick and strike again.... Wind and strike! Keep it up till he shows!"

Despite my intense excitement, I was calm enough to follow directions. But when I struck I felt no weight at all—no strain on the line. Frantically I wound and jerked—again and again! I never felt him at all. Suddenly my line rose—and then, bewilderingly near the boat, when I was looking far off, the water split with a roar and out shot a huge, gleaming, white-and-purple fish. He blurred in my sight. Down he went with a crash. I wound the reel like a madman, but I never even half got up the slack line. The swordfish had run straight toward the boat. He leaped again, in a place I did not expect, and going down, instantly came up in another direction. His speed, his savageness, stunned me. I could not judge of his strength, for I never felt his weight. The next leap I saw him sling the hook. It was a great performance. Then that swordfish, finding himself free, leaped for the open sea, and every few yards he came out in a clean jump. I watched him, too fascinated to count the times he broke water, but he kept it up till he was out of sight on the horizon.

At first Captain Dan took the loss harder than I took it. But gradually I realized what had happened, and, though I made a brave effort to be game and cheerful, I was sick. It did seem hard that, after all those twenty-five days of patience and hope and toil, I could not have hooked the swordfish. I see now that it was nothing, only an incident, but I shall never forget the pang.

That day ended my 1914 experience. The strain had been too hard on me. It had taken all this time for me to appreciate what swordfishing might be. I assured Captain Dan I would come back in 1915, but at the time he did not believe me. He said:

"If you hadn't stuck it out so long I wouldn't care. Most of the fishermen try only a few days and never come back. Don't quit now!"

But I did go back in 1915. Long ago on my lonely desert trips I learned the value of companions and I dreaded the strain of this swordfishing game. I needed some one to help lessen it. Besides that, I needed snapshot pictures of leaping swordfish, and it was obvious that Captain Dan and I would have our hands full when a fish got hooked. We had music, books, magazines—everything that could be thought of.

Murphy, the famous old Avalon fisherman and tackle-maker, had made me a double split-bamboo rod, and I had brought the much-talked-of B-Ocean reel. This is Boschen's invention—one he was years in perfecting. It held fifteen hundred feet of No. 24 line. And I will say now that it is a grand reel, the best on the market. But I did not know that then, and had to go through the trip with it, till we were both tried out. Lastly, and most important, I had worked to get into condition to fight swordfish. For weeks I rowed a boat at home to get arms and back in shape, and especially my hands. Let no fisherman imagine he can land a fighting swordfish with soft hands!

So, prepared for a long, hard strain, like that of 1914, I left Avalon hopeful, of course, but serious, determined, and alive to the possibilities of failure.

I did not troll across the channel between the islands. There was a big swell running, and four hours of it gave me a disagreeable feeling. Now and then I got up to see how far off Clemente was. And upon the last of these occasions I saw the fins of a swordfish right across our bow. I yelled to Captain Dan. He turned the boat aside, almost on top of the swordfish. Hurriedly I put a bait on my hook and got it overboard, and let the line run. Then I looked about for the swordfish. He had gone down.

It seemed then that, simultaneously with the recurrence of a peculiar and familiar disappointment, a heavy and powerful fish viciously took my bait and swept away. I yelled to Captain Dan:

"He's got it!" ...

Captain Dan stopped the engine and came to my side. "No!" he exclaimed.

Then I replied, "Look at that line!" ...

It seemed like a dream. Too good to be true! I let out a shout when I hooked him and a yell of joy when he broke water—a big swordfish, over two hundred pounds. What really transpired on Captain Dan's boat the following few moments I cannot adequately describe. Suffice to say that it was violent effort, excitement, and hilarity. I never counted the leaps of the swordfish. I never clearly saw him after that first leap. He seemed only a gleam in flying spray. Still, I did not make any mistakes.

At the end of perhaps a quarter of an hour the swordfish quit his surface work and settled down to under-water fighting, and I began to find myself. Captain Dan played the phonograph, laughed, and joked while I fought the fish. My companions watched my rod and line and the water, wide-eyed and mute, as if they could not believe what seemed true.

In about an hour and a half the swordfish came up and, tired out, he rolled on the top of the great swells. But he could not be drawn near the boat. One little wave of his tail made my rod bend dangerously. Still, I knew I had him beaten, and I calculated that in another hour, perhaps, I could lead him alongside.

Then, like thunder out of a clear sky, something went wrong with the great B-Ocean reel. It worked hard. When a big swell carried the swordfish up, pulling out line, the reel rasped.

"It's freezing on you!" shouted Captain Dan, with dark glance.

A new reel sometimes clogs and stops from friction and heat. I had had von Hofe and other reels freeze. But in this instance, it seemed that for the reel to freeze would be simply heartbreaking. Well—it froze, tight as a shut vise! I sat there, clutching the vibrating rod, and I watched the swordfish as the swells lifted him. I expected the line to break, but, instead, the hook tore out.

Next day we sighted four swordfish and tried in vain to coax one to bite.

Next day we sighted ten swordfish, which is a record for one day. They were indifferent.

The next three. The next one, with like result. The next day no fish were sighted, and that fact encouraged Captain Dan.

The next day, late in the afternoon, I had a strike and hooked a swordfish. He leaped twice and threw the hook.

The next day I got eleven jumps out of another before he gracefully flung the hook at the boat.

The next day, a big swordfish, with a ragged purple fin, took my bait right astern of the boat and sounded deep. I hooked him. Time and time again I struck with all my might. The fish did not seem to mind that. He swam along with the boat. He appeared very heavy. I was elated and curious.

"What's he going to do?" I kept asking Captain Dan.

"Wait!" he exclaimed.

After six minutes the swordfish came up, probably annoyed by the hook fast in him. When he showed his flippers, as Captain Dan called them, we all burst out with wonder and awe. As yet I had no reason to fear a swordfish.

"He's a whale!" yelled Captain Dan.

Probably this fish measured eight feet between his dorsal fin and the great curved fluke of his tail, and that would make his total length over twelve feet.

No doubt the swordfish associated the thing fast in his jaw with the boat, for he suddenly awoke. He lifted himself, wagging his sword, showing his great silvery side. Then he began to thresh. I never felt a quarter of such power at the end of a line. He went swift as a flash. Then he leaped sheer ahead, like a porpoise, only infinitely more active. We all yelled. He was of great size, over three hundred, broad, heavy, long, and the most violent and savage fish I ever had a look at. Then he rose half—two-thirds out of the water, shaking his massive head, jaws open, sword sweeping, and seemed to move across the water in a growing, boiling maelstrom of foam. This was the famous "walking on his tail" I had heard so much about. It was an incredible feat. He must have covered fifty yards. Then he plunged down, and turned swiftly in a curve toward the boat. He looked threatening to me. I could not manage the slack line. One more leap and he threw the hook. I found the point of the hook bent. It had never been embedded in his jaw. And also I found that his violent exercise had lasted just one minute. I wondered how long I would have lasted had the hook been deep-set.

Next day I had a swordfish take my bait, swim away on the surface, showing the flying-fish plainly between his narrow beak, and after fooling with it for a while he ejected it.

Next day I got a great splashing strike from another, without even a sight of the fish.

Next day I hooked one that made nineteen beautiful leaps straightaway before he got rid of the hook.

And about that time I was come to a sad pass. In fact, I could not sleep, eat, or rest. I was crazy on swordfish.

Day after day, from early morning till late afternoon, aboard on the sea, trolling, watching, waiting, eternally on the alert, I had kept at the game. My emotional temperament made this game a particularly trying one. And every possible unlucky, unforeseen, and sickening thing that could happen to a fisherman had happened. I grew morbid, hopeless. I could no longer see the beauty of that wild and lonely island, nor the wonder of that smooth, blue Pacific, nor the myriad of strange sea-creatures. It was a bad state of mind which I could not wholly conquer. Only by going at it so hard, and sticking so long, without any rests, could I gain the experience I wanted. A man to be a great fisherman should have what makes Stewart White a great hunter—no emotions. If a lion charged me I would imagine a million things. Once when a Mexican tigre, a jaguar, charged me I—But that is not this story. Boschen has the temperament for a great fisherman. He is phlegmatic. All day—and day after day—he sits there, on trigger, so to speak, waiting for the strike that will come. He is so constituted that it does not matter to him how soon or how late the strike comes. To me the wait, the suspense, grew to be maddening. Yet I stuck it out, and in this I claim a victory, of which I am prouder than I am of the record that gave me more swordfish to my credit than any other fisherman has taken.

On the next day, August 11th, about three o'clock, I saw a long, moving shadow back of my bait. I jumped up. There was the purple, drifting shape of a swordfish. I felt a slight vibration when he hit the bait with his sword. Then he took the bait. I hooked this swordfish. He leaped eight times before he started out to sea. He took us three miles. In an hour and five minutes I brought him to gaff—a small fish. Captain Dan would take no chances of losing him. He risked much when he grasped the waving sword with his right hand, and with the gaff in his left he hauled the swordfish aboard and let him slide down into the cockpit. For Captain Dan it was no less an overcoming of obstinate difficulty than for me. He was as elated as I, but I forgot the past long, long siege, while he remembered it.

That swordfish certainly looked a tiger of the sea. He had purple fins, long, graceful, sharp; purple stripes on a background of dark, mottled bronze green; mother-of-pearl tint fading into the green; and great opal eyes with dark spots in the center. The colors came out most vividly and exquisitely, the purple blazing, just as the swordfish trembled his last and died. He was nine feet two inches long and weighed one hundred and eighteen pounds.

I caught one the next day, one hundred and forty-four pounds. Fought another the next day and he threw the hook after a half-hour. Caught two the following day—one hundred and twenty, and one hundred and sixty-six pounds. And then, Captain Dan foreshadowing my remarkable finish, exclaimed:

"I'm lookin' for busted records now!"

One day about noon the sea was calm except up toward the west end, where a wind was whipping the water white. Clemente Island towered with its steep slopes of wild oats and its blue cañons full of haze.

Captain Dan said he had seen a big swordfish jump off to the west, and we put on full speed. He must have been a mile out and just where the breeze ruffled the water. As good luck would have it, we came upon the fish on the surface. I consider this a fine piece of judgment for Captain Dan, to locate him at that distance. He was a monster and fresh run from the outside sea. That is to say, his great fin and tail were violet, almost pink in color. They had not had time to get sunburnt, as those of fish earlier arrived at Clemente.

We made a wide circle round him, to draw the flying-fish bait near him. But before we could get it near he went down. The same old story, I thought, with despair—these floating fish will not bite. We circled over the place where he had gone down, and I watched my bait rising and falling in the low swells.

Suddenly Captain Dan yelled and I saw a great blaze of purple and silver green flashing after my bait. It was the swordfish, and he took the bait on the run. That was a moment for a fisherman! I found it almost impossible to let him have enough line. All that I remember about the hooking of him was a tremendous shock. His first dash was irresistibly powerful, and I had a sensation of the absurdity of trying to stop a fish like that. Then the line began to rise on the surface and to lengthen in my sight, and I tried to control my rapture and fear enough to be able to see him clearly when he leaped. The water split, and up he shot—a huge, glittering, savage, beautiful creature, all purple and opal in the sunlight. He did not get all the way out of the water, but when he dropped back he made the water roar.

Then, tearing off line, he was out of the water in similar leaps—seven times more. Captain Dan had his work cut out for him as well as I had mine. It was utterly impossible to keep a tight line, and when I felt the slacking of weight I grew numb and sick—thinking he was gone. But he suddenly straightened the line with a jerk that lifted me, and he started inshore. He had about four hundred feet of line out, and more slipping out as if the drag was not there. Captain Dan headed the boat after him at full speed. Then followed a most thrilling race. It was over very quickly, but it seemed an age. When he stopped and went down he had pulled thirteen hundred feet off my reel while we were chasing him at full speed. While he sounded I got back half of this line. I wish I could give some impression of the extraordinary strength and speed of this royal purple fish of the sea. He came up again, in two more leaps, one of which showed me his breadth of back, and then again was performed for me the feature of which I had heard so much and which has made the swordfish the most famous of all fish—he rose two-thirds out of the water, I suppose by reason of the enormous power of his tail, though it seemed like magic, and then he began to walk across the sea in a great circle of white foam, wagging his massive head, sword flying, jaws wide, dorsal fin savagely erect, like a lion's mane. He was magnificent. I have never seen fury so expressed or such an unquenchable spirit. Then he dropped back with a sudden splash, and went down and down and down.

All swordfish fight differently, and this one adopted tuna tactics. He sounded and began to plug away and bang the leader with his tail. He would take off three hundred feet of line, and then, as he slowed up, I, by the labor of Hercules, pulled and pumped and wound most of it back on the reel. This kept up for an hour—surely the hardest hour's work of my life.

But a swordfish is changeable. That is the beauty of his gameness. He left off sounding and came up to fight on the surface. In the next hour he pulled us from the Fence to Long Point, a distance of four miles.

Once off the Point, where the tide rip is strong, he began to circle in great, wide circles. Strangely, he did not put out to sea. And here, during the next hour, I had the finest of experiences I think that ever befell a fisherman. I was hooked to a monster fighting swordfish; I was wet with sweat, and salt water that had dripped from my reel, and I was aching in every muscle. The sun was setting in banks of gold and silver fog over the west end, and the sea was opalescent—vast, shimmering, heaving, beautiful. And at this sunset moment, or hour—for time seemed nothing—a school of giant tuna began leaping around us, smashing the water, making the flying-fish rise in clouds, like drifting bees. I saw a whole flock of flying-fish rise into the air with that sunset glow and color in the background, and the exquisite beauty of life and movement was indescribable. Next a bald eagle came soaring down, and, swooping along the surface, he lowered his talons to pick up a crippled flying-fish. And when the hoary-headed bird rose, a golden eagle, larger and more powerful, began to contest with him for the prey.

Then the sky darkened and the moon whitened—and my fight went on. I had taken the precaution to work for two months at rowing to harden my hands for just such a fight as this. Yet my hands suffered greatly. A man who is not in the best of physical trim, with his hands hard, cannot hope to land a big swordfish.

I was all afternoon at this final test, and all in, too, but at last I brought him near enough for Captain Dan to grasp the leader.... Then there was something doing around that boat for a spell! I was positive a German torpedo had hit us. But the explosion was only the swordfish's tail and Dan's voice yelling for another gaff. When Captain Dan got the second gaff in him there was another submarine attack, but the boat did not sink.

Next came the job of lassoing the monster's tail. Here I shone, for I had lassoed mountain-lions with Buffalo Jones, and I was efficient and quick. Captain Dan and I were unable to haul the fish on board, and we had to get out the block and tackle and lift the tail on deck, secure that, and then pull up the head from the other side. After that I needed some kind of tackle to hold me up.

We were miles from camp, and I was wet and cold and exhausted, and the pain in my blistered hands was excruciating. But not soon shall I forget that ride down the shore with the sea so rippling and moon-blanched, and the boom of the surf on the rocks, and the peaks of the island standing bold and dark against the white stars.

This swordfish weighed three hundred and sixteen pounds on faulty scales at Clemente. He very likely weighed much more. He was the largest Captain Dan ever saw, up to that time. Al Shade guessed his weight at three hundred and sixty. The market fishermen, who put in at the little harbor the next day, judged him way over three hundred, and these men are accurate. The fish hung head down for a day and night, lost all the water and blood and feed in him, and another day later, when landed at Avalon, he had lost considerable. There were fishermen who discredited Captain Dan and me, who in our enthusiasm claimed a record.

But—that sort of thing is one of the aspects of the sport. I was sorry, for Captain Dan's sake. The rivalries between boatmen are keen and important, and they are fostered by unsportsman-like fishermen. And fishermen live among past associations; they grow to believe their performances unbeatable and they hate to see a new king crowned. This may be human, since we are creatures who want always to excel, but it is irritating to the young fishermen. As for myself, what did I care how much the swordfish weighed? He was huge, magnificent, beautiful, and game to the end of that four-hour battle. Who or what could change that—or the memory of those schools of flying-fish in the sunset glow—or the giant tuna, smashing the water all about me—or the eagles fighting over my head—or the beauty of wild and lonely Clemente under its silver cloud-banks?

I went on catching one or two swordfish every day, and Captain Dan averred that the day would come when we would swamp the boat. These days were fruitful of the knowledge of swordfish that I had longed to earn.

They are indeed "queer birds." I learned to recognize the sharp vibration of my line when a swordfish rapped the bait with his sword. No doubt he thought he thus killed his prey. Then the strike would come invariably soon after. No two swordfish acted or fought alike. I hooked one that refused to stand the strain of the line. He followed the boat, and was easily gaffed. I hooked another, a heavy fish, that did not show for two hours. We were sure we had a broadbill, and were correspondingly worried. The broadbill swordfish is a different proposition. He is larger, fiercer, and tireless. He will charge the boat, and nothing but the churning propeller will keep him from ramming the boat. There were eight broadbill swordfish hooked at Avalon during the summer, and not one brought to gaff. This is an old story. Only two have been caught to date. They are so powerful, so resistless, so desperate, and so cunning that it seems impossible to catch them. They will cut bait after bait off your hook as clean as if it had been done with a knife. For that matter, their broad bill is a straight, long, powerful two-edged sword. And the fish perfectly understands its use.

This matter of swordfish charging the boat is apt to be discredited by fishermen. But it certainly is not doubted by the few who know. I have seen two swordfish threaten my boat, and one charge it. Walker, an Avalon boatman, tells of a prodigious battle his angler had with a broadbill giant calculated to weigh five hundred pounds. This fight lasted eight hours. Many times the swordfish charged the boat and lost his nerve. If that propeller had stopped he would have gone through the boat as if it had been paper. After this fish freed himself he was so mad that he charged the boat repeatedly. Boschen fought a big broadbill for eleven hours. And during this fight the swordfish sounded to the bottom forty-eight times, and had to be pumped up; he led the boat almost around Catalina Island—twenty-nine miles; and he had gotten out into the channel, headed for Clemente, when he broke away. This fish did everything. I consider this battle the greatest on record. Only a man of enormous strength and endurance could have lasted so long—not to speak of the skill and wits necessary on the part of both fisherman and boatman. All fishermen fish for the big fish, though it is sport to catch any game fish, irrespective of size. But let any fisherman who has nerve see and feel a big swordfish on his line, and from that moment he is obsessed. Why, a tarpon is child's play compared to holding a fast swordfish.

It is my great ambition now to catch a broadbill. That would completely round out my fishing experience. And I shall try. But I doubt that I will be so fortunate. It takes a long time. Boschen was years catching his fish. Moreover, though it is hard to get a broadbill to bite—and harder to hook him—it is infinitely harder to do anything with him after you do get fast to him.

A word about Avalon boatmen. They are a fine body of men. I have heard them maligned. Certainly they have petty rivalries and jealousies, but this is not their fault. They fish all the seasons around and have been there for years. Boatmen at Long Key and other Florida resorts—at Tampico, Aransas Pass—are not in the same class with the Avalon men. They want to please and to excel, and to number you among their patrons for the future. And the boats—nowhere are there such splendid boats. Captain Danielson's boat had utterly spoiled me for fishing out of any other. He had it built, and the ideas of its construction were a product of fifteen years' study. It is thirty-eight feet long, and wide, with roomy, shaded cockpit and cabin, and comfortable revolving chairs to fish from. These chairs have moving sockets into which you can jam the butt of your rod; and the backs can be removed in a flash. Then you can haul at a fish! The boat lies deep, with heavy ballast in the stern. It has a keel all the way, and an enormous rudder. Both are constructed so your line can slip under the boat without fouling. It is equipped with sail and a powerful engine. Danielson can turn this boat, going at full speed, in its own length! Consider the merit of this when a tuna strikes, or a swordfish starts for the open sea. How many tarpon, barracuda, amberjack, and tuna I have lost on the Atlantic seaboard just because the boat could not be turned in time!

Clemente Island is a mountain of cliffs and caves. It must be of volcanic origin, and when the lava rose, hot and boiling, great blow-holes formed, and hardened to make the caves. It is an exceedingly beautiful island. The fishing side is on the north, or lee, shore, where the water is very deep right off the rocks. There are kelp-beds along the shore, and the combination of deep water, kelp, and small fish is what holds the swordfish there in August and September. I have seen acres of flying-fish in the air at once, and great swarms of yellowtail, basking on the surface. The color of the water is indigo blue, clear as crystal. Always a fascinating thing for me was to watch the water for new and different fish, strange marine creatures, life of some kind. And the watching was always rewarded. I have been close to schools of devilish blackfish, and I have watched great whales play all around me. What a spectacle to see a whale roll and dip his enormous body and bend and sound, lifting the huge, glistening flukes of his tail, wide as a house! I hate sharks and have caught many, both little and big. When you are watching for swordfish it is no fun to have a big shark break for your bait, throw the water, get your hook, and lift you from your seat. It happened often. But sometimes when I was sure it was a shark it was really a swordfish! I used to love to watch the sunfish leap, they are so round and glistening and awkward. I could tell one two miles away. The blue shark leaps often and he always turns clear over. You cannot mistake it. Nor can you mistake a swordfish when he breaks, even though you only see the splash. He makes two great sheets of water rise and fall. Probably all these fish leap to shake off the remoras. A remora is a parasite, a queer little fish, pale in color, because he probably lives inside the gills of the fish he preys upon, with the suckers on top of his head, arranged in a shield, ribbed like a washboard. This little fish is as mysterious as any creature of the sea. He is as swift as lightning. He can run over the body of a swordfish so quickly you can scarcely follow his movement, and at all times he is fast to the swordfish, holding with that flat sucker head. Mr. Holder wrote years ago that the remora sticks to a fish just to be carried along, as a means of travel, but I do not incline to this belief. We found many remoras inside the gills of swordfish, and their presence there was evidence of their blood-sucking tendencies. I used to search every swordfish for these remoras, and I would keep them in a bucket till we got to our anchorage. A school of tame rock-bass there, and tame yellowtail, and a few great sea-bass were always waiting for us—for our discarded bait or fish of some kind. But when I threw in a live remora, how these hungry fish did dart away! Life in the ocean is strange, complex, ferocious, and wonderful.

Al Shade keeps the only camp at Clemente. It is a clean, comfortable, delightful place. I have found no place where sleep is so easy, so sweet, so deep. Shade lives a lonely life there ten months in the year. And it is no wonder that when a fisherman arrives Al almost kills himself in his good humor and kindness and usefulness. Men who live lonely lives are always glad to see their fellow-men. But he loves Clemente Island. Who would not?

When I think of it many pictures come to mind—evening with the sea rolling high and waves curving shoreward in great dark ripples, that break and spread white and run up the strand. The sky is pale blue above, a green sheen low down, with white stars blinking. The promontories run down into the sea, sheer, black, rugged, bold, mighty. The surf is loud and deep, detonating, and the pebbles scream as the waves draw them down. Strange to realize that surf when on the morrow the sea will be like glass—not a wave nor a ripple under the gray fog! Wild and beautiful Clemente—the island of caves and cañons and cliffs—lilac and cactus and ice-plant and arbor-vitæ and ironwood, with the wild goats silhouetted dark against the bold sky-line!

There came that day of all days. I never believed Captain Dan, but now I shall never forget. The greatest day that ever befell me! I brought four swordfish to gaff and whipped another, the biggest one of the whole trip, and saw him tear away from the hook just at the last—in all, nine hours of strenuous hanging on to a rod.

I caught the first one before six o'clock, as the sun was rising red-gold, dazzling, glorious. He leaped in the sun eleven times. He weighed one hundred and eighty-seven.

After breakfast we sighted two swordfish on the smooth sea. Both charged the bait. I hooked one of these and he leaped twenty-three times. He weighed one hundred and sixty-eight.

Then off the east end we saw a big swordfish leap five times. We went out toward the open sea. But we never got anywhere near him. I had three strikes, one after another, when we were speeding the boat. Then we shut down and took to slow trolling. I saw another swordfish sail for my bait, and yelled. He shot off with the bait and his dorsal fin stuck out of the water. I hooked him. He leaped thirty-eight times. How the camera did snap during this fight! He weighed two hundred and ten.

I had a fierce strike on the way in. Too fast! We lost him.

"The sea's alive with swordfish!" cried Captain Dan. "It's the day!"

Then I awoke to my opportunity.

Round the east end, close to the great black bluff, where the swells pile up so thunderously, I spied the biggest purple fin I had ever seen. This fellow came to meet us—took my bait. I hooked at him, but did not hurt or scare him. Finally I pulled the hook out of him. While I was reeling in my line suddenly a huge purple shadow hove in sight. It was the swordfish—and certainly one of immense size—the hugest yet.

"He's following the boat!" yelled Captain Dan, in great excitement.

So I saw, but I could not speak or yell. All was intense excitement on that boat. I jumped up on the stern, holding the bait Captain Dan had put on my hook. Then I paused to look. We all looked, spellbound. That was a sight of a lifetime. There he swam, the monster, a few feet under the surface, only a rod back of the boat. I had no calm judgment with which to measure his dimensions. I only saw that he was tremendous and beautiful. His great, yard-wide fins gleamed royal purple. And the purple strips crossed his silver sides. He glowed in the water, changed color like a chameleon, and drifted, floated after us. I thought of my brother Reddy—how he would have gloried in that sight! I thought of Dilg, of Bob Davis, of Professor Kellogg—other great fishermen, all in a flash. Indeed, though I gloated over my fortune, I was not selfish. Then I threw in the flying-fish bait. The swordfish loomed up, while my heart ceased to beat. There, in plain sight, he took the bait, as a trout might have taken a grasshopper. Slowly he sank. The line began to slip off the reel. He ceased to be a bright purple mass—grew dim—then vague—and disappeared.

I sat down, jammed the rod in the socket, and got ready. For the life of me I could not steady my legs.

"What'll he weigh?" I gasped.

"O Lord! he looked twice as big as the big one you got," replied Dan.

"Stand by with the cameras!" I said to my companions, and as they lined up, two on one side and one on the other, I began to strike at that fish with all my might and main. I must have had at least twelve powerful strikes before he began to wake up.

Then!

He came up, throwing the water in angry spouts. If he did not threaten the boat I was crazy. He began an exhibition that dwarfed any other I had seen, and it was so swift that I could scarcely follow him. Yet when I saw the line rise, and then the wonderful, long, shiny body, instinct with fury, shoot into the air, I yelled the number of the leap, and this was the signal for the camera-workers. They held the cameras close, without trying to focus, facing the fish, and they snapped when I yelled. It was all gloriously exciting. I could never describe that exhibition. I only know that he leaped clear forty-six times, and after a swift, hard hour for me he got away. Strangely, I was almost happy that he had shaken loose, for he had given such remarkable opportunities for pictures.

Captain Dan threw the wheel hard over and the boat turned. The swordfish, tired out and unconscious of freedom, was floating near the surface, a drifting blaze of purple. The boat sheered close to him. Captain Dan reached over with a gaff—and all but gaffed that swordfish before he sank too deep. Captain Dan was white with disappointment. That more than anything showed me his earnestness, what it all meant to him.

On the way in, for we had been led out a couple of miles, I saw a blue streak after my bait, and I was ready before the swordfish got to it. He struck viciously and I dared not let him have much line. When I hooked him he started out to sea at a clip that smoked the line off my reel. Captain Dan got the boat turned before the swordfish began to leap. Then it was almost a straightaway race. This fellow was a greyhound leaper. He did not churn the water, nor dash to and fro on the surface, but kept steadily leaping ahead. He cleared the water thirty-nine times before he gave up leaping. Then he sounded. The line went slack. I thought he was gone. Suddenly he showed again, in a white splash, and he was not half as far away as when he went down. Then I felt the pull on the line. It was heavy, for he had left a great bag in it. I endeavored to recover line, but it came in very slowly. The swordfish then threshed on the surface so that we could hear the water crack. But he did not leap again. He had gone mad with rage. He seemed to have no sense of direction. He went down again, only to rush up, still closer to us. Then it was plain he saw the nature of his foe. Splitting water like a swift motor-boat, he charged us.

I had a cold sensation, but was too excited to be afraid. Almost I forgot to reel in.

"He's after us!" I said, grimly.

Captain Dan started the boat ahead fast. The swordfish got out of line with the boat. But he was close, and he made me think of the charging rhinoceros Dugmore photographed. And then I yelled for the cameras to be snapped. They all clicked—and then, when the swordfish shot close behind us, presenting the most magnificent picture, no one was ready!

As he passed I thought I saw the line round his body. Then he sounded and began to plug. He towed us six miles out to sea. I could not stop him. I had begun to weaken. My hands were sights. My back hurt. But I stayed with him. He felt like a log and I could not recover line. Captain Dan said it was because I was almost all in, but I did not think that. Presently this swordfish turned inshore and towed us back the six miles. By this time it was late and I was all in. But the swordfish did not seem nearer the boat. I got mad and found some reserve strength. I simply had to bring him to gaff. I pulled and pumped and wound until I was blind and could scarcely feel. My old blisters opened and bled. My left arm was dead. I seemed to have no more strength than a kitten. I could not lead the fish nor turn him. I had to drag and drag, inch by inch. It was agonizing. But finally I was encouraged by sight of him, a long, fine, game fellow. A hundred times I got the end of the double line near the leader in sight, only to lose it.

Seven o'clock passed. I had fought this swordfish nearly three hours. I could not last much longer. I rested a little, holding hard, and then began a last and desperate effort to bring him to gaff. I was absolutely dripping with sweat, and red flashes passed before my eyes, and queer dots. The last supreme pull—all I had left—brought the end of the leader to Captain Dan's outstretched hand.

The swordfish came in broadside. In the clear water we saw him plainly, beautifully striped tiger that he was! And we all saw that he had not been hooked. He had been lassoed. In some way the leader had looped around him with the hook catching under the wire. No wonder it had nearly killed me to bring him to the boat, and surely I never would have succeeded had it not been for the record Captain Dan coveted. That was the strangest feature in all my wonderful Clemente experience—to see that superb swordfish looped in a noose of my long leader. He was without a scratch. It may serve to give some faint idea of the bewildering possibilities in the pursuit of this royal purple game of the Pacific.

CHAPTER IV

TWO FIGHTS WITH SWORDFISH

My first day at Avalon, 1916, was one likely to be memorable among my fishing experiences.

The weather (August 2d) was delightful—smooth, rippling sea, no wind, clear sky and warm. The Sierra Nevada Mountains shone dark above the horizon.

A little before noon we passed my friend Lone Angler, who hailed us and said there was a big broadbill swordfish off in the steamer-course. We steered off in that direction.

There were sunfish and sharks showing all around. Once I saw a whale. The sea was glassy, with a long, heaving swell. Birds were plentiful in scattered groups.

We ran across a shark of small size and tried to get him to take a bait. He refused. A little later Captain Dan espied a fin, and upon running up we discovered the huge, brown, leathery tail and dorsal of a broadbill swordfish.

Captain Dan advised a long line out so that we could circle the fish from a distance and not scare him. I do not remember any unusual excitement. I was curious and interested. Remembering all I had heard about these fish, I did not anticipate getting a strike from him.

We circled him and drew the flying-fish bait so that he would swim near it. As it was, I had to reel in some. Presently we had the bait some twenty yards ahead of him. Then Captain Dan slowed down. The broadbill wiggled his tail and slid out of sight. Dan said he was going for my bait. But I did not believe so. Several moments passed. I had given up any little hope I might have had when I received a quick, strong, vibrating strike—different from any I had ever experienced. I suppose the strangeness was due to the shock he gave my line when he struck the bait with his sword. The line paid out unsteadily and slowly. I looked at Dan and he looked at me. Neither of us was excited nor particularly elated. I guess I did not realize what was actually going on.

I let him have about one hundred and fifty feet of line.

When I sat down to jam the rod-butt in the socket I had awakened to possibilities. Throwing on the drag and winding in until my line was taut, I struck hard—four times. He made impossible any more attempts at this by starting off on a heavy, irresistible rush. But he was not fast, or so it seemed to me. He did not get more than four hundred feet of line before we ran up on him. Presently he came to the surface to thresh around. He did not appear scared or angry. Probably he was annoyed at the pricking of the hook. But he kept moving, sometimes on the surface and sometimes beneath. I did not fight him hard, preferring to let him pull out the line, and then when he rested I worked on him to recover it. My idea was to keep a perpetual strain upon him.

I do not think I had even a hope of bringing this fish to the boat.

It was twelve o'clock exactly when I hooked him, and a quarter of an hour sped by. My first big thrill came when he leaped. This was a surprise. He was fooling round, and then, all of a sudden, he broke water clear. It was an awkward, ponderous action, and looked as if he had come up backward, like a bucking bronco. His size and his long, sinister sword amazed me and frightened me. It gave me a cold sensation to realize I was hooked to a huge, dangerous fish. But that in itself was a new kind of thrill. No boatman fears a Marlin as he does the true broadbill swordfish.

My second thrill came when the fish lunged on the surface in a red foam. If I had hooked him so he bled freely there was a chance to land him! This approach to encouragement, however, was short-lived. He went down, and if I had been hooked to a submarine I could scarcely have felt more helpless. He sounded about five hundred feet and then sulked. I had the pleasant task of pumping him up. This brought the sweat out upon me and loosened me up. I began to fight him harder. And it seemed that as I increased the strain he grew stronger and a little more active. Still there was not any difference in his tactics. I began to get a conception of the vitality and endurance of a broadbill in contrast with the speed and savageness of his brother fish, the Marlin, or roundbill.

At two o'clock matters were about the same. I was not tired, but certainly the fish was not tired, either. He came to the surface just about as much as he sounded. I had no difficulty at all in getting back the line he took, at least all save a hundred feet or so. When I tried to lead him or lift him—then I got his point of view. He would not budge an inch. There seemed nothing to do but let him work on the drag, and when he had pulled out a few hundred feet of line we ran up on him and I reeled in the line. Now and then I put all the strain I could on the rod and worked him that way.

At three o'clock I began to get tired. My hands hurt. And I concluded I had been rather unlucky to start on a broadbill at the very beginning.

From that time he showed less frequently, and, if anything, he grew slower and heavier. I felt no more rushes. And along about this time I found I could lead him somewhat. This made me begin to work hard. Yet, notwithstanding, I had no hope of capturing the fish. It was only experience.

Captain Dan kept saying: "Well, you wanted to hook up with a broadbill! Now how do you like it?" He had no idea I would ever land him. Several times I asked him to give an opinion as to the size of the swordfish, but he would not venture that until he had gotten a good close view of him.

At four o'clock I made the alarming discovery that the great B-Ocean reel was freezing, just as my other one had frozen on my first swordfish the year previous. Captain Dan used language. He threw up his hands. He gave up. But I did not.

"Dan, see here," I said. "We'll run up on him, throw off a lot of slack line, then cut it and tie it to another reel!"

"We might do that. But it'll disqualify the fish," he replied.

Captain Dan, like all the boatmen at Avalon, has fixed ideas about the Tuna Club and its records and requirements. It is all right, I suppose, for a club to have rules, and not count or credit an angler who breaks a rod or is driven to the expedient I had proposed. But I do not fish for clubs or records. I fish for the fun, the excitement, the thrill of the game, and I would rather let my fish go than not. So I said:

"We'll certainly lose the fish if we don't change reels. I am using the regulation tackle, and to my mind the more tackle we use, provided we land the fish, the more credit is due us. It is not an easy matter to change reels or lines or rods with a big fish working all the time."

Captain Dan acquiesced, but told me to try fighting him a while with the light drag and the thumb-brake. So far only the heavy drag had frozen. I tried Dan's idea, to my exceeding discomfort; and the result was that the swordfish drew far away from us. Presently the reel froze solid. The handle would not turn. But with the drag off the spool ran free.

Then we ran away from the fish, circling and letting out slack line. When we came to the end of the line we turned back a little, and with a big slack we took the risk of cutting the line and tying it on the other reel. We had just got this done when the line straightened tight! I wound in about twelve hundred feet of line and was tired and wet when I had gotten in all I could pull. This brought us to within a couple of hundred feet of our quarry. Also it brought us to five o'clock. Five hours!... I began to have queer sensations—aches, pains, tremblings, saggings. Likewise misgivings!

About this period I determined to see how close to the boat I could pull him. I worked. The word "worked" is not readily understood until a man has tried to pull a big broadbill close to the boat. I pulled until I saw stars and my bones cracked. Then there was another crack. The rod broke at the reel seat! And the reel seat was bent. Fortunately the line could still pay out. And I held the tip while Dan pried and hammered the reel off the broken butt on to another one. Then he put the tip in that butt, and once more I had to reel in what seemed miles and miles of line.

Five thirty! It seemed around the end of the world for me. We had drifted into a tide-rip about five miles east of Avalon, and in this rough water I had a terrible time trying to hold my fish. When I discovered that I could hold him—and therefore that he was playing out—then there burst upon me the dazzling hope of actually bringing him to gaff. It is something to fight a fish for more than five hours without one single hope of his capture. I had done that. And now, suddenly, to be fired with hope gave me new strength and spirit to work. The pain in my hands was excruciating. I was burning all over; wet and slippery, and aching in every muscle. These next few minutes seemed longer than all the hours. I found that to put the old strain on the rod made me blind with pain. There was no fun, no excitement, no thrill now. As I labored I could not help marveling at the strange, imbecile pursuits of mankind. Here I was in an agony, absolutely useless. Why did I keep it up? I could not give up, and I concluded I was crazy.

I conceived the most unreasonable hatred for that poor swordfish that had done nothing to me and that certainly would have been justified in ramming the boat.

To my despair the fish sounded deep, going down and down. Captain Dan watched the line. Finally it ceased to pay out.

"Pump him up!" said Dan.

This was funny. It was about as funny as death.

I rested awhile and meditated upon the weakness of the flesh. The thing most desirable and beautiful in all the universe was rest. It was so sweet to think of that I was hard put to it to keep from tossing the rod overboard. There was something so desperately trying and painful in this fight with a broadbill. At last I drew a deep, long breath, and, with a pang in my breast and little stings all over me, I began to lift on him. He was at the bottom of the ocean. He was just as unattainable as the bottom of the ocean. But there are ethics of a sportsman!

Inch by inch and foot by foot I pumped up this live and dragging weight. I sweat, I panted, I whistled, I bled—and my arms were dead, and my hands raw and my heart seemed about to burst.

Suddenly Captain Dan electrified me.

"There's the end of the double line!" he yelled.

Unbelievable as it was, there the knot in the end of the short six feet of double line showed at the surface. I pumped and I reeled inch by inch.

A long dark object showed indistinctly, wavered as the swells rose, then showed again. As I strained at the rod so I strained my eyes.

"I see the leader!" yelled Dan, in great excitement.

I saw it, too, and I spent the last ounce of strength left in me. Up and up came the long, dark, vague object.

"You've got him licked!" exclaimed Dan. "Not a wag left in him!"

It did seem so. And that bewildering instant saw the birth of assurance in me. I was going to get him! That was a grand instant for a fisherman. I could have lifted anything then.

The swordfish became clear to my gaze. He was a devilish-looking monster, two feet thick across the back, twelve feet long over all, and he would have weighed at the least over four hundred pounds. And I had beaten him! That was there to be seen. He had none of the beauty and color of the roundbill swordfish. He was dark, almost black, with huge dorsal and tail, and a wicked broad sword fully four feet long. What terrified me was his enormous size and the deadly look of him. I expected to see him rush at the boat.

Watching him thus, I reveled in my wonderful luck. Up to this date there had been only three of these rare fish caught in twenty-five years of Avalon fishing. And this one was far larger than those that had been taken.

"Lift him! Closer!" called Captain Dan. "In two minutes I'll have a gaff in him!"

I made a last effort. Dan reached for the leader.

Then the hook tore out.

My swordfish, without a movement of tail or fin, slowly sank—to vanish in the blue water.

After resting my blistered hands for three days, which time was scarcely long enough to heal them, I could not resist the call of the sea.

We went off Seal Rocks and trolled about five miles out. We met a sand-dabber who said he had seen a big broadbill back a ways. So we turned round. After a while I saw a big, vicious splash half a mile east, and we made for it. Then I soon espied the fish.

We worked around him awhile, but he would not take a barracuda or a flying-fish.

It was hard to keep track of him, on account of rough water. Soon he went down.

Then a little later I saw what Dan called a Marlin. He had big flippers, wide apart. I took him for a broadbill.

We circled him, and before he saw a bait he leaped twice, coming about half out, with belly toward us. He looked huge, but just how big it was impossible to say.

After a while he came up, and we circled him. As the bait drifted round before him—twenty yards or more off—he gave that little wiggle of the tail sickle, and went under. I waited. I had given up hope when I felt him hit the bait. Then he ran off, pretty fast. I let him have a long line. Then I sat down and struck him. He surged off, and we all got ready to watch him leap. But he did not show.

He swam off, sounded, came up, rolled around, went down again. But we did not get a look at him. He fought like any other heavy swordfish.

In one and one-half hours I pulled him close to the boat, and we all saw him. But I did not get a good look at him as he wove to and fro behind the boat.

Then he sounded.

I began to work on him, and worked harder. He seemed to get stronger all the time.

"He feels like a broadbill, I tell you," I said to Captain Dan.

Dan shook his head, yet all the same he looked dubious.

Then began a slow, persistent, hard battle between me and the fish, the severity of which I did not realize at the time. In hours like those time has wings. My hands grew hot. They itched, and I wanted to remove the wet gloves. But I did not, and sought to keep my mind off what had been half-healed blisters. Neither the fish nor I made any new moves, it all being plug on his part and give and take on mine. Slowly and doggedly he worked out toward the sea, and while the hours passed, just as persistently he circled back.

Captain Dan came to stand beside me, earnestly watching the rod bend and the line stretch. He shook his head.

"That's a big Marlin and you've got him foul-hooked," he asserted. This statement was made at the end of three hours and more. I did not agree. Dan and I often had arguments. He always tackled me when I was in some such situation as this—for then, of course, he had the best of it. My brother Rome was in the boat that day, an intensely interested observer. He had not as yet hooked a swordfish.

"It's a German submarine!" he declared.

My brother's wife and the other ladies with us on board were inclined to favor my side; at least they were sorry for the fish and said he must be very big.

"Dan, I could tell a foul-hooked fish," I asserted, positively. "This fellow is too alive—too limber. He doesn't sag like a dead weight."

"Well, if he's not foul-hooked, then you're all in," replied the captain.

Cheerful acquiescence is a desirable trait in any one, especially an angler who aspires to things, but that was left out in the ordering of my complex disposition. However, to get angry makes a man fight harder, and so it was with me.

At the end of five hours Dan suggested putting the harness on me. This contrivance, by the way, is a thing of straps and buckles, and its use is to fit over an angler's shoulders and to snap on the rod. It helps him lift the fish, puts his shoulders more into play, rests his arms. But I had never worn one. I was afraid of it.

"Suppose he pulls me overboard, with that on!" I exclaimed. "He'll drown me!"

"We'll hold on to you," replied Dan, cheerily, as he strapped it around me.

Later it turned out that I had exactly the right view concerning this harness, for Dustin Farnum was nearly pulled overboard and—But I have not space for that story here. My brother Rome wants to write that story, anyhow, because it is so funny, he says.

On the other hand, the fact soon manifested itself to me that I could lift a great deal more with said harness to help. The big fish began to come nearer and also he began to get mad. Here I forgot the pain in my hands. I grew enthusiastic. And foolishly I bragged. Then I lifted so hard that I cracked the great Conroy rod.

Dan threw up his hands. He quit, same as he quit the first day out, when I hooked the broadbill and the reel froze.

"Disqualified fish, even if you ketch him—which you won't," he said, dejectedly.

"Crack goes thirty-five dollars!" exclaimed my brother. "Sure is funny, brother, how you can decimate good money into the general atmosphere!"

If there really is anything fine in the fighting of a big fish, which theory I have begun to doubt, certainly Captain Dan and Brother R. C. did not know it.

Remarks were forthcoming from me, I am ashamed to state, that should not have been. Then I got Dan to tie splints on the rod, after which I fought my quarry some more. The splints broke. Dan had to bind the cracked rod with heavy pieces of wood and they added considerable weight to what had before felt like a ton.

The fish had been hooked at eleven o'clock and it was now five. We had drifted or been pulled into the main channel, where strong currents and a choppy sea made the matter a pretty serious and uncomfortable one. Here I expended all I had left in a short and furious struggle to bring the fish up, if not to gaff, at least so we could see what he looked like. How strange and unfathomable a feeling this mystery of him gave rise to! If I could only see him once, then he could get away and welcome. Captain Dan, in anticipation of a need of much elbow room in that cockpit, ordered my brother and the ladies to go into the cabin or up on top. And they all scrambled up and lay flat on the deck-roof, with their heads over, watching me. They had to hold on some, too. In fact, they were having the time of their lives.

My supreme effort brought the fish within the hundredth foot length of line—then my hands and my back refused any more.

"Dan, here's the great chance you've always hankered for!" I said. "Now let's see you pull him right in!"

And I passed him the rod and got up. Dan took it with the pleased expression of a child suddenly and wonderfully come into possession of a long-unattainable toy. Captain Dan was going to pull that fish right up to the boat. He was! Now Dan is big—he weighs two hundred; he has arms and hands like the limbs of a Vulcan. Perhaps Dan had every reason to believe he would pull the fish right up to the boat. But somehow I knew that he would not.

My fish, perhaps feeling a new and different and mightier hand at the rod, showed how he liked it by a magnificent rush—the greatest of the whole fight—and he took about five hundred feet of line.

Dan's expression changed as if by magic.

"Steer the boat! Port! Port!" he yelled.

Probably I could not run a boat right with perfectly fresh and well hands, and with my lacerated and stinging ones I surely made a mess of it. This brought language from my boatman—well, to say the least, quite disrespectable. Fortunately, however, I got the boat around and we ran down on the fish. Dan, working with long, powerful sweeps of the rod, got the line back and the fish close. The game began to look great to me. All along I had guessed this fish to be a wonder; and now I knew it.

Hauling him close that way angered him. He made another rush, long and savage. The line smoked off that reel. Dan's expression was one of utmost gratification to me. A boatman at last cornered—tied up to a whale of a fish!

Somewhere out there a couple of hundred yards the big fish came up and roared on the surface. I saw only circling wake and waves like those behind a speedy motor-boat. But Dan let out a strange shout, and up above the girls screamed, and brother Rome yelled murder or something. I gathered that he had a camera.

"Steady up there!" I called out. "If you fall overboard it's good night!... For we want this fish!"

I had all I could do. Dan would order me to steer this way and that—to throw out the clutch—to throw it in. Still I was able to keep track of events. This fish made nineteen rushes in the succeeding half-hour. Never for an instant did Captain Dan let up. Assuredly during that time he spent more force on the fish than I had in six hours.

The sea was bad, the boat was rolling, the cockpit was inches deep under water many a time. I was hard put to it to stay at my post; and what saved the watchers above could not be explained by me.

"Mebbe I can hold him now—a little," called Dan once, as he got the hundred-foot mark over the reel. "Strap the harness on me!"

I fastened the straps round Dan's broad shoulders. His shirt was as wet as if he had fallen overboard. Maybe some of that wet was spray. His face was purple, his big arms bulging, and he whistled as he breathed.

"Good-by, Dan. This will be a fitting end for a boatman," I said, cheerfully, as I dove back to the wheel.

At six o'clock our fish was going strong and Dan was tiring fast. He had, of course, worked too desperately hard.

Meanwhile the sun sank and the sea went down. All the west was gold and red, with the towers of Church Rock spiring the horizon. A flock of gulls were circling low, perhaps over a school of tuna. The white cottages of Avalon looked mere specks on the dark island.

Captain Dan had the swordfish within a hundred feet of the boat and was able to hold him. This seemed hopeful. It looked now just a matter of a little more time. But Dan needed a rest.

I suggested that my brother come down and take a hand in the final round, which I frankly confessed was liable to be hell.

"Not on your life!" was the prompt reply. "I want to begin on a little swordfish!... Why, that—that fish hasn't waked up yet!"

And I was bound to confess there seemed to me to be a good deal of sense in what he said.

"Dan, I'll take the rod—rest you a bit—so you can finish him," I offered.

The half-hour Dan recorded as my further work on this fish will always be a dark and poignant blank in my fishing experience. When it was over twilight had come and the fish was rolling and circling perhaps fifty yards from the boat.

Here Dan took the rod again, and with the harness on and fresh gloves went at the fish in grim determination.

Suddenly the moon sailed out from behind a fog-bank and the sea was transformed. It was as beautiful as it was lucky for us.

By Herculean effort Dan brought the swordfish close. If any angler doubts the strength of a twenty-four thread line his experience is still young. That line was a rope, yet it sang like a banjo string.

Leaning over the side, with two pairs of gloves on, I caught the double line, and as I pulled and Dan reeled the fish came up nearer. But I could not see him. Then I reached the leader and held on as for dear life.

"I've got the leader!" I yelled. "Hurry, Dan!"

Dan dropped the rod and reached for his gaff. But he had neglected to unhook the rod from the harness, and as the fish lunged and tore the leader away from me there came near to being disaster. However,

Dan got straightened out and anchored in the chair and began to haul away again. It appeared we had the fish almost done, but he was so big that a mere movement of his tail irresistibly drew out the line.

Then the tip of the rod broke off short just even with the splints and it slid down the line out of sight. Dan lowered the rod so most of the strain would come on the reel, and now he held like grim death.

"Dan, if we don't make any more mistakes we'll get that fish!" I declared.

The sea was almost calm now, and moon-blanched so that we could plainly see the line. Despite Dan's efforts, the swordfish slowly ran off a hundred feet more of line. Dan groaned. But I yelled with sheer exultation. For, standing up on the gunwale, I saw the swordfish. He had come up. He was phosphorescent—a long gleam of silver—and he rolled in the unmistakable manner of a fish nearly beaten.

Suddenly he headed for the boat. It was a strange motion. I was surprised—then frightened. Dan reeled in rapidly. The streak of white gleamed closer and closer. It was like white fire—a long, savage, pointed shape.

"Look! Look!" I yelled to those above. "Don't miss it!... Oh, great!"

"He's charging the boat!" hoarsely shouted Dan.

"He's all in!" yelled my brother.

I jumped into the cockpit and leaned over the gunwale beside the rod. Then I grasped the line, letting it slip through my hands. Dan wound in with fierce energy. I felt the end of the double line go by me, and at this I let out another shout to warn Dan. Then I had the end of the leader—a good strong grip—and, looking down, I saw the clear silver outline of the hugest fish I had ever seen short of shark or whale. He made a beautiful, wild, frightful sight. He rolled on his back. Roundbill or broadbill, he had an enormous length of sword.

"Come, Dan—we've got him!" I panted.

Dan could not, dare not get up then.

The situation was perilous. I saw how Dan clutched the reel, with his big thumbs biting into the line. I did my best. My sight failed me for an instant. But the fish pulled the leader through my hands. My brother leaped down to help—alas, too late!

"Let go, Dan! Give him line!"

But Dan was past that. Afterward he said his grip was locked. He held, and not another foot did the swordfish get. Again I leaned over the gunwale. I saw him—a monster—pale, wavering. His tail had an enormous spread. I could no longer see his sword. Almost he was ready to give up.

Then the double line snapped. I fell back in the boat and Dan fell back in the chair.

Nine hours!

CHAPTER V

SAILFISH—THE ATLANTIC BROTHER TO THE PACIFIC SWORDFISH

In the winter of 1916 I persuaded Captain Sam Johnson, otherwise famous as Horse-mackerel Sam, of Seabright, New Jersey, to go to Long Key with me and see if the two of us as a team could not outwit those illusive and strange sailfish of the Gulf Stream.

Sam and I have had many adventures going down to sea. At Seabright we used to launch a Seabright skiff in the gray gloom of early morning and shoot the surf, and return shoreward in the afternoon to ride a great swell clear till it broke on the sand. When I think of Sam I think of tuna—those torpedoes of the ocean. I have caught many tuna with Sam, and hooked big ones, but these giants are still roving the blue deeps. Once I hooked a tuna off Sandy Hook, out in the channel, and as I was playing him the Lusitania bore down the channel. Like a mountain she loomed over us. I felt like an atom looking up and up. Passengers waved down to us as the tuna bent my rod. The great ship passed on in a seething roar—passed on to her tragic fate. We rode the heavy swells she lifted—and my tuna got away.

Sam Johnson is from Norway. His ancestors lived by fishing. Sam knows and loves the sea. He has been a sailor before the mast, but he is more fisherman than sailor. He is a stalwart man, with an iron, stern, weather-beaten face and keen blue eyes, and he has an arm like the branch of an oak. For many years he has been a market fisherman at Seabright, where on off days he pursued the horse-mackerel for the fun of it, and which earned him his name. Better than any man I ever met Sam knows the sea; he knows fish, he knows boats and engines. And I have reached a time in my experience of fishing where I want that kind of a boatman.

Sam and I went after sailfish at Long Key and we got them. But I do not consider the experience conclusive. If it had not been for my hard-earned knowledge of the Pacific swordfish, and for Sam's keenness on the sea, we would not have been so fortunate. We established the record, but, what is more important, we showed what magnificent sport is possible. This advent added much to the attractiveness of Long Key for me. And Long Key was attractive enough before.

Sailfish had been caught occasionally at Long Key, during every season. But I am inclined to believe that, in most instances, the capture of sailfish had been accident—mere fisherman's luck. Anglers have fished along the reef and inside, trolling with heavy tackle for anything that might strike, and once in a while a sailfish has somehow hooked himself. Mr. Schutt tells of hooking one on a Wilson spoon, and I know of another angler who had this happen. I know of one gentleman who told me he hooked a fish that he supposed was a barracuda, and while he was fighting this supposed barracuda he was interested in the leaping of a sailfish near his boat. His boatman importuned him to hurry in the barracuda so there would be a chance to go after the leaping sailfish. But it turned out that the sailfish was on his hook. Another angler went out with heavy rod, the great B-Ocean reel, and two big hooks (which is an outfit suitable only for large tuna or swordfish), and this fellow hooked a sailfish which had no chance and was dead in less than ten minutes. A party of anglers were out on the reef, fishing for anything, and they decided to take a turn outside where I had been spending days after sailfish. Scarcely had these men left the reef when five sailfish loomed up and all of them, with that perversity and capriciousness which makes fish so incomprehensible, tried to climb on board the boat. One, a heavy fish, did succeed in hooking himself and getting aboard. I could multiply events of this nature, but this is enough to illustrate my point—that there is a vast difference between several fishermen out of thousands bringing in several sailfish in one season and one fisherman deliberately going after sailfish with light tackle and eventually getting them.

It is not easy. On the contrary, it is extremely hard. It takes infinite patience, and very much has to be learned that can be learned only by experience. But it is magnificent sport and worth any effort. It makes tarpon-fishing tame by comparison. Tarpon-fishing is easy. Anybody can catch a tarpon by going after him. But not every fisherman can catch a sailfish. One fisherman out of a hundred will get his sailfish, but only one out of a thousand will experience the wonder and thrill and beauty of the sport.

Sailfishing is really swordfishing, and herein lies the secret of my success at Long Key. I am not satisfied that the sailfish I caught were all Marlin and brothers to the Pacific Marlin. The Atlantic fish are very much smaller than those of the Pacific, and are differently marked and built. Yet they are near enough alike to be brothers.

There are three species that I know of in southern waters. The Histiophorus, the sailfish about which I am writing and of which descriptions follow. There is another species, Tetrapturus albidus, that is not uncommon in the Gulf Stream. It is my impression that this species is larger. The Indians, with whom I fished in the Caribbean, tell of a great swordfish—in Spanish the Aguja de casta, and this species must be related to Xiphias, the magnificent flatbilled swordfish of the Atlantic and Pacific.

The morning of my greatest day with sailfish I was out in the Gulf Stream, seven miles offshore, before the other fishermen had gotten out of bed. We saw the sun rise ruddy and bright out of the eastern sea, and we saw sailfish leap as if to welcome the rising of the lord of day. A dark, glancing ripple wavered over the water; there was just enough swell to make seeing fish easy.

I was using a rod that weighed nine ounces over all, and twelve hundred feet of fifteen-thread line. I was not satisfied then that the regular light outfit of the Tuna Club, such as I used at Avalon, would do for sailfish. No. 9 breaks of its own weight. And I have had a sailfish run off three hundred yards of line and jump all the time he was doing it. Besides, nobody knows how large these sailfish grow. I had hold of one that would certainly have broken my line if he had not thrown the hook.

On this memorable day I had scarcely trolled half a mile out into the Stream before I felt that inexplicable rap at my bait which swordfish and sailfish make with their bills. I jumped up and got ready. I saw a long bronze shape back of my bait. Then I saw and felt him take hold. He certainly did not encounter the slightest resistance in running out my line. He swam off slowly. I never had Sam throw out the clutch and stop the boat until after I had hooked the fish. I wanted the boat to keep moving, so if I did get a chance to strike at a fish it would be with a tight line. These sailfish are wary and this procedure is difficult. If the fish had run off swiftly I would have struck sooner. Everything depends on how he takes the bait. This fellow took fifty feet of line before I hooked him.

He came up at once, and with two-thirds of his body out of the water he began to skitter toward us. He looked silver and bronze in the morning light. There was excitement on board. Sam threw out the clutch. My companions dove for the cameras, and we all yelled. The sailfish came skittering toward us. It was a spectacular and thrilling sight. He was not powerful enough to rise clear on his tail and do the famous trick of the Pacific swordfish—"walking on the water." But he gave a mighty good imitation. Then before the cameras got in a snap he went down. And he ran, to come up far astern and begin to leap. I threw off the drag and yelled, "Go!"

This was pleasant for Sam, who kept repeating, "Look at him yump!"

The sailfish evidently wanted to pose for pictures, for he gave a wonderful exhibition of high and lofty tumbling, with the result, of course, that he quickly exhausted himself. Then came a short period during which he sounded and I slowly worked him closer. Presently he swam toward the boat—the old swordfish trick. I never liked it, but with the sailfish at least was not nervous about him attacking the boat. Let me add here that this freedom from dread—which is never absent during the fighting of a big swordfish—is one of the features so attractive in sailfishing. Besides, fish that have been hooked for any length of time, if they are going to shake or break loose, always do so near the boat. We moved away from this fellow, and presently he came up again, and leaped three more times clear, making nineteen leaps in all. That about finished his performance, so regretfully I led him alongside; and Sam, who had profited by our other days of landing sailfish, took him cautiously by the sword, and then by the gills, and slid him into the boat.

Sailfish are never alike, except in general outline. This one was silver and bronze, with green bars, rather faint, and a dark-blue sail without any spots. He measured seven feet one inch. But we measured his quality by his leaps and nineteen gave him the record for us so far.

We stowed him up in the bow and got under way again, and scarcely had I let my bait far enough astern when a sailfish hit it. In fact, he rushed it. Quick as I was, which was as quick as a flash, I was not quick enough for that fish. He felt the hook and he went away. But he had been there long enough to get my bait.

Just then Sam pointed. I saw a sailfish break water a hundred yards away.

"Look at him yump!" repeated Sam, every time the fish came out, which, to be exact, was five times.

"We'll go over and pick him up," I said.

Sam and I always argue a little about the exact spot where a fish has broken water. I never missed it far, but Sam seldom missed it at all. He could tell by a slight foam always left by the break. We had two baits out, as one or another of my companions always holds a rod. The more baits out the better! We had two vicious, smashing strikes at the same time. The fish on the other rod let go just as I hooked mine.

He came up beautifully, throwing the spray, glinting in the sun, an angry fish with sail spread and his fins going. Then on the boat was the same old thrilling bustle and excitement and hilarity I knew so well and which always pleased me so much. This sailfish was a jumper.

"Look at him yump!" exclaimed Sam, with as much glee as if he had not seen it before.

The cameras got busy. Then I was attracted by something flashing in the water nearer the boat than my fish. Suddenly a sailfish leaped, straightaway, over my line. Then two leaped at once, both directly over my line.

"Sam, they'll cut my line!" I cried. "What do you think of that?"

Suddenly I saw sharp, dark, curved tails cutting the water. All was excitement on board that boat then.

"A school of sailfish! Look! Look!" I yelled.

I counted ten tails, but there were more than that, and if I had been quicker I could have counted more. Presently they went down. And I, returning to earth and the business of fishing, discovered that during the excitement my sailfish had taken advantage of a perfectly loose line to free himself. Nine leaps we recorded him!

Assuredly we all felt that there would be no difficulty in soon hooking up with another sailfish. And precisely three minutes later I was standing up, leaning forward, all aquiver, watching my line fly off the reel. I hooked that fellow hard. He was heavy, and he did not come up or take off any length of line. Settling down slowly, he descended three or four hundred feet, or so it seemed, and began to plug, very much like an albacore, only much heavier. He fooled around down there for ten minutes, with me jerking at him all the time to irritate him, before he showed any sign of rising. At last I worried him into a fighting mood, and up he came, so fast that I did not even try to take up the slack, and he shot straight up. This jump, like that of a kingfish, was wonderful. But it was so quick that the cameras could not cover it, and we missed a great picture. He went down, only to leap again. I reeled in the slack line and began to jerk at him to torment him, and I got him to jumping and threshing right near the boat. The sun was in the faces of the cameras and that was bad. And as it turned out not one of these exposures was good. What a chance missed! But we did not know that then, and we kept on tormenting him and snapping pictures of his leaps. In this way, which was not careless, but deliberate, I played with him until he shook out the hook. Fifteen leaps was his record.

Then it was interesting to see how soon I could raise another fish. I was on the qui vive for a while, then settled back to the old expectant watchfulness. And presently I was rewarded by that vibrating rap at my bait. I stood up so the better to see. The swells were just right and the sun was over my shoulder. I spied the long, dark shape back of my bait, saw it slide up and strike, felt the sharp rap—and again. Then came the gentle tug. I let out line, but he let go. Still I could see him plainly when the swell was right. I began to jerk my bait, to give it a jumping motion, as I had so often done with flying-fish bait when after swordfish. He sheered off, then turned with a rush, broadside on, with his sail up. I saw him clearly, his whole length, and he appeared blue and green and silver. He took the bait and turned away from me, and when I struck the hook into his jaw I felt that it would stay. He was not a jumper—only breaking clear twice. I could not make him leap. He fought hard enough, however, and with that tackle took thirty minutes to land.

It was eight o'clock. I had two sailfish in the boat and had fought two besides. And at that time I sighted the first fishing-boat coming out toward the reef. Before that boat got out near us I had struck and lost three more sailfish, with eleven leaps in all to my credit. This boatman had followed Sam and me the day before and he appeared to be bent upon repeating himself. I thought I would rather enjoy that, because he had two inexperienced anglers aboard, and they, in the midst of a school of striking sailfish, would be sure to afford some fun. Three other boats came out across the reef, ventured a little way in the Gulf Stream, and then went back to grouper and barracuda. But that one boatman, B., stuck to us. And right away things began to happen to his anglers. No one so lucky in strikes as a green hand! I saw them get nine strikes without hooking a fish. And there appeared to be a turmoil on board that boat. I saw B. tearing his hair and the fishermen frantically jerking, and then waving rods and arms. Much as I enjoyed it, Sam enjoyed it more. But I was not mean enough to begrudge them a fish and believed that sooner or later they would catch one.

Presently, when B.'s boat was just right for his anglers to see everything my way, I felt a tug on my line. I leaped up, let the reel run. Then I threw on my drag and leaned over to strike. But he let go. Quickly I threw off the drag. The sailfish came back. Another tug! I let him run. Then threw on the drag and got ready. But, no, he let go. Again I threw off the drag and again he came back. He was hungry, but he was cunning, too, and too far back for me to see. I let him run fifty feet, threw on the drag, and struck hard. No go! I missed him. But again I threw off the drag, let out more line back to him, and he took the bait the fourth time, and harder than ever. I let him run perhaps a hundred feet. All the time, of course, my boat was running. I had out a long line—two hundred yards. Then I threw on the drag and almost cracked the rod. This time I actually felt the hook go in.

How heavy and fast he was! The line slipped off and I was afraid of the drag. I threw it off—no easy matter with that weight on it—and then the line whistled. The sailfish was running straight toward B.'s boat and, I calculated, should be close to it.

"Sam," I yelled, "watch him! If he jumps he'll jump into that boat!"

Then he came out, the biggest sailfish I ever saw, and he leaped magnificently, not twenty yards back of that boat. He must have been beyond the lines of the trolling anglers. I expected him to cross them or cut himself loose. We yelled to B. to steer off, and while we yelled the big sailfish leaped and leaped, apparently keeping just as close to the boat. He certainly was right upon it and he was a savage leaper. He would shoot up, wag his head, his sail spread like the ears of a mad elephant, and he would turn clear over to alight with a smack and splash that we plainly heard. And he had out nine hundred feet of line. Because of his size I wanted him badly, but, badly as that was, I fought him without a drag, let him run and leap, and I hoped he would jump right into that boat. Afterward these anglers told me they expected him to do just that and were scared to death. Also they said a close sight of him leaping was beautiful and thrilling in the extreme.

I did not keep track of all this sailfish's leaps, but Sam recorded twenty-three, and that is enough for any fisherman. I venture to state that it will not be beaten very soon. When he stopped leaping we drew him away from the other boat, and settled down to a hard fight with a heavy, stubborn, game fish. In perhaps half an hour I had him twenty yards away, and there he stayed while I stood up on the stern to watch him and keep clear of the propeller. He weaved from side to side, exactly like a tired swordfish, and every now and then he would stick out his bill and swish! he would cut at the leader. This fish was not only much larger than any I had seen, but also more brilliantly colored. There were suggestions of purple that reminded me of the swordfish—that royal purple game of the Pacific. Another striking feature was that in certain lights he was a vivid green, and again, when deeper, he assumed a strange, triangular shape, much like that of a kite. That, of course, was when he extended the wide, waving sail. I was not able to see that this sail afforded him any particular aid. It took me an hour to tire out this sailfish, and when we got him in the boat he measured seven feet and six inches, which was four inches longer than any record I could find then.

At eleven o'clock I had another in the boat, making four sailfish in all. We got fourteen jumps out of this last one. That was the end of my remarkable luck, though it was luck to me to hook other sailfish during the afternoon, and running up the number of leaps. I am proud of that, anyway, and to those who criticized my catch as unsportsman-like I could only say that it was a chance of a lifetime and I was after photographs of leaping sailfish. Besides, I had a great opportunity to beat my record of four swordfish in one day at Clemente Island in the Pacific. But I was not equal to it.

I do not know how to catch sailfish yet, though I have caught a good many. The sport is young and it is as difficult as it is trying. This catch of mine made fishermen flock to the Stream all the rest of the season, and more fish were caught than formerly. But the proportion held about the same, although I consider that fishing for a sailfish and catching one is a great gain in point. Still, we do not know much about sailfish or how to take them. If I got twenty strikes and caught only four fish, very likely the smallest that bit, I most assuredly was not doing skilful fishing as compared with other kinds of fishing. And there is the rub. Sailfish are not any other kind of fish. They have a wary and cunning habit, with an exceptional occasion of blind hunger, and they have small, bony jaws into which it is hard to sink a hook. Not one of my sailfish was hooked deep down. Yet I let nearly all of them run out a long line. Moreover, as I said before, if a sailfish is hooked there are ten chances to one that he will free himself.

This one thing, then, I believe I have proved to myself—that the sailfish is the gamest, the most beautiful and spectacular, and the hardest fish to catch on light tackle, just as his brother, the Pacific swordfish, is the grandest fish to take on the heaviest of tackle.

Long Key, indeed, has its charm. Most all the anglers who visit there go back again. Only the queer ones—and there are many—who want three kinds of boats, and nine kinds of bait, and a deep-sea diver for a boatman, and tackle that cannot be broken, and smooth, calm seas always, and five hundred pounds of fish a day—only that kind complain of Long Key and kick—and yet go back again!

Sailfish will draw more and finer anglers down to the white strip of color that shines white all day under a white sun and the same all night under white stars. But it is not alone the fish that draws real sportsmen to a place and makes them love it and profit by their return. It is the spirit of the place—the mystery, like that of the little hermit-crab, which crawls over the coral sand in his stolen shell, and keeps to his lonely course, and loves his life so well—sunshine, which is best of all for men; and the wind in the waving palms; and the lonely, wandering coast with the eternal moan out on the reefs, the sweet, fresh tang, the clear, antiseptic breath of salt, and always by the glowing, hot, colorful day or by the soft dark night with its shadows and whisperings on the beach, that significant presence—the sense of something vaster than the heaving sea.

Light Tackle in the Gulf Stream

In view of the present controversy between light tackle and heavy tackle champions, I think it advisable for me to state more definitely my stand on the matter of light tackle before going on with a story about it.

There is a sharp line to be drawn between light tackle that is right and light tackle that is wrong. So few anglers ever seem to think of the case of the poor fish! In Borneo there is a species of lightning-bug that tourists carry around at night on spits, delighted with the novelty. But is that not rather hard on the lightning-bugs? As a matter of fact, if we are to develop as anglers who believe in conservation and sportsmanship, we must consider the fish—his right to life, and, especially if he must be killed, to do it without brutality.

Brutal it is to haul in a fish on tackle so heavy that he has no chance for his life; likewise it is brutal to hook a fish on tackle so light that, if he does not break it, he must be followed around and all over, chased by a motor-boat hour after hour, until he practically dies of exhaustion.

I have had many tarpon and many tuna taken off my hooks by sharks because I was using tackle too light. It never appeared an impossible feat to catch Marlin swordfish on a nine-thread line, nor sailfish on a six-thread line. But those lines are too light.

My business is to tell stories. If I can be so fortunate as to make them thrilling and pleasing, for the edification of thousands who have other business and therefore less leisure, then that is a splendid thing for me. It is a responsibility that I appreciate. But on the other hand I must tell the truth, I must show my own development, I must be of service to the many who have so much more time to read than fish. It is not enough to give pleasure merely; a writer should instruct. And if what I say above offends any fisherman, I am sorry, and I suggest that he read it twice.

What weight tackle to use is not such a hard problem to decide. All it takes is some experience. To quote Mr. Bates, "The principle is that the angler should subdue the fish by his skill with rod and line, and put his strength into the battle to end it, and not employ a worrying process to a frightened fish that does not know what it is fighting."

CHAPTER VI

GULF STREAM FISHING

Some years have passed since I advocated light tackle fishing at Long Key. In the early days of this famous resort most fishermen used hand lines or very heavy outfits. The difficulties of introducing a sportsman-like ideal have been manifold. A good rule of angling philosophy is not to interfere with any fisherman's peculiar ways of being happy, unless you want to be hated. It is not easy to influence a majority of men in the interests of conservation. Half of them do not know the conditions and are only out for a few days' or weeks' fun; the rest do not care. But the facts are that all food fish and game fish must be conserved. The waste has been enormous. If fishermen will only study the use of light tackle they will soon appreciate a finer sport, more fun and gratification, and a saving of fish.

Such expert and fine anglers as Crowninshield, Heilner, Cassiard, Lester, Conill, and others are all enthusiastic about light tackle and they preach the gospel of conservation.

But the boatmen of Long Key, with the exception of Jordon, are all against light tackle. I must say that James Jordon is to be congratulated and recommended. The trouble at Long Key is that new boatmen are hired each season, and, as they do not own their boats, all their interest centers in as big a catch as possible for each angler they take out, in the hope and expectation, of course, of a generous tip. Heavy tackle means a big catch and light tackle the reverse. And so tons of good food and game fish are brought in only to be thrown to the sharks. I mention this here to give it a wide publicity. It is criminal in these days and ought to be stopped.

The season of 1918 was a disappointment in regard to any great enthusiasm over the use of light tackle. We have tried to introduce principles of the Tuna Club of Avalon. President Coxe of the Pacific organization is doing much to revive the earlier ideals of Doctor Holder, founder of the famous club. This year at Long Key a number of prizes were offered by individual members. The contention was that the light tackle specified was too light. This is absolutely a mistake. I have proved that the regulation Tuna

Club nine-thread line and six-ounce tip are strong enough, if great care and skill be employed, to take the tricky, hard-jawed, wild-leaping sailfish.

And for bonefish, that rare fighter known to so few anglers, the three-six tackle—a three-ounce tip and six-thread line—is just the ideal rig to make the sport exceedingly difficult, fascinating, and thrilling. Old bonefishermen almost invariably use heavy tackle—stiff rods and twelve-or fifteen-thread lines. They have their arguments, and indeed these are hard nuts to crack. They claim three-six for the swift and powerful bonefish is simply absurd. No! I can prove otherwise. But that must be another story.

Some one must pioneer these sorely needed reforms. It may be a thankless task, but it is one that some of us are standing by. We need the help of brother anglers.

One morning in February there was a light breeze from the north and the day promised to be ideal. We ran out to the buoy and found the Gulf Stream a very dark blue, with a low ripple and a few white-caps here and there.

Above the spindle we began to see sailfish jumping everywhere. One leaped thirteen times, and another nineteen. Many of them came out sidewise, with a long, sliding plunge, which action at first I took to be that made by a feeding fish. After a while, however, and upon closer view, I changed my mind about this.

My method, upon seeing a fish jump, was to speed up the boat until we were in the vicinity where the fish had come up. Then we would slow down and begin trolling, with two baits out, one some forty or fifty feet back and the other considerably farther.

We covered several places where we had seen the sheetlike splashes; and at the third or fourth I felt the old electrifying tap at my bait. I leaped up and let my bait run back. The sailfish tapped again, then took hold so hard and ran off so swiftly that I jerked sooner than usual. I pulled the bait away from him. All this time the boat was running. Instead of winding in I let the bait run back. Suddenly the sailfish took it fiercely. I let him run a long way before I struck at him, and then I called to the boatman to throw out the clutch. When the boat is moving there is a better chance of a tight line while striking, and that is imperative if an angler expects to hook the majority of these illusive sailfish. I hooked this fellow, and he showed at once, a small fish, and began to leap toward the boat, making a big bag in the line. I completely lost the feel of his weight. When he went down, and with all that slack line, I thought he was gone. But presently the line tightened and he began to jump in another direction. He came out twice with his sail spread, a splendid, vivid picture; then he took to skittering, occasionally throwing himself clear, and he made some surface runs, splashing and threshing, and then made some clean greyhound-like leaps. In all he cleared the water eleven times before he settled down. After that it took me half an hour to land him. He was not hurt and we let him go.

Soon after we got going again we raised a school of four or more sailfish. And when a number rush for the baits it is always exciting. The first fish hit my bait and the second took R. C.'s. I saw both fish in action, and there is considerable difference between the hitting and the taking of a bait. R. C. jerked his bait away from his fish and I yelled for him to let it run back. He did so. A bronze and silver blaze and a boil on the water told me how hungry R. C.'s sailfish was. "Let him run with it!" I yelled. Then I attended to my own troubles. There was a fish rapping at my bait. I let out line, yard after yard, but he would not take hold, and, as R. C.'s line was sweeping over mine, I thought best to reel in.

"Hook him now!" I yelled.

I surely did shiver at the way my brother came up with that light tackle. But he hooked the sailfish, and nothing broke. Then came a big white splash on the surface, but no sign of the fish. R. C.'s line sagged down.

"Look out! Wind in! He's coming at us!" I called.

"He's off!" replied my brother.

That might well have been, but, as I expected, he was not. He broke water on a slack line and showed us all his dripping, colorful body nearer than a hundred feet. R. C. thereupon performed with incredible speed at the reel and quickly had a tight line. Mr. Sailfish did not like that. He slid out, wrathfully wagging his bill, and left a seamy, foamy track behind him, finally to end that play with a splendid long leap. He was headed away from us now, with two hundred yards of line out, going hard and fast, and we had to follow him. We had a fine straightaway run to recover the line. This was a thrilling chase, and one, I think, we never would have had if R. C. had been using heavy tackle. The sailfish led us out half a mile before he sounded.

Then in fifteen minutes more R. C. had him up where we could see his purple and bronze colors and the strange, triangular form of him, which peculiar shape came mostly from the waving sail. I thought I saw other shapes and colors with him, and bent over the gunwale to see better.

"He's got company. Two sharks!—You want to do some quick work now or good-by sailfish!"

A small gray shark and a huge yellow shark were coming up with our quarry. R. C. said things, and pulled hard on the light tackle. I got hold of the leader and drew the sailfish close to the boat. He began to thresh, and the big shark came with a rush. Instinctively I let go of the leader, which action was a blunder. The sailfish saw the shark and, waking up, he fought a good deal harder than before the sharks appeared upon the scene. He took off line, and got so far away that I gave up any hope that the sharks might not get him. There was a heavy commotion out in the water. The shark had made a rush. So had the sailfish, and he came right back to the boat. R. C. reeled in swiftly.

"Hold him hard now!" I admonished, and I leaped up on the stern. The sailfish sheered round on the surface, with tail and bill out, while the shark swam about five feet under him. He was a shovel-nosed, big-finned yellow shark, weighing about five hundred pounds. He saw me. I waved my hat at him, but he did not mind that. He swam up toward the surface and his prey. R. C. was now handling the light tackle pretty roughly. It is really remarkable what can be done with nine-thread. In another moment we would have lost the sailfish. The boatman brought my rifle and a shot scared the shark away. Then we got the sailfish into the boat. He was a beautiful specimen for mounting, weighing forty-five pounds, the first my brother had taken.

After that we had several strikes, but not one of them was what I could call a hungry, smashing strike. These sailfish are finicky biters. I had one rap at my bait with his bill until he knocked the bait off.

I think the feature of the day was the sight of two flying-fish that just missed boarding the boat. They came out to the left of us and sailed ahead together. Then they must have been turned by the wind, for they made a beautiful, graceful curve until they came around so that I was sure they would fly into the boat. Their motion was indescribably airy and feathery, buoyant and swift, with not the slightest quiver of fins or wings as they passed within five feet of me. I could see through the crystal wings. Their bodies were white and silvery, and they had staring black eyes. They were not so large as the California flying-fish, nor did they have any blue color. They resembled the California species, however, in that same strange, hunted look which always struck me. To see these flying-fish this way was provocative of thought. They had been pursued by some hungry devil of a fish, and with a birdlike swiftness with which nature had marvelously endowed them they had escaped the enemy. Here I had at once the wonder and beauty and terror of the sea. These fish were not leaping with joy. I have not often seen fish in the salt water perform antics for anything except flight or pursuit. Sometimes kingfish appear to be playing when they leap so wonderfully at sunset hour, but as a rule salt-water fish do not seem to be playful.

At Long Key the Gulf Stream is offshore five miles. The water shoals gradually anywhere from two feet near the beach to twenty feet five miles out on the reef. When there has been no wind for several days, which is a rare thing for Long Key, the water becomes crystal clear and the fish and marine creatures are an endless source of interest to the fisherman. Of course a large boat, in going out on the reef, must use the channel between the keys, but a small boat or canoe can go anywhere. It is remarkable how the great game fish come in from the Stream across the reef into shoal water. Barracuda come right up to the shore, and likewise the big sharks. The bottom is a clean, white, finely ribbed coral sand, with patches of brown seaweed here and there and golden spots, and in the shallower water different kinds of sponges. Out on the reef the water is a light green. The Gulf Stream runs along the outer edge of the reef, and here between Tennessee Buoy and Alligator Light, eighteen miles, is a feeding-ground for sailfish, kingfish, amberjack, barracuda, and other fishes. The ballyhoo is the main feed of these fishes, and it is indeed a queer little fish. He was made by nature, like the sardine and mullet and flying-fish, to serve as food for the larger fishes. The ballyhoo is about a foot long, slim and flat, shiny and white on the sides and dark green on the back, with a sharp-pointed, bright-yellow tail, the lower lobe of which is developed to twice the length of the upper. He has a very strange feature in the fact that his lower jaw resembles the bill of a snipe, being several inches long, sharp and pointed and hard; but he has no upper lip or beak at all. This half-bill must be used in relation to his food, but I do not have any idea how this is done.

One day I found the Gulf Stream a mile off Tennessee Buoy, whereas on other days it would be close in. On this particular day the water was a dark, clear, indigo blue and appreciably warmer than the surrounding sea. This Stream has a current of several miles an hour, flowing up the coast. Everywhere we saw the Portuguese men-of-war shining on the waves. There was a slight, cool breeze blowing, rippling the water just enough to make fishing favorable. I saw a big loggerhead turtle, weighing about three hundred pounds, coming around on the surface among these Portuguese men-of-war, and as we ran up I saw that he was feeding on these queer balloon-like little creatures. Sometimes he would come up under one and it would stick on his back, and he would turn laboriously around from under it, and submerge his back so he had it floating again. Then he would open his cavernous mouth and take it in. Considering the stinging poison these Portuguese men-of-war secrete about them, the turtle must have had a very tabasco-sauce meal. Right away I began to see evidence of fish on the surface, which is always a good sign. We went past a school of bonita breaking the water up into little swirls. Then I saw a smashing break of a sailfish coming out sideways, sending the water in white sheets. We slowed down the boat and got our baits overboard at once. I was using a ballyhoo bait hooked by a small hook through the lips, with a second and larger hook buried in the body. R. C. was using a strip of mullet, which for obvious reasons seems to be the preferred bait from Palm Beach to Long Key. And the obvious reason is that nobody seems to take the trouble to get what might be proper bait for sailfish. Mullet is an easy bait to get and commands just as high a price as anything else, which, as a matter of fact, is highway robbery. With a bait like a ballyhoo or a shiner I could get ten bites to one with mullet.

We trolled along at slow speed. The air was cool, the sun pleasant, the sea beautiful, and this was the time to sit back and enjoy a sense of freedom and great space of the ocean, and watch for leaping fish or whatever might attract the eye.

Here and there we passed a strange jellyfish, the like of which I had never before seen. It was about as large as a good-sized cantaloup, and pale, clear yellow all over one end and down through the middle, and then commenced a dark red fringe which had a waving motion. Inside this fringe was a scalloped circular appendage that had a sucking motion, which must have propelled it through the water, and it made quite fair progress. Around every one of these strange jellyfish was a little school of tiny minnows, as clear-colored as crystals. These all swam on in the same direction as the drift of the Gulf Stream.

When we are fishing for sailfish everything that strikes we take to be a sailfish until we find out it is something else. They are inconsistent and queer fish. Sometimes they will rush a bait, at other times they will tug at it and then chew at it, and then they will tap it with their bills. I think I have demonstrated that they are about the hardest fish to hook that swims, and also on light tackle they are one of the gamest and most thrilling. However, not one in a hundred fishermen who come to Long Key will go after them with light tackle. And likewise not one out of twenty-five sailfish brought in there is caught by a fisherman who deliberately went out after sailfish. Mostly they are caught by accident while drags are set for kingfish or barracuda. At Palm Beach I believe they fish for them quite persistently, with a great deal of success. But it is more a method of still fishing which has no charms for me.

Presently my boatman yelled, "Sailfish!" We looked off to port and saw a big sailfish break water nine times. He was perhaps five hundred yards distant. My boatman put on speed, and, as my boat is fast, it did not take us long to get somewhere near where this big fish broke. We did our best to get to the exact spot where he came up, then slowed down and trolled over the place. In this instance I felt a light tap on my bait and I jumped up quickly, both to look and let him take line. But I did not see him or feel him any more. We went on. I saw a flash of bright silver back of my brother's bait. At the instant he hooked a kingfish. And then I felt one cut my bait off. Kingfish are savage strikers and they almost invariably hook themselves when the drag is set. But as I fish for sailfish with a free-running reel, of course I am exasperated when a kingfish takes hold. My brother pulled in this kingfish, which was small, and we rebaited our hooks and went on again. I saw more turtles, and one we almost ran over, he was so lazy in getting down. These big, cumbersome sea animals, once they get headed down and started, can disappear with remarkable rapidity. I rather enjoy watching them, but my boatman, who is a native of these parts and therefore a turtle-hunter by instinct, always wore a rather disappointed look when we saw one. This was because I would not allow him to harpoon it.

The absence of gulls along this stretch of reef is a feature that struck me. So that once in a while when I did see a lonely white gull I watched him with pleasure. And once I saw a cero mackerel jump way in along the reef, and even at a mile's distance I could see the wonderful curve he made.

The wind freshened, and all at once it seemed leaping sailfish were all around us. Then as we turned the boat this way and that we had thrills of anticipation. Suddenly R. C. had a strike. The fish took the bait hungrily and sheered off like an arrow and took line rapidly. When R. C. hooked him he came up with a big splash and shook himself to free the hook. He jumped here and there and then went down deep. And then he took a good deal of line off the reel. I was surprised to see a sailfish stick his bill out of the water very much closer to the boat than where R. C.'s fish should have been. I had no idea then that this was a fish other than the one R. C. had hooked. But when he cut the line either with his bill or his tail, and R. C. wound it in, we very soon discovered that it was not the fish that he had hooked. This is one of the handicaps of light tackle.

We went on fishing. Sailfish would jump around us for a while and then they would stop. We would not see one for several minutes. It is always very exciting to be among them this way. Presently I had one take hold to run off slowly and steadily, and I let him go for fifty feet, and when I struck I tore the hook away from him. Quickly I let slack line run back to him ten or fifteen feet at a time, until I felt him take it once more. He took it rather suspiciously, I felt, and I honestly believe that I could tell that he was mouthing or chewing the bait, which made me careful to let the line run off easily to him. Suddenly he rushed off, making the reel smoke. I let him run one hundred and fifty feet and then stood up, throwing on the drag, and when the line straightened tight I tried to jerk at him as hard as the tackle would stand. As a matter of fact, however, he was going so fast and hard that he hooked himself. It is indeed seldom that I miss one when he runs like this. This fellow came up two hundred yards from the boat and slid along the water with half of his body raised, much like one of those coasting-boards I have seen bathers use, towed behind a motor-launch. He went down and came up in a magnificent sheer leap, with his broad sail shining in the sun. Very angry he was, and he reminded me of a Marlin swordfish. Next he went down, and came up again bent in a curve, with the big sail stretched again. He skittered over the water, going down and coming up, until he had leaped seven times. This was a big, heavy fish, and on the light six-ounce tip and nine-thread line I had my work cut out for me. We had to run the boat toward him so I could get back my line. Here was the advantage of having a fast boat with a big rudder. Otherwise I would have lost my fish. After some steady deep plugging he came up again and set my heart aflutter by a long surface play in which he took off one hundred yards of line and then turned, leaping straight for the boat. Fortunately the line was slack and I could throw off the drag and let him run. Slack line never bothers me when I really get one of these fish well hooked. If he is not well hooked he is going to get away, anyhow. After that he went down into deep water and I had one long hour of hard work in bringing him to the boat. Six hours later he weighed fifty-eight and a half pounds, and as he had lost a good deal of blood and dried out considerably, he would have gone over sixty pounds, which, so far, is the largest sailfish I know of caught on light tackle.

The sailfish were still leaping around us and we started off again. The captain called our attention to a tail and a sail a few yards apart not far from the boat. We circled around them to drive them down. I saw a big wave back of R. C.'s bait and I yelled, "Look out!" I felt something hit my bait and then hit it again. I knew it was a sailfish rapping at it. I let the line slip off the reel. Just then R. C. had a vicious strike and when he hooked the fish the line snapped. He claimed that he had jerked too hard. This is the difficulty with light tackle—to strike hard, yet not break anything. I was standing up and leaning forward, letting my line slip off the reel, trying to coax that sailfish to come back. Something took hold and almost jerked the rod out of my hands. That was a magnificent strike, and of course I thought it was one of the sailfish. But when I hooked him I had my doubts. The weight was heavy and ponderous and tugging. He went down and down and down. The boatman said amberjack. I was afraid so, but I still had my hopes. For a while I could not budge him, and at last, when I had given up hope that it was a sailfish, I worked a good deal harder than I would have otherwise. It took me twenty-five minutes to subdue a forty-pound amberjack. Here was proof of what could be done with light tackle.

About ten-thirty of this most delightful and favorable day we ran into a school of barracuda. R. C. hooked a small one, which was instantly set upon by its voracious comrades and torn to pieces. Then I had a tremendous strike, hard, swift, long—everything to make a tingle of nerve and blood. The instant I struck, up out of a flying splash rose a long, sharp, silver-flashing tiger of the sea, and if he leaped an inch he leaped forty feet. On that light tackle he was a revelation. Five times more he leaped, straight up, very high, gills agape, jaws wide, body curved—a sight for any angler. He made long runs and short runs and all kinds of runs, and for half an hour he defied any strain I dared put on him. Eventually I captured him, and I considered him superior to a tarpon of equal or even more weight.

Barracuda are a despised fish, apparently because of their voracious and murderous nature. But I incline to the belief that it is because the invariable use of heavy tackle has blinded the fishermen to the wonderful leaping and fighting qualities of this long-nosed, long-toothed sea-tiger. The few of us who have hooked barracuda on light tackle know him as a marvelous performer. Van Campen Heilner wrote about a barracuda he caught on a bass rod, and he is not likely to forget it, nor will the reader of his story forget it.

R. C. had another strike, hooked his fish, and brought it in readily. It was a bonita of about five pounds, the first one my brother had ever caught. We were admiring his beautiful, subdued colors as he swam near the boat, when up out of the blue depths shot a long gray form as swift as lightning. It was a big barracuda. In his rush he cut that bonita in two. The captain grasped the line and yelled for us to get the gaffs. R. C. dropped the rod and got the small gaff, and as I went for the big one I heard them both yell. Then I bent over to see half a dozen big gray streaks rush for what was left of that poor little bonita. The big barracuda with incredible speed and unbelievable ferocity rushed right to the side of the boat at the bonita. He got hold of it and R. C. in striking at him to gaff him hit him over the head several times. Then the gaff hook caught him and R. C. began to lift. The barracuda looked to me to be fully seven feet long and half as big around as a telegraph pole. He made a tremendous splash in the water. R. C. was deluged. He and the boatman yelled in their excitement. But R. C. was unable to hold the big fish on this small gaff, and I got there too late. The barracuda broke loose. Then, equally incredibly, he turned with still greater ferocity and rushed the bonita again, but before he could get to it another and smaller barracuda had hold of it. At this instant I leaned over with a club. With one powerful sweep I hit one of the barracuda on the head. When I reached over again the largest one was contending with a smaller one for the remains of the bonita. I made a vicious pass at the big one, missing him. Quick as I was, before I could get back, the big fellow had taken the head of the bonita and rushed off with it, tearing the line out of the captain's hands. Then we looked at one another. It had all happened in a minute. We were all wringing wet and panting from excitement and exertion. This is a gruesome tale of the sea and I put it here only to illustrate the incomparable savageness of these tigers of the Gulf Stream.

The captain put the fish away and cleaned up the boat and we resumed fishing. I ate lunch holding the rod in one hand, loath to waste any time on this wonderful day. Sailfish were still jumping here and there and far away. The next thing to happen was that R. C. hooked a small kingfish, and at the same instant a big one came clear out in an unsuccessful effort to get my bait. This happened to be near the reef, and as we were going out I hooked a big grouper that tried out my small tackle for all it was worth. But I managed to keep him from getting on the bottom, and at length brought him in. The little six-ounce tip now looked like a buggy-whip that was old and worn out. After that nothing happened for quite a little spell. We had opportunity to get rested. Presently R. C. had a sailfish tap his bait and tap it again and tug at it and then take hold and start away. R. C. hooked him and did it carefully, trying not to put too much strain on the line. Here is where great skill is required. But the line broke. After that he took one of my other tackles. Something went wrong with the engine and the captain had to shut down and we drifted. I had a long line out and it gradually sank. Something took hold and I hooked it and found myself fast to a deep-sea, hard-fighting fish of some kind. I got him up eventually, and was surprised to see a great, broad, red-colored fish, which turned out to be a mutton-fish, much prized for food. I had now gotten six varieties of fish in the Gulf Stream and we were wondering what next. I was hoping it would be a dolphin or a waahoo. It happened, however, to be a beautiful cero mackerel, one of the shapeliest and most attractive fish in these waters. He is built something like the brook-trout, except for a much sharper head and wider fins and tail. But he is speckled very much after the manner of the trout. We trolled on, and all of a sudden raised a school of sailfish. They came up with a splashing rush very thrilling to see. One hit R. C.'s bait hard, and then another, by way of contrast, began to tug and chew at mine. I let the line out slowly. And as I did so I saw another one follow R. C.'s mutilated bait which he was bringing toward the boat. He was a big purple-and-bronze fellow and he would have taken a whole bait if it could have been gotten to him. But he sheered away, frightened by the boat. I failed to hook my fish. It was getting along pretty well into the afternoon by this time and the later it got the better the small fish and kingfish seemed to bite. I caught one barracuda and six kingfish, while R. C. was performing a somewhat similar feat. Then he got a smashing strike from a sailfish that went off on a hard, fast rush, so that he hooked it perfectly. He jumped nine times, several of which leaps I photographed. He was a good-sized fish and active and strong. R. C. had him up to the boat in thirty minutes, which was fine work for the light tackle. I made sure that the fish was as good as caught and I did not look to see where he was hooked. My boatman is not skilled in the handling of the fish when they are brought in. Few boatmen are. He took hold of the leader, and as he began to lift I saw that the hook was fast in the bill of the sailfish fully six inches from his mouth. At that instant the sailfish began to thresh. I yelled to the boatman to let go, but either I was not quick enough or he did not obey, for the hook snapped free and the sailfish slowly swam away, his great purple-and-blue spotted sail waving in the water, and his bronze sides shining. And we were both glad that he had gotten away, because we had had the fun out of him and had taken pictures of him jumping, and he was now alive and might make another fisherman sport some day.

CHAPTER VII

BONEFISH

In my experience as a fisherman the greatest pleasure has been the certainty of something new to learn, to feel, to anticipate, to thrill over. An old proverb tells us that if you wish to bring back the wealth of the Indias you must go out with its equivalent. Surely the longer a man fishes the wealthier he becomes in experience, in reminiscence, in love of nature, if he goes out with the harvest of a quiet eye, free from the plague of himself.

As a boy, fishing was a passion with me, but no more for the conquest of golden sunfish and speckled chubs and horny catfish than for the haunting sound of the waterfall and the color and loneliness of the cliffs. As a man, and a writer who is forever learning, fishing is still a passion, stronger with all the years, but tempered by an understanding of the nature of primitive man, hidden in all of us, and by a keen reluctance to deal pain to any creature. The sea and the river and the mountain have almost taught me not to kill except for the urgent needs of life; and the time will come when I shall have grown up to that. When I read a naturalist or a biologist I am always ashamed of what I have called a sport. Yet one of the truths of evolution is that not to practise strife, not to use violence, not to fish or hunt—that is to say, not to fight—is to retrograde as a natural man. Spiritual and intellectual growth is attained at the expense of the physical.

Always, then, when I am fishing I feel that the fish are incidental, and that the reward of effort and endurance, the incalculable and intangible knowledge emanate from the swelling and infinite sea or from the shaded and murmuring stream. Thus I assuage my conscience and justify the fun, the joy, the excitement, and the violence.

Five years ago I had never heard of a bonefish. The first man who ever spoke to me about this species said to me, very quietly with serious intentness: "Have you had any experience with bonefish?" I said no, and asked him what kind that was. His reply was enigmatical. "Well, don't go after bonefish unless you can give up all other fishing." I remember I laughed. But I never forgot that remark, and now it comes back to me clear in its significance. That fisherman read me as well as I misunderstood him.

Later that season I listened to talk of inexperienced bonefishermen telling what they had done and heard. To me it was absurd. So much fishing talk seems ridiculous, anyway. And the expert fishermen, wherever they were, received the expressive titles: "Bonefish Bugs and Bonefish Nuts!" Again I heard arguments about tackle rigged for these mysterious fish and these arguments fixed my vague impression. By and by some bonefishermen came to Long Key, and the first sight of a bonefish made me curious. I think it weighed five pounds—a fair-sized specimen. Even to my prejudiced eye that fish showed class. So I began to question the bonefishermen.

At once I found this type of angler to be remarkably reticent as to experience and method. Moreover, the tackle used was amazing to me. Stiff rods and heavy lines for little fish! I gathered another impression, and it was that bonefish were related to dynamite and chain lightning. Everybody who would listen to my questions had different things to say. No two men agreed on tackle or bait or ground or anything. I enlisted the interest of my brother R. C., and we decided, just to satisfy curiosity, to go out and catch some bonefish. The complacent, smug conceit of fishermen! I can see now how funny ours was. Fortunately it is now past tense. If I am ever conceited again I hope no one will read my stories.

My brother and I could not bring ourselves to try for bonefish with heavy tackle. It was preposterous. Three—four—five-pound fish! We had seen no larger. Bass tackle was certainly heavy enough for us. So in the innocence of our hearts and the assurance of our vanity we sallied forth to catch bonefish.

That was four years ago. Did we have good luck? No! Luck has nothing to do with bonefishing. What happened? For one solid month each winter of those four years we had devoted ourselves to bonefishing with light tackle. We stuck to our colors. The space of this whole volume would not be half enough to tell our experience—the amaze, the difficulty, the perseverance, the defeat, the wonder, and at last the achievement. The season of 1918 we hooked about fifty bonefish on three-six tackles—that is, three-ounce tips and six-thread lines—and we landed fourteen of them. I caught nine and R. C. caught five. R. C.'s eight-pound fish justified our contention and crowned our efforts.

To date, in all my experience, I consider this bonefish achievement the most thrilling, fascinating, difficult, and instructive. That is a broad statement and I hope I can prove it. I am prepared to state that I feel almost certain, if I spent another month bonefishing, I would become obsessed and perhaps lose my enthusiasm for other kinds of fish.

Why?

There is a multiplicity of reasons. My reasons range from the exceedingly graceful beauty of a bonefish to the fact that he is the best food fish I ever ate. That is a wide range. He is the wisest, shyest, wariest, strangest fish I ever studied; and I am not excepting the great Xiphias gladius—the broadbill swordfish. As for the speed of a bonefish, I claim no salmon, no barracuda, no other fish celebrated for swiftness of motion, is in his class. A bonefish is so incredibly fast that it was a long time before I could believe the evidence of my own eyes. You see him; he is there perfectly still in the clear, shallow water, a creature of fish shape, pale green and silver, but crystal-like, a phantom shape, staring at you with strange black eyes; then he is gone. Vanished! Absolutely without your seeing a movement, even a faint streak! By peering keenly you may discern a little swirl in the water. As for the strength of a bonefish, I actually hesitate to give my impressions. No one will ever believe how powerful a bonefish is until he has tried to stop the rush and heard the line snap. As for his cunning, it is utterly baffling. As for his biting, it is almost imperceptible. As for his tactics, they are beyond conjecture.

I want to append here a few passages from my note-books, in the hope that a bare, bald statement of fact will help my argument.

First experience on a bonefish shoal. This wide area of coral mud was dry at low tide. When we arrived the tide was rising. Water scarcely a foot deep, very clear. Bottom white, with patches of brown grass. We saw bonefish everywhere and expected great sport. But no matter where we stopped we could not get any bites. Schools of bonefish swam up to the boat, only to dart away. Everywhere we saw thin white tails sticking out, as they swam along, feeding with noses in the mud. When we drew in our baits we invariably found them half gone, and it was our assumption that the blue crabs did this.

At sunset the wind quieted. It grew very still and beautiful. The water was rosy. Here and there we saw swirls and tails standing out, and we heard heavy thumps of plunging fish. But we could not get any bites.

When we returned to camp we were told that the half of our soldier-crab baits had been sucked off by bonefish. Did not believe that.

Tide bothered us again this morning. It seems exceedingly difficult to tell one night before what the tide is going to do the next morning. At ten o'clock we walked to the same place we were yesterday. It was a bright, warm day, with just enough breeze to ruffle the water and make fishing pleasant, and we certainly expected to have good luck. But we fished for about three hours without any sign of a fish. This was discouraging and we could not account for it.

So we moved. About half a mile down the beach I thought I caught a glimpse of a bonefish. It was a likely-looking contrast to the white marl all around. Here I made a long cast and sat down to wait. My brother lagged behind. Presently I spied two bonefish nosing along not ten feet from the shore. They saw me, so I made no attempt to drag the bait near them, but I called to my brother and told him to try to get a bait ahead of them. This was a little after flood-tide. It struck me then that these singular fish feed up the beach with one tide and down with another.

Just when my brother reached me I got a nibble. I called to him and then stood up, ready to strike. I caught a glimpse of the fish. He looked big and dark. He had his nose down, fooling with my bait. When I struck him he felt heavy. I put on the click of the reel, and when the bonefish started off he pulled the rod down hard, taking the line fast. He made one swirl on the surface and then started up-shore. He seemed exceedingly swift. I ran along the beach until presently the line slackened and I felt that the hook had torn out. This was disappointment. I could not figure that I had done anything wrong, but I decided in the future to use a smaller and sharper hook. We went on down the beach, seeing several bonefish on the way, and finally we ran into a big school of them. They were right alongshore, but when they saw us we could not induce them to bite.

Every day we learn something. It is necessary to keep out of sight of these fish. After they bite, everything depends upon the skilful hooking of the fish. Probably it will require a good deal of skill to land them after you have hooked them, but we have had little experience at that so far. When these fish are along the shore they certainly are feeding, and presumably they are feeding on crabs of some sort. Bonefish appear to be game worthy of any fisherman's best efforts.

It was a still, hot day, without any clouds. We went up the beach to a point opposite an old construction camp. To-day when we expected the tide to be doing one thing it was doing another. Ebb and flow and flood-tide have become as difficult as Sanskrit synonyms for me. My brother took an easy and comfortable chair and sat up the beach, and I, like an ambitious fisherman, laboriously and adventurously waded out one hundred and fifty feet to an old platform that had been erected there. I climbed upon this, and found it a very precarious place to sit. Come to think about it, there is something very remarkable about the places a fisherman will pick out to sit down on. This place was a two-by-four plank full of nails, and I cheerfully availed myself of it and, casting my bait out as far as I could, I calmly sat down to wait for a bonefish. It has become a settled conviction in my mind that you have to wait for bonefish. But all at once I got a hard bite. It quite excited me. I jerked and pulled the bait away from the fish and he followed it and took it again. I saw this fish and several others in the white patch of ground where there were not any weeds. But in my excitement I did not have out a long enough line, and when I jerked the fish turned over and got away. This was all right, but the next two hours sitting in the sun on that seat with a nail sticking into me were not altogether pleasurable. When I thought I had endured it as long as I could I saw a flock of seven bonefish swimming past me, and one of them was a whopper. The sight revived me. I hardly breathed while that bunch of fish swam right for my bait, and for all I could see they did not know it was there. I waited another long time. The sun was hot—there was no breeze—the heat was reflected from the water. I could have stood all this well enough, but I could not stand the nails. So I climbed down off my perch, having forgotten that all this time the tide had been rising. And as I could not climb back I had to get wet, to the infinite amusement of my brother. After that I fished from the shore.

Presently my brother shouted and I looked up to see him pulling on a fish. There was a big splash in the water and then I saw his line running out. The fish was heading straight for the framework on which I had been seated and I knew if he ever did get there he would break the line. All of a sudden I saw the fish he had hooked. And he reached the framework all right!

I had one more strike this day, but did not hook the fish. It seems this bonefishing takes infinite patience. For all we can tell, these fish come swimming along with the rising tide close in to shore and they are exceedingly shy and wary. My brother now has caught two small bonefish and each of them gave a good strong bite, at once starting off with the bait. We had been under the impression that it was almost impossible to feel the bonefish bite. It will take work to learn this game.

Yesterday we went up on the north side of the island to the place near the mangroves where we had seen some bonefish. Arriving there, we found the tide almost flood, with the water perfectly smooth and very clear and about a foot deep up at the mangrove roots. Here and there at a little distance we could see splashes. We separated, and I took the outside, while R. C. took the inside close to the mangroves. We waded along. Before I had time to make a cast I saw a three-pound bonefish come sneaking along, and when he saw me he darted away like an arrow. I made a long cast and composed myself to wait. Presently a yell from R. C. electrified me with the hope that he had hooked a fish. But it turned out that he had only seen one. He moved forward very cautiously in the water and presently made a cast. He then said that a big bonefish was right near his hook, and during the next few minutes this fish circled his bait twice, crossing his line. Then he counted out loud: one, two, three, four, five bonefish right in front of him, one of which was a whopper. I stood up myself and saw one over to my right, of about five pounds, sneaking along with his nose to the bottom. When I made a cast over in his direction he disappeared as suddenly as if he had dissolved in the water. Looking out to my left, I saw half a dozen bonefish swimming toward me, and they came quite close. When I moved they vanished. Then I made a cast over in this direction. The bonefish came back and swam all around my bait, apparently not noticing it. They were on the feed, and the reason they did not take our bait must have been that they saw us. We fished there for an hour without having a sign of a bite, and then we gave it up.

To-day about flood-tide I had a little strike. I jerked hard, but failed to see the fish, and then when I reeled in I found he still had hold of it. Then I struck him, and in one little jerk he broke the leader.

I just had a talk with a fellow who claims to know a good deal about bonefishing. He said he had caught a good many ranging up to eight pounds. His claim was that soldier crabs were the best bait. He said he had fished with professional boatmen who knew the game thoroughly. They would pole the skiff alongshore and keep a sharp lookout for what he called bonefish mud. And I assume that he meant muddy places in the water that had been stirred up by bonefish. Of course, any place where these little swirls could be seen was very likely to be a bonefish bank. He claimed that it was necessary to hold the line near the reel between the forefingers, and to feel for the very slightest vibration. Bonefish have a sucker-like mouth. They draw the bait in, and smash it. Sometimes, of course, they move away, drawing out the line, but that kind of a bite is exceptional. It is imperative to strike the fish when this vibration is felt. Not one in five bonefish is hooked.

We have had two northers and the water grew so cold that it drove the fish out. The last two or three days have been warm and to-day it was hot. However, I did not expect the bonefish in yet, and when we went in bathing at flood-tide I was very glad to see two fish. I hurried out and got my rod and began to try. Presently I had a little strike. I waited and it was repeated; then I jerked and felt the fish. He made a wave and that was the last I knew of him.

Reeling in, I looked at my bait, to find that it had been pretty badly chewed, but I fastened it on again and made another cast. I set down the rod. Then I went back after the bucket for the rest of the bait. Upon my return I saw the line jerking and I ran to the rod. I saw a little splash, and a big white tail of a bonefish stick out of the water. I put my thumb on the reel and jerked hard. Instantly I felt the fish, heavy and powerful. He made a surge and then ran straight out. The line burned my thumb so I could not hold it. I put on the click and the fish made a swifter, harder run for at least a hundred yards, and he tore the hook out.

This makes a number of fish that have gotten away from me in this manner. It is exasperating and difficult to explain. I have to use a pretty heavy sinker in order to cast the bait out. I have arranged this sinker, which has a hole through it, so that the line will run freely. This seems to work all right on the bite, but I am afraid it does not work after the fish is hooked. That sinker drags on the bottom. This is the best rigging that I can plan at the present stage of the game. I have an idea now that a bonefish should be hooked hard and then very carefully handled.

I fished off the beach awhile in front of the cabin. We used both kinds of crabs, soldier and hermit. I fished two hours and a half, from the late rising tide to the first of the ebb, without a sign or sight of a fish. R. C. finally got tired and set his rod and went in bathing. Then it happened. I heard his reel singing and saw his rod nodding; then I made a dash for it. The fish was running straight out, heavy and fast, and he broke the line.

This may have been caused by the heavy sinker catching in the weeds. We must do more planning to get a suitable rig for these bonefish.

Day before yesterday R. C. and I went up to the Long Key point, and rowed in on the mangrove shoal where once before I saw so many bonefish. The tide was about one-quarter in, and there was a foot of water all over the flats. We anchored at the outer edge and began to fish. We had made elaborate preparations in the way of tackle, bait, canoe, etc., and it really would have been remarkable if we had had any luck. After a little while I distinctly felt something at my hook, and upon jerking I had one splendid surge out of a good, heavy bonefish. That was all that happened in that place.

It was near flood-tide when we went back. I stood up and kept a keen watch for little muddy places in the water, also bonefish. At last I saw several fish, and there we anchored. I fished on one side of the boat, and R. C. on the other. On two different occasions, feeling a nibble on his line, he jerked, all to no avail. The third time he yelled as he struck, and I turned in time to see the white thresh of a bonefish. He made a quick dash off to the side and then came in close to the boat, swimming around with short runs two or three times, and then, apparently tired, he came close. I made ready to lift him into the boat, when, lo and behold! he made a wonderful run of fully three hundred feet before R. C. could stop him. Finally he was led to the boat, and turned out to be a fish of three and a half pounds. It simply made R. C. and me gasp to speak of what a really large bonefish might be able to do. There is something irresistible about the pursuit of these fish, and perhaps this is it. We changed places, and as a last try anchored in deeper water, fishing as before. This time I had a distinct tug at my line and I hooked a fish. He wiggled and jerked and threshed around so that I told R. C. that it was not a bonefish, but R. C. contended it was. Anyway, he came toward the boat rather easily until we saw him and he saw us, and then he made a dash similar to that of R. C.'s fish and he tore out the hook. This was the extent of our adventure that day, and we were very much pleased.

Next morning we started out with a high northeast trade-wind blowing. Nothing could dampen our ardor.

It was blowing so hard up at No. 2 viaduct that we decided to stay inside. There is a big flat there cut up by channels, and it is said to be a fine ground for bonefish. The tide was right and the water was clear, but even in the lee of the bank the wind blew pretty hard. We anchored in about three feet of water and began to fish.

After a while we moved. The water was about a foot deep, and the bottom clean white marl, with little patches of vegetation. Crabs and crab-holes were numerous. I saw a small shark and a couple of rays. When we got to the middle of a big flat I saw the big, white, glistening tails of bonefish sticking out of the water. We dropped anchor and, much excited, were about to make casts, when R. C. lost his hat. He swore. We had to pull up anchor and go get the hat. Unfortunately this scared the fish. Also it presaged a rather hard-luck afternoon. In fishing, as in many other things, if the beginning is tragedy all will be tragedy, growing worse all the time. We moved around up above where I had seen these bonefish, and there we dropped anchor. No sooner had we gotten our baits overboard than we began to see bonefish tails off at quite some distance. The thing to do, of course, was to sit right there and be patient, but this was almost impossible for us. We moved again and again, but we did not get any nearer to the fish. Finally I determined that we would stick in one place. This we did, and the bonefish began to come around. When they would swim close to the boat and see us they would give a tremendous surge and disappear, as if by magic. But they always left a muddy place in the water. The speed of these fish is beyond belief. I could not cast where I wanted to; I tried again and again. When I did get my bait off at a reasonable distance, I could feel crabs nibbling at it. These pests robbed us of many a good bait. One of them cut my line right in two. They seemed to be very plentiful, and that must be why the bonefish were plentiful, too. R. C. kept losing bait after bait, which he claimed was the work of crabs, but I rather believed it to be the work of bonefish. It was too windy for us to tell anything about the pressure of the line. It had to be quite a strong tug to be felt at all. Presently I felt one, and instead of striking at once I waited to see what would happen. After a while I reeled in to find my bait gone. Then I was consoled by the proof that a bonefish had taken the bait off for me. Another time three bonefish came along for my bait and stuck their tails up out of the water, and were evidently nosing around it, but I felt absolutely nothing on the line. When I reeled in the bait was gone.

We kept up this sort of thing for two hours. I knew that we were doing it wrong. R. C. said bad conditions, but I claimed that these were only partly responsible for our failure. I knew that we moved about too much, that we did not cast far enough and wait long enough, and that by all means we should not have cracked bait on the bottom of the boat, and particularly we did not know when we had a bite! But it is one thing to be sure of a fact and another to be able to practise it. At last we gave up in despair, and upon paddling back toward the launch we saw a school of bonefish with their tails in the air. We followed them around for a while, apparently very much to their amusement. At sunset we got back to the launch and started for camp.

This was a long, hard afternoon's work for nothing. However, it is my idea that experience is never too dearly bought. I will never do some things again, and the harder these fish are to catch, the more time and effort it takes—the more intelligence and cunning—all the more will I appreciate success if it ever does come. It is in the attainment of difficult tasks that we earn our reward. There are several old bonefish experts here in camp, and they laughed when I related some of our experiences. Bonefishermen are loath to tell anything about their methods. This must be a growth of the difficult game. I had an expert bonefisherman tell me that when he was surprised while fishing on one of the shoals, he always dropped his rod and pretended to be digging for shells. And it is a fact that the bonefish guides at Metacumbe did not let any one get a line on their methods. They will avoid a bonefishing-ground while others are there, and if they are surprised there ahead of others, they will pull up anchor and go away. May I be preserved from any such personal selfishness and reticence as this! One of these bonefish experts at the camp told me that in all his years of experience he had never gotten a bonefish bite. If you feel a tug, it is when the bonefish is ejecting the hook. Then it is too late. The bonefish noses around the bait and sucks it in without any apparent movement of the line. And that can be detected first by a little sagging of the line or by a little strain upon it. That is the time to strike. He also said that he always broke his soldier crabs on a piece of lead to prevent the jar from frightening the fish.

Doctor B. tells a couple of interesting experiences with bonefish. On one occasion he was fishing near another boat in which was a friend. The water was very clear and still, and he could see his friend's bait lying upon the sand. An enormous bonefish swam up and took the bait, and Doctor B. was so thrilled and excited that he could not yell. When the man hooked the fish it shot off in a straightaway rush, raising a ridge upon the water. It ran the length of the line and freed itself. Later Doctor B.'s friend showed the hook, that had been straightened out. They measured the line and found it to be five hundred and fifty-five feet. The bonefish had gone the length of this in one run, and they estimated that he would have weighed not less than fifteen pounds.

On another occasion Dr. B. saw a heavy bonefish hooked. It ran straight off shore, and turning, ran in with such speed that it came shooting out upon dry land and was easily captured. These two instances are cases in point of the incredible speed and strength of this strange fish.

R. C. had a splendid fight with a bonefish to-day. The wind was blowing hard and the canoe was not easy to fish out of. We had great difficulty in telling when we did have a bite. I had one that I know of. When R. C. hooked his fish it sheered off between the canoe and the beach and ran up-shore quite a long way. Then it headed out to sea and made a long run, and then circled. It made short, quick surges, each time jerking R. C.'s rod down and pulling the reel handle out of his fingers. He had to put on a glove. We were both excited and thrilled with the gameness of this fish. It circled the canoe three times, and tired out very slowly. When he got it close the very thing happened that I feared. It darted under the anchor rope and we lost it. This battle lasted about fifteen minutes, and afforded us an actual instance of the wonderful qualities of this fish.

Yesterday R. C. hooked a bonefish that made a tremendous rush straight offshore, and never stopped until he had pulled out the hook. This must have been a very heavy and powerful fish.

I had my taste of the same dose to-day. I felt a tiny little tug upon my line that electrified me and I jerked as hard as I dared. I realized that I had hooked some kind of fish, but, as it was wiggling and did not feel heavy, I concluded that I had hooked one of those pesky blowfish. But all of a sudden my line cut through the water and fairly whistled. I wound in the slack and then felt a heavy fish. He made a short plunge and then a longer one, straight out, making my reel scream. I was afraid to thumb the line, so I let him go. With these jerky plunges he ran about three hundred feet. Then I felt my line get fast, and, handing my rod to R. C., I slipped off my shoes and went overboard. I waded out, winding as I went, to find that the bonefish had fouled the line on a sponge on the bottom, and he had broken free just above the hook.

Yesterday the fag end of the northeast gale still held on, but we decided to try for bonefish. Low tide at two o'clock.

I waded up-shore with the canoe, and R. C. walked. It was a hard job to face the wind and waves and pull the canoe. It made me tired and wet.

When we got above the old camp the tide had started in. We saw bonefish tails standing up out of the water. Hurriedly baiting our hooks, we waded to get ahead of them. But we could not catch them wading, so went back to the canoe and paddled swiftly ahead, anchored, and got out to wade once more.

R. C. was above me. We saw the big tail of one bonefish and both of us waded to get ahead of him. At last I made a cast, but did not see him any more. The wind was across my line, making a big curve in it, and I was afraid I could not tell a bite if I had one. Was about to reel in when I felt the faint tug. I swept my rod up and back, hard as I dared. The line came tight, I felt a heavy weight; a quiver, and then my rod was pulled down. I had hooked him. The thrill was remarkable. He took a short dash, then turned. I thought I had lost him. But he was running in. Frantically I wound the reel, but could not get in the slack. I saw my line coming, heard it hiss in the water, then made out the dark shape of a bonefish. He ran right at me—almost hit my feet. When he saw me he darted off with incredible speed, making my reel scream. I feared the strain on the line, and I plunged through the water as fast as I could after him. He ran four hundred feet in that dash, and I ran fifty. Not often have I of late years tingled and thrilled and panted with such excitement. It was great. It brought back the days of boyhood. When he stopped that run I was tired and thoroughly wet. He sheered off as I waded and wound in. I got him back near me. He shot off in a shoal place of white mud where I saw him plainly, and he scared a school of bonefish that split and ran every way. My fish took to making short circles; I could not keep a tight line. Lost! I wound in fast, felt him again, then absolutely lost feel of him or sight of him. Lost again! My sensations were remarkable, considering it was only a fish of arm's-length at the end of the line. But these bonefish rouse an angler as no other fish can. All at once I felt the line come tight. He was still on, now running inshore.

The water was about a foot deep. I saw the bulge, or narrow wave, he made. He ran out a hundred feet, and had me dashing after him again. I could not trust that light line at the speed he swam, so I ran to release the strain. He led me inshore, then up-shore, and out toward sea again, all the time fighting with a couple of hundred feet of line out. Occasionally he would make a solid, thumping splash. He worked offshore some two hundred yards, where be led me in water half to my hips. I had to try to stop him here, and with fear and trepidation I thumbed the reel. The first pressure brought a savage rush, but it was short. He turned, and I wound him back and waded inshore.

From that moment I had him beaten, although I was afraid of his short thumps as he headed away and tugged. Finally I had him within twenty feet circling around me, tired and loggy, yet still strong enough to require careful handling.

He looked short and heavy, pale checked green and silver; and his staring black eye, set forward in his pointed white nose, could be plainly seen. This fish made a rare picture for an angler.

So I led him to the canoe and, ascertaining that I had him well hooked, I lifted him in.

Never have I seen so beautiful a fish. A golden trout, a white sea-bass, a dolphin, all are beautiful, but not so exquisite as this bonefish. He seemed all bars of dazzling silver. His tail had a blue margin and streaks of lilac. His lower (anal) fins were blazing with opal fire, and the pectoral fins were crystal white. His eye was a dead, piercing black, staring and deep. We estimated his weight. I held for six pounds, but R. C. shook his head. He did not believe that. But we agreed on the magnificent fight he had made.

Then we waded up-shore farther and began to fish. In just five minutes I had the same kind of strike, slight, almost imperceptible, vibrating, and I hooked a fish exactly as I had the first one. He was light of weight, but swift as a flash. I played him from where I stood. This time I essayed with all skill to keep a taut line. It was impossible. Now I felt his weight and again only a slack line. This fish, too, ran right to my feet, then in a boiling splash sheered away. But he could not go far. I reeled him back and led him to the canoe. He was small, and the smallness of him was such a surprise in contrast to what his fight had led me to imagine he was.

R. C. had one strike and broke his line on the jerk. We had to give up on account of sunset at hand.

There was another hard thunder-storm last night. The last few days have begun the vernal equinox. It rained torrents all night and stopped at dawn. The wind was northeast and cool. Cloudy overhead, with purple horizon all around—a forbidding day. But we decided to go fishing, anyhow. We had new, delicate three-six tackles to try. About seven the wind died away. There was a dead calm, and the sun tried to show. Then another breeze came out of the east.

We went up on the inside after bait, and had the luck to find some. Crossing the island, we came out at the old construction camp where we had left the canoe. By this time a stiff breeze was blowing and the tide was rising fast. We had our troubles paddling and poling up to the grove of cocoanuts. Opposite this we anchored and began to fish.

Conditions were not favorable. The water was choppy and roily, the canoe bobbed a good deal, the anchors dragged, and we did not see any fish. All the same, we persevered. At length I had a bite, but pulled too late. We tried again for a while, only to be disappointed. Then we moved.

We had to put the stern anchor down first and let it drag till it held and the canoe drifted around away from the wind, then we dropped the bow anchor. After a time I had a faint feeling at the end of my line—an indescribable feeling. I jerked and hooked a bonefish. He did not feel heavy. He ran off, and the wind bagged my line and the waves also helped to pull out the hook.

Following that we changed places several times, in one of which R. C. had a strike, but failed to hook the fish. Just opposite the old wreck on the shore I had another fish take hold, and, upon hooking him, had precisely the same thing happen as in the first instance. I think the bag of my line, which I could not avoid, allowed the lead to sag down and drag upon the bottom. Of course when it caught the bonefish pulled free.

In some places we found the water clearer than in others. Flood-tide had long come when we anchored opposite the old camp. R. C. cast out upon a brown patch of weeds where we have caught some fine fish, and I cast below. Perhaps in five minutes or less R. C. swept up his rod. I saw it bend forward, down toward the water. He had hooked a heavy fish. The line hissed away to the right, and almost at once picked up a good-sized piece of seaweed.

"It's a big fish!" I exclaimed, excitedly. "Look at him go!... That seaweed will make you lose him. Let me wade out and pull it off?"

"No! Let's take a chance.... Too late, anyhow! Gee! He's going!... He's got two hundred yards out!"

Two-thirds of the line was off the reel, and the piece of seaweed seemed to be a drag on the fish. He slowed up. The line was tight, the rod bent. Suddenly the tip sprang back. We had seen that often before.

"Gone!" said R. C., dejectedly.

But I was not so sure of that, although I was hopeless. R. C. wound in, finding the line came slowly, as if weighted. I watched closely. We thought that was on account of the seaweed. But suddenly the reel began to screech.

"I've got him yet!" yelled R. C., with joy.

I was overjoyed, too, but I contained myself, for I expected dire results from that run.

Zee! Zee! Zee! went the reel, and the rod nodded in time.

"We must get rid of that seaweed or lose him.... Pull up your anchor with one hand.... Careful now."

He did so, and quickly I got mine up. What ticklish business!

"Keep a tight line!" I cautioned, as I backed the canoe hard with all my power. It was not easy to go backward and keep head on to the wind. The waves broke over the end of the canoe, splashing me in the face so I could taste and smell the salt. I made half a dozen shoves with the paddle. Then, nearing the piece of seaweed, I dropped my anchor.

In a flash I got that dangerous piece of seaweed off R. C.'s line.

"Good work!... Say, but that helps.... We'd never have gotten him," said R. C., beaming. I saw him look then as he used to in our sunfish, bent-pin days.

"We've not got him yet," I replied, grimly. "Handle him as easily as you can."

Then began a fight. The bonefish changed his swift, long runs, and took to slow sweeps to and fro, and whenever he was drawn a few yards closer he would give a solid jerk and get that much line back. There was much danger from other pieces of floating weed. R. C. maneuvered his line to miss them. All the time the bonefish was pulling doggedly. I had little hope we might capture him. At the end of fifteen minutes he was still a hundred yards from the canoe and neither of us had seen him. Our excitement grew tenser every moment. The fish sheered to and fro, and would not come into shallower water. He would not budge. He took one long run straight up the shore, in line with us, and then circled out. This alarmed me, but he did not increase his lead. He came slowly around, yard by yard. R. C. reeled carefully, not hard enough to antagonize him, and after what seemed a long time got him within a hundred feet, and I had a glimpse of green and silver. Then off he ran again. How unbelievably swift! He had been close—then almost the same instant he was far off.

"I saw him! On a wave!" yelled R. C. "That's no bonefish! What can he be, anyhow? I believe I've got a barracuda!"

I looked and looked, but I could not see him.

"No matter what you think you saw, that fish is a bonefish," I declared, positively. "The runs he made! I saw silver and green! Careful now. I know he's a bonefish. And he must be big."

"Maybe it's only the wind and waves that make him feel so strong," replied R. C.

"No! You can't fool me! Play him for a big one. He's been on twenty-three minutes now. Stand up—I'll steady the canoe—and watch for that sudden rush when he sees the canoe. The finish is in sight."

It was an indication of a tiring fish that he made his first circle of the canoe, but too far out for us to see him. This circling a boat is a remarkable feature, and I think it comes from the habit of a bonefish of pulling broadside. I cautioned R. C. to avoid the seaweed and to lead him a little more, but to be infinitely careful not to apply too much strain. He circled us again, a few yards closer. The third circle he did not gain a foot. Then he was on his fourth lap around the canoe, drawing closer. On his fifth lap clear round us he came near as fifty feet. I could not resist standing up to see. I got a glimpse of him and he looked long. But I did not say anything to R. C. We had both hooked too many big bonefish that got away immediately. This was another affair.

He circled us the sixth time. Six times! Then he came rather close. On this occasion he saw the canoe. He surged and sped out so swiftly that I was simply paralyzed. R. C. yelled something that had a note of admiration of sheer glory in the spirit of that fish.

"Here's where he leaves us!" I echoed.

But, as luck would have it, he stopped that run short of two hundred yards; and turned broadside to circle slowly back, allowing R. C. to get in line. He swam slower this time, and did not make the heavy tugs. He came easily, weaving to and fro. R. C. got him to within twenty-five feet of the boat, yet still could not see him. It was my job to think quick and sit still with ready hands on the anchor rope. He began to plunge, taking a little line each time. Then suddenly I saw R. C.'s line coming toward us. I knew that would happen.

"Now! Look out! Reel in fast!" I cried, tensely.

As I leaned over to heave up the anchor, I saw the bonefish flashing nearer. At that instant of thrilling excitement and suspense I could not trust my eyesight. There he was, swimming heavily, and he looked three feet long, thick and dark and heavy. I got the anchor up just as he passed under the canoe. Maybe I did not revel in pride of my quickness of thought and action!

"Oh! He's gone under the rope!" gasped R. C.

"No!" I yelled, sharply. "Let your line run out! Put your tip down! We'll drift over your line."

R. C. was dominated to do so, and presently the canoe drifted over where the line was stretched. That second ticklish moment passed. It had scared me. But I could not refrain from one sally.

"I got the anchor up. What did you think I'd do?"

R. C. passed by my remark. This was serious business for him. He looked quite earnest and pale.

"Say! did you see him?" he ejaculated, looking at me.

"Wish I hadn't," I replied.

We were drifting inshore, which was well, provided we did not drift too hard to suit the bonefish. He swam along in plain sight, and he seemed so big that I would not have gazed any longer if I could have helped it.

I kept the canoe headed in, and we were not long coming to shallow water. Here the bonefish made a final dash for freedom, but it was short and feeble, compared with his first runs. He got about twenty feet away, then sheered, showing his broad, silver side. R. C. wound him in close, and an instant later the bow of the canoe grated on shore.

"Now what?" asked R. C. as I stepped out into the water. "Won't it be risky to lift him into the canoe?"

"Lift nothing! I have this all figured out. Lead him along."

R. C. stepped out upon the beach while I was in the water. The bonefish lay on his side, a blaze of silver. I took hold of the line very gently and led the fish a little closer in. The water was about six inches deep. There were waves beating in—a miniature surf. And I calculated on the receding of a wave. Then with one quick pull I slid our beautiful quarry up on the coral sand. The instant he was out of the water the leader snapped. I was ready for this, too. But at that it was an awful instant! As the wave came back, almost deep enough to float the bonefish, I scooped him up.

"He's ours!" I said, consulting my watch. "Thirty-three minutes! I give you my word that fight was comparable to ones I've had with a Pacific swordfish."

"Look at him!" R. C. burst out. "Look at him! When the leader broke I thought he was lost. I'm sick yet. Didn't you almost bungle that?"

"Not a chance, R. C.," I replied. "Had that all figured. I never put any strain on your line until the wave went back. Then I slid him out, the leader broke, and I scooped him up."

R. C. stood gazing down at the glistening, opal-spotted fish. What a contrast he presented to any other kind of a fish! How many beautiful species have we seen lying on sand or moss or ferns, just come out of the water! But I could remember no other so rare as this bonefish. The exceeding difficulty of the capture of this, our first really large bonefish, had a great deal to do with our admiration and pride. For the hard work of any achievement is what makes it worth while. But this had nothing to do with the exquisite, indescribable beauty of the bonefish. He was long, thick, heavy, and round, with speed and power in every line; a sharp white nose and huge black eyes. The body of him was live, quivering silver, molten silver in the sunlight, crossed and barred with blazing stripes. The opal hues came out upon the anal fin, and the broad tail curled up, showing lavender tints on a background of brilliant blue. He weighed eight pounds. Symbolic of the mysterious life and beauty in the ocean! Wonderful and prolific as nature is on land, she is infinitely more so in the sea. By the sun and the sea we live; and I shall never tire of seeking and studying the manifold life of the deep.

CHAPTER VIII

SOME RARE FISH

It is very strange that the longer a man fishes the more there seems to be to learn. In my case this is one of the secrets of the fascination of the game. Always there will be greater fish in the ocean than I have ever caught.

Five or six years ago I heard the name "waahoo" mentioned at Long Key. The boatmen were using it in a way to make one see that they did not believe there was such a fish as a waahoo. The old conch fishermen had never heard the name. For that matter, neither had I.

Later I heard the particulars of a hard and spectacular fight Judge Shields had had with a strange fish which the Smithsonian declared to be a waahoo. The name waahoo appears to be more familiarly associated with a shrub called burning-bush, also a Pacific coast berry, and again a small tree of the South called winged elm. When this name is mentioned to a fisherman he is apt to think only fun is intended. To be sure, I thought so.

In February, 1915, I met Judge Shields at Long Key, and, remembering his capture of this strange fish some years previous, I questioned him. He was singularly enthusiastic about the waahoo, and what he said excited my curiosity. Either the genial judge was obsessed or else this waahoo was a great fish. I was inclined to believe both, and then I forgot all about the matter.

This year at Long Key I was trolling for sailfish out in the Gulf Stream, a mile or so southeast of Tennessee Buoy. It was a fine day for fishing, there being a slight breeze and a ripple on the water. My boatman, Captain Sam, and I kept a sharp watch on all sides for sailfish. I was using light tackle, and of course trolling, with the reel free running, except for my thumb.

Suddenly I had a bewildering swift and hard strike. What a wonder that I kept the reel from over-running! I certainly can testify to the burn on my thumb.

Sam yelled "Sailfish!" and stooped for the lever, awaiting my order to throw out the clutch.

Then I yelled: "Stop the boat, Sam!... It's no sailfish!"

That strike took six hundred feet of line quicker than any other I had ever experienced. I simply did not dare to throw on the drag. But the instant the speed slackened I did throw it on, and jerked to hook the fish. I felt no weight. The line went slack.

"No good!" I called, and began to wind in.

At that instant a fish savagely broke water abreast of the boat, about fifty yards out. He looked long, black, sharp-nosed. Sam saw him, too. Then I felt a heavy pull on my rod and the line began to slip out. I jerked and jerked, and felt that I had a fish hooked. The line appeared strained and slow, which I knew to be caused by a long and wide bag in it.

"Sam," I yelled, "the fish that jumped is on my line!"

"No," replied Sam.

It did seem incredible. Sam figured that no fish could run astern for two hundred yards and then quick as a flash break water abreast of us. But I knew it was true. Then the line slackened just as it had before. I began to wind up swiftly.

"He's gone," I said.

Scarcely had I said that when a smashing break in the water on the other side of the boat alarmed and further excited me. I did not see the fish. But I jumped up and bent over the stern to shove my rod deep into the water back of the propeller. I did this despite the certainty that the fish had broken loose. It was a wise move, for the rod was nearly pulled out of my hands. I lifted it, bent double, and began to wind furiously. So intent was I on the job of getting up the slack line that I scarcely looked up from the reel.

"Look at him yump!" yelled Sam.

I looked, but not quickly enough.

"Over here! Look at him yump!" went on Sam.

That fish made me seem like an amateur. I could not do a thing with him. The drag was light, and when I reeled in some line the fish got most of it back again. Every second I expected him to get free for sure. It was a miracle he did not shake the hook, as he certainly had a loose rein most all the time. The fact was he had such speed that I was unable to keep a strain upon him. I had no idea what kind of a fish it was. And Sam likewise was nonplussed.

I was not sure the fish tired quickly, for I was so excited I had no thought of time, but it did not seem very long before I had him within fifty yards, sweeping in wide half-circles back of the boat. Occasionally I saw a broad, bright-green flash. When I was sure he was slowing up I put on the other drag and drew him closer. Then in the clear water we saw a strange, wild, graceful fish, the like of which we had never beheld. He was long, slender, yet singularly round and muscular. His color appeared to be blue, green, silver crossed by bars. His tail was big like that of a tuna, and his head sharper, more wolfish than a barracuda. He had a long, low, straight dorsal fin. We watched him swimming slowly to and fro beside the boat, and we speculated upon his species. But all I could decide was that I had a rare specimen for my collection.

Sam was just as averse to the use of the gaff as I was. I played the fish out completely before Sam grasped the leader, pulled him close, lifted him in, and laid him down—a glistening, quivering, wonderful fish nearly six feet long.

He was black opal blue; iridescent silver underneath; pale blue dorsal; dark-blue fins and copper-bronze tail, with bright bars down his body.

I took this thirty-six pound fish to be a sea-roe, a game fish lately noticed on the Atlantic seaboard. But I was wrong. One old conch fisherman who had been around the Keys for forty years had never seen such a fish. Then Mr. Schutt came and congratulated me upon landing a waahoo.

The catching of this specimen interested me to inquire when I could, and find out for myself, more about this rare fish.

Natives round Key West sometimes take it in nets and with the grains, and they call it "springer." It is well known in the West Indies, where it bears the name "queenfish." After studying this waahoo there were boatmen and fishermen at Long Key who believed they had seen schools of them. Mr. Schutt had observed schools of them on the reef, low down near the coral—fish that would run from forty to one hundred pounds. It made me thrill just to think of hooking a waahoo weighing anywhere near a hundred pounds. Mr. Shannon testified that he had once observed a school of waahoo leaping in the Gulf

Stream—all very large fish. And once, on a clear, still day, I drifted over a bunch of big, sharp-nosed, game-looking fish that I am sure belonged to this species.

The waahoo seldom, almost never, is hooked by a fisherman. This fact makes me curious. All fish have to eat, and at least two waahoo have been caught. Why not more? I do not believe that it is just a new fish. I see Palm Beach notices printed to the effect that sailfish were never heard of there before the Russo-Japanese War, and that the explosions of floating mines drove them from their old haunts. I do not take stock in such theory as that. As a matter of fact, Holder observed the sailfish (Histiophorus) in the Gulf Stream off the Keys many years ago. Likewise the waahoo must always have been there, absent perhaps in varying seasons. It is fascinating to ponder over tackle and bait and cunning calculated to take this rare denizen of the Gulf Stream.

During half a dozen sojourns at Long Key I had heard of two or three dolphin being caught by lucky anglers who were trolling for anything that would bite. But until 1916 I never saw a dolphin. Certainly I never hoped to take one of these rare and beautiful deep-sea fish. Never would have the luck. But in February I took two, and now I am forbidden the peculiar pleasure of disclaiming my fisherman's luck.

Dolphin seems a singularly attractive name. It always made me think of the deep blue sea, of old tars, and tall-sparred, white-sailed brigs. It is the name of a fish beloved of all sailors. I do not know why, but I suspect that it is because the dolphin haunts ships and is an omen of good luck, and probably the most exquisitely colored fish in the ocean.

One day, two miles out in the Gulf Stream, I got a peculiar strike, quite unlike any I had ever felt. A fisherman grows to be a specialist in strikes. This one was quick, energetic, jerky, yet strong. And it was a hungry strike. A fish that is hungry can almost always be hooked. I let this one run a little and then hooked him. He felt light, but savage. He took line in short, zigzag rushes. I fancied it was a bonita, but Sam shook his head. With about a hundred yards of line out, the fish leaped. He was golden. He had a huge, blunt, bow-shaped head and a narrow tail. The distance was pretty far, and I had no certainty to go by, yet I yelled:

"Dolphin!"

Sam was not so sure, but he looked mighty hopeful. The fish sounded and ran in on me, then darted here and there, then began to leap and thresh upon the surface. He was hard to lead—a very strong fish for his light weight. I never handled a fish more carefully. He came up on a low swell, heading toward us, and he cut the water for fifty feet, with only his dorsal, a gleam of gold, showing in the sunlight.

Next he jumped five times, and I could hear the wrestling sound he made when he shook himself. I had no idea what he might do next, and if he had not been securely hooked would have gotten off. I tried hard to keep the line taut and was not always successful. Like the waahoo, he performed tricks new to me. One was an awkward diving leap that somehow jerked the line in a way to alarm me. When he quit his tumbling and rushing I led him close to the boat.

This has always been to me one of the rewards of fishing. It quite outweighs that doubtful moment for me when the fish lies in the boat or helpless on the moss. Then I am always sorry, and more often than not let the fish go alive.

My first sight of a dolphin near at hand was one to remember. The fish flashed gold—deep rich gold—with little flecks of blue and white. Then the very next flash there were greens and yellows—changing, colorful, brilliant bars. In that background of dark, clear, blue Gulf Stream water this dolphin was radiant, golden, exquisitely beautiful. It was a shame to lift him out of the water. But—

The appearance of the dolphin when just out of the water beggars description. Very few anglers in the world have ever had this experience. Not many anglers, perhaps, care for the beauty of a fish. But I do. And for the sake of those who feel the same way I wish I could paint him. But that seems impossible. For even while I gazed the fish changed color. He should have been called the chameleon of the ocean. He looked a quivering, shimmering, changeful creature, the color of golden-rod. He was the personification of beautiful color alive. The fact that he was dying made the changing hues. It gave me a pang—that I should be the cause of the death of so beautiful a thing.

If I caught his appearance for one fleeting instant here it is: Vivid green-gold, spotted in brilliant blue, and each blue spot was a circle inclosing white. The long dorsal extending from nose to tail seemed black and purple near the head, shading toward the tail to rich olive green with splashes of blue. Just below the dorsal, on the background of gold, was a line of black dots. The fins were pearly silver beneath, and dark green above. All the upper body was gold shading to silver, and this silver held exquisite turquoise-blue spots surrounded with white rings, in strange contrast to those ringed dots above. There was even a suggestion of pink glints. And the eyes were a deep purple with gold iris.

The beauty of the dolphin resembled the mystery of the Gulf Stream—too illusive for the eye of man.

More than once some benighted angler had mentioned bonefish to me. These individuals always appeared to be quiet, retiring fishermen who hesitated to enlarge upon what was manifestly close to their hearts. I had never paid any attention to them. Who ever heard of a bonefish, anyway? The name itself did not appeal to my euphonious ear.

But on this 1916 trip some faint glimmering must have penetrated the density of my cranium. I had always prided myself upon my conviction that I did not know it all, but, just the same, I had looked down from my lofty height of tuna and swordfish rather to despise little salt-water fish that could not pull me out of the boat. The waahoo and the dolphin had opened my eyes. When some mild, quiet, soft-voiced gentleman said bonefish to me again I listened. Not only did I listen, I grew interested. Then I saw a couple of bonefish. They shone like silver, were singularly graceful in build, felt heavy as lead, and looked game all over. I made the mental observation that the man who had named them bonefish should have had half of that name applied to his head.

After that I was more interested in bonefish. I never failed to ask questions. But bonefishermen were scarce and as reticent as scarce. To sum up all of my inquiries, I learned or heard a lot that left me completely bewildered, so that I had no idea whether a bonefish was a joke or the grandest fish that swims. I deducted from the amazing information that if a fisherman sat all day in the blazing sun and had the genius to discover when he had a bite he was learning. No one ever caught bonefish without days and days of learning. Then there were incidents calculated to disturb the peace of a contemplative angler like myself.

One man with heavy tackle yanked some bonefish out of the tide right in front of my cabin, quite as I used to haul out suckers. Other men tried it for days without success, though it appeared bonefish were passing every tide. Then there was a loquacious boatman named Jimmy, who, when he had spare time, was always fishing for bonefish. He would tell the most remarkable tales about these fish. So finally I drifted to that fatal pass where I decided I wanted to catch bonefish. I imagined it would be easy for me. So did Captain Sam. Alas! the vanity of man!

Forthwith Captain Sam and I started out to catch soldier-crabs for bait. The directions we got from conch fishermen and others led us to assume that it would be an easy matter to find crabs. It was not! We had to go poking round mangrove roots until we learned how to catch the soldiers. If this had not been fun for me it would have been hard work. But ever since I was a little tad I have loved to chase things in the water. And upon this occasion it was with great satisfaction that I caught more bait than Captain Sam. Sam is something of a naturalist and he was always spending time over a curious bug or shell or object he found. Eventually we collected a bucketful of soldier-crabs.

Next day, about the last of the ebb-tide, we tied a skiff astern and went up the Key to a cove where there were wide flats. While working our way inshore over the shoals we hit bottom several times and finally went aground. This did not worry us, for we believed the rising tide would float us.

Then we got in the skiff and rowed toward the flats. I was rather concerned to see that apparently the tide was just about as high along this shore as it ever got. Sam shook his head. The tides were strange around the Keys. It will be high on the Gulf side and low on the Atlantic side, and sometimes it will run one way through the channels for thirty-six hours. But we forgot this as soon as we reached the bonefish shoals.

Sam took an oar and slowly poled inshore, while I stood up on a seat to watch for fish. The water was from six to eighteen inches deep and very clear and still. The bottom appeared to be a soft mud, gray, almost white in color, with patches of dark grass here and there. It was really marl, which is dead and decayed coral.

Scarcely had we gotten over the edge of this shoal when we began to see things—big blue crabs, the kind that can pinch and that play havoc with the fishermen's nets, and impudent little gray crabs, and needle-fish, and small chocolate-colored sharks—nurse sharks, Sam called them—and barracuda from one foot to five feet in length, and whip-rays and sting-rays. It was exceedingly interesting and surprising to see all these in such shallow water. And they were all tame.

Here and there we saw little boils of the water, and then a muddy patch where some fish had stirred the marl. Sam and I concluded these were made by bonefish. Still, we could not be sure. I can see a fish a long way in the water and I surely was alert. But some time elapsed and we had poled to within a few rods of the mangroves before I really caught sight of our coveted quarry. Then I saw five bonefish, two of them large, between the boat and the mangroves. They were motionless. Somehow the sight of them was thrilling. They looked wary, cunning, game, and reminded me of gray wolves I had seen on the desert. Suddenly they vanished. It was incredible the way they disappeared. When we got up to the place where they had been there were the little swirls in the roiled water.

Then Sam sighted two more bonefish that flashed away too swiftly for me to see. We stuck an oar down in the mud and anchored the boat. It seemed absolutely silly to fish in water a foot deep. But I meant to try it. Putting a crab on my hook, I cast off ten or a dozen yards, and composed myself to rest and watch.

Certainly I expected no results. But it was attractive there. The wide flat stretched away, bordered by the rich, dark mangroves. Cranes and pelicans were fishing off the shoals, and outside rippled the green channel, and beyond that the dark-blue sea. The sun shone hot. There was scarcely any perceptible breeze. All this would have been enjoyable and fruitful if there had not been a fish within a mile.

Almost directly I felt a very faint vibration of my line. I waited, expectantly, thinking that I might be about to have a bite. But the line slackened and nothing happened.

There were splashes all around us and waves and ripples here and there, and occasionally a sounding thump. We grew more alert and interested. Sam saw a bonefish right near the boat. He pointed, and the fish was gone. After that we sat very still, I, of course, expecting a bite every moment. Presently I saw a bonefish not six feet from the boat. Where he came from was a mystery, but he appeared like magic, and suddenly, just as magically, he vanished.

"Funny fish," observed Sam, thoughtfully. Something had begun to dawn upon Sam, as it had upon me.

No very long time elapsed before we had seen a dozen bonefish, any one of which I could have reached with my rod. But not a bite! I reeled in to find my bait gone.

"That bait was eaten off by crabs," I said to Sam, as I put on another.

Right away after my cast I felt, rather than saw, that slight vibration of my line. I waited as before, and just as before the line almost imperceptibly slackened and nothing happened.

Presently I did see a blue crab deliberately cut my line. We had to move the boat, pick up the lost piece of line, and knot it to the other. Then I watched a blue crab tear off my bait. But I failed to feel or see that faint vibration of my line. We moved the boat again, and again my line was cut. These blue crabs were a nuisance. Sam moved the boat again. We worked up the flat nearer where the little mangroves, scarce a foot high, lifted a few leaves out of the water. Whenever I stood up I saw bonefish, and everywhere we could hear them. Once more we composed ourselves to watch and await developments.

In the succeeding hour I had many of the peculiar vibrations of my line, and, strange to see, every time I reeled in, part of my bait or all of it was gone. Still I fished on patiently for a bonefish bite.

Meanwhile the sun lost its heat, slowly slanted to the horizon of mangroves, and turned red. It was about the hour of sunset and it turned out to be a beautiful and memorable one. Not a breath of air stirred. There was no sound except the screech of a gull and the distant splashes of wading birds. I had not before experienced silence on or near salt water. The whole experience was new. We remarked that the tide had not seemed to rise any higher. Everywhere were little swells, little waves, little wakes, all made by bonefish. The sun sank red and gold, and all the wide flat seemed on fire, with little mangroves standing clear and dark against the ruddy glow. And about this time the strangest thing happened. It might have been going on before, but Sam and I had not seen it. All around us were bonefish tails lifted out of the water. They glistened like silver. When a bonefish feeds his head is down and his tail is up, and, the water being shallow, the upper fluke of his tail stands out. If I saw one I saw a thousand. It was particularly easy to see them in the glassy water toward the sunset.

A school of feeding bonefish came toward us. I counted eleven tails out of the water. They were around my bait. Now or never, I thought, waiting frantically! But they went on feeding—passed over my line— and came so near the boat that I could plainly see the gray shadow shapes, the long, sharp noses, the dark, staring eyes. I reeled in to find my bait gone, as usual. It was exasperating.

We had to give up then, as darkness was not far off. Sam was worried about the boat. He rowed while I stood up. Going back, I saw bonefish in twos and fours and droves. We passed school after school. They had just come in from the sea, for they were headed up the flat. I saw many ten-pound fish, but I did not know enough about bonefish then to appreciate what I saw. However, I did appreciate their keen sight and wariness and wonderful speed and incredible power. Some of the big surges made me speculate what a heavy bonefish might do to light tackle. Sam and I were disappointed at our luck, somewhat uncertain whether it was caused by destructive work of crabs or the wrong kind of bait or both. It scarcely occurred to us to inquire into our ignorance.

We found the boat hard and fast in the mud. Sam rowed me ashore. I walked back to camp, and he stayed all night, and all the next day, waiting for the tide to float the boat.

After that on several days we went up to the flat to fish for bonefish. But we could not hit the right tide or the fish were not there. At any rate, we did not see any or get any bites.

Then I began to fish for bonefish in front of my cottage. Whenever I would stick my rod in the sand and go in out of the hot sun a bonefish would take my bait and start off to sea. Before I could get back he would break something.

This happened several times before I became so aroused that I determined to catch one of these fish or die. I fished and fished. I went to sleep in a camp-chair and absolutely ruined my reputation as an ardent fisherman. One afternoon, just after I had made a cast, I felt the same old strange vibration of my line. I was not proof against it and I jerked. Lo! I hooked a fish that made a savage rush, pulled my bass-rod out of shape, and took all my line before I could stop him. Then he swept from side to side. I reeled him in, only to have him run out again and again and yet again. I knew I had a heavy fish. I expected him to break my line. I handled him gingerly. Imagine my amaze to beach a little fish that weighed scarcely more than two pounds! But it was a bonefish—a glistening mother-of-pearl bonefish. Somehow the obsession of these bonefishermen began to be less puzzling to me. Sam saw me catch this bonefish, and he was as amazed as I was at the gameness and speed and strength of so small a fish.

Next day a bonefisherman of years' experience answered a few questions I put to him. No, he never fished for anything except bonefish. They were the hardest fish in the sea to make bite, the hardest to land after they were hooked. Yes, that very, very slight vibration of the line—that strange feeling rather than movement—was the instant of their quick bite. An instant before or an instant after would be fatal.

It dawned upon me then that on my first day I must have had dozens of bonefish bites, but I did not know it! I was humiliated—I was taken down from my lofty perch—I was furious. I thanked the gentleman for his enlightenment and went away in search of Sam. I told Sam, and he laughed—laughed at me and at himself. After all, it was a joke. And I had to laugh too. It is good for a fisherman to have the conceit taken out of him—if anything can accomplish that. Then Sam and I got our heads together. What we planned and what we did must make another story.

CHAPTER IX

SWORDFISH

From records of the New York Bureau of Fisheries, by G. B. Goode

The swordfish, Xiphias gladius, ranges along the Atlantic coast of America from Jamaica (latitude 18° N.), Cuba, and the Bermudas, to Cape Breton (latitude 47° N.). It has not been seen at Greenland, Iceland, or Spitzbergen, but occurs, according to Collett, at the North Cape (latitude 71°). It is abundant along the coasts of western Europe, entering the Baltic and the Mediterranean. I can find no record of the species on the west coast of Africa south of Cape Verde, though Lutken, who may have access to facts unknown to me, states that they occur clear down to the Cape of Good Hope, South Atlantic in mid-ocean, to the west coast of South America and to southern California (latitude 34°), New Zealand, and in the Indian Ocean off Mauritius.

The names of the swordfish all have reference to that prominent feature, the prolonged snout. The "swordfish" of our own tongue, the "zwardfis" of the Hollander, the Italian "sofia" and "pesce-spada," the Spanish "espada" and "espadarte," varied by "pez do spada" in Cuba, and the French "espadon," "dard," and "epee de mer," are simply variations of one theme, repetitions of the "gladius" of ancient Italy and "xiphius," the name by which Aristotle, the father of zoology, called the same fish twenty-three hundred years ago. The French "empereur" and the "imperador" and the "ocean kingfish" of the Spanish and French West Indies, carry out the same idea, for the Roman Emperor was always represented holding a drawn sword in his hand. The Portuguese names are "aguhao," meaning "needle," or "needle-fish."

This species has been particularly fortunate in escaping the numerous redescriptions to which almost all widely distributed forms have been subjected. By the writers of antiquity it was spoken of under its Aristotelian name, and in the tenth edition of his Systema Naturæ, at the very inception of binomial nomenclative, Linnaeus called it Xiphias gladius. By this name it has been known ever since, and only one additional name is included in its synonym, Xiphias rondeletic of Leach.

The swordfish has been so long and so well known that its right to its peculiar name has seldom been infringed upon. The various species of Tetrapturus have sometimes shared its title, and this is not to be wondered at, since they closely resemble Xiphias gladius, and the appellative has frequently been applied to the family Xiphiidæ—the swordfish—which includes them all.

The name "bill-fish," usually applied to our Tetrapturus albidus, a fish of the swordfish family, often taken on our coast, must be pronounced objectionable, since it is in many districts used for various species of Belonidæ, the garfishes or green-bones (Belone truncata and others), which are members of the same faunas. Spear-fish is a much better name.

The "sailfish," Histiophorus americanus, is called by sailors in the South the "boohoo" or "woohoo." This is evidently a corrupted form of "guebum," a name, apparently of Indian origin, given to the same fish in Brazil. It is possible that Tetrapturus is also called "boohoo," since the two genera are not sufficiently unlike to impress sailors with their differences. Blecker states that in Sumatra the Malays call the related species, H. gladius, by the name "Joohoo" (Juhu), a curious coincidence. The names may have been carried from the Malay Archipelago to South America, or vice versa, by mariners.

In Cuba the spear-fish are called "aguja" and "aguja de palada"; the sailfish, "aguja prieta" or "aguja valadora"; Tetrapturus albidus especially known as the "aguja blanca," T. albidus as the "aguja de castro."

In the West Indies and Florida the scabbard-fish or silvery hairy-tail, Trichiurus lepturus, a form allied to the Xiphias, though not resembling it closely in external appearance, is often called "swordfish." The body of this fish is shaped like the blade of a saber, and its skin has a bright, metallic luster like that of polished steel, hence the name.

Swordfish are most abundant on the shoals near the shore and on the banks during the months of July and August; that they make their appearance on the frequented cruising-grounds between Montauk Point and the eastern part of Georges Banks sometime between the 25th of May and the 20th of June, and that they remain until the approach of cold weather in October and November. The dates of the first fish on the cruising-grounds referred to are recorded for three years, and are reasonably reliable: in 1875, June 20th; in 1877, June 10th; in 1878, June 14th.

South of the cruising-grounds the dates of arrival and departure are doubtless farther apart, the season being shorter north and east. There are no means of obtaining information, since the men engaged in this fishery are the only ones likely to remember the dates when the fish are seen.

The swordfish comes into our waters in pursuit of its food. At least this is the most probable explanation of its movements, since the duties of reproduction appear to be performed elsewhere. Like the tuna, the bluefish, the bonito, and the squiteague, they pursue and prey upon the schools of menhaden and mackerel, which are so abundant in the summer months. "When you see swordfish, you may know that mackerel are about," said an old fisherman to me. "When you see the fin-back whale following food, there you may find swordfish," said another. The swordfish also feeds upon squid, which are at times abundant on our banks.

To what extent this fish is amenable to the influences of temperature is an unsolved problem. We are met at the outset by the fact that they are frequently taken on trawl lines which are set at the depth of one hundred fathoms or more, on the offshore banks. We know that the temperature of the water in these localities and at that depth is sure to be less than 40° Fahr. How is this fact to be reconciled with the known habits of the fish, that it prefers the warmest weather of summer and swims at the surface in water of temperature ranging from 55° to 70°, sinking when cool winds blow below? The case seemed clear enough until the inconvenient discovery was made that swordfish are taken on bottom trawl lines. In other respects their habits agree closely with those of the mackerel tribe, all the members of which seem sensitive to slight changes in temperature, and which, as a rule, prefer temperature in the neighborhood of 50° or more.

The appearance of the fish at the surface depends largely upon the temperature. They are seen only upon quiet summer days, in the morning before ten or eleven o'clock, and in the afternoon about four o'clock. Old fishermen say that they rise when the mackerel rise, and when the mackerel go down they go down also.

Regarding the winter abode of the swordfish, conjecture is useless. I have already discussed this question at length with reference to the menhaden and mackerel. With the swordfish the conditions are very different. The former are known to spawn in our waters, and the schools of young ones follow the old ones in toward the shores. The latter do not spawn in our waters. We cannot well believe that they hibernate, nor is the hypothesis of a sojourn in the middle strata of mid-ocean exactly tenable. Perhaps they migrate to some distant region, where they spawn. But then the spawning-time of this species in the Mediterranean, as is related in a subsequent paragraph, appears to occur in the summer months, at the very time when the swordfish are most abundant in our own waters, apparently feeling no responsibility for the perpetuation of their species.

The swordfish, when swimming at the surface, usually allows its dorsal fin and the upper lobe of its caudal fin to be visible, projecting out of the water. It is this habit which enables the fisherman to detect the presence of the fish. It swims slowly along, and the fishing-schooner with a light breeze finds no difficulty in overtaking it. When excited its motions are very rapid and nervous. Swordfish are sometimes seen to leap entirely out of the water. Early writers attributed this habit to the tormenting presence of parasites, but this theory seems hardly necessary, knowing what we do of its violent exertions at other times. The pointed head, the fins of the back and abdomen snugly fitting into grooves, the absence of ventrals, the long, lithe, muscular body, sloping slowly to the tail, fits it for the most rapid and forceful movement through the water. Prof. Richard Owen, testifying in an England court in regard to its power, said:

"It strikes with the accumulated force of fifteen double-handed hammers. Its velocity is equal to that of a swivel shot, and is as dangerous in its effect as a heavy artillery projectile."

Many very curious instances are on record of the encounter of this fish with other fishes, or of their attacks upon ships. What can be the inducement for it to attack objects so much larger than itself is hard to surmise. We are all familiar with the couplet from Oppian:

Nature her bounty to his mouth confined,
Gave him a sword, but left unarmed his mind.

It surely seems as if temporary insanity sometimes takes possession of the fish. It is not strange that when harpooned it should retaliate by attacking its assailant. An old swordfisherman told Mr. Blackman that his vessel had been struck twenty times. There are, however, many instances of entirely unprovoked assaults on vessels at sea. Many of these are recounted in a later portion of this memoir. Their movements when feeding are discussed below as well as their alleged peculiarities of movement during breeding season.

It is the universal testimony of our fishermen that two are never seen swimming close together. Captain Ashby says that they are always distant from each other at least thirty or forty feet.

The pugnacity of the swordfish has become a byword. Without any special effort on my part, numerous instances of their attacks upon vessels have in the last ten years found their way into the pigeonhole labeled "Swordfish."

Ælian says (b. XXXII, c. 6) that the swordfish has a sharp-pointed snout with which it is able to pierce the sides of a ship and send it to the bottom, instances of which have been known near a place in Mauritania known as Cotte, not far from the river Sixus, on the African side of the Mediterranean. He describes the sword as like the beak of the ship known as the trireme, which was rowed with three banks of oars.

The London Daily News of December 11, 1868, contained the following paragraph, which emanated, I suspect, from the pen of Prof. R. A. Proctor.

Last Wednesday the court of common pleas—rather a strange place, by the by, for inquiring into the natural history of fishes—was engaged for several hours in trying to determine under what circumstances a swordfish might be able to escape scot-free after thrusting his snout into the side of a ship. The gallant ship Dreadnought, thoroughly repaired and classed A1 at Lloyd's, had been insured for £3,000 against all risks of the sea. She sailed on March 10, 1864, from Columbo for London. Three days later the crew, while fishing, hooked a swordfish. Xiphias, however, broke the line, and a few moments after leaped half out of the water, with the object, it should seem, of taking a look at his persecutor, the Dreadnaught. Probably he satisfied himself that the enemy was some abnormally large cetacean, which it was his natural duty to attack forthwith. Be this as it may, the attack was made, and the next morning the captain was awakened with the unwelcome intelligence that the ship had sprung a leak. She was taken back to Columbo, and thence to Cochin, where she hove down. Near the keel was found a round hole, an inch in diameter, running completely through the copper sheathing and planking.

As attacks by swordfish are included among sea risks, the insurance company was willing to pay the damages claimed by the owners of the ship, if only it could be proved that the hole had been really made by aswordfish. No instances had ever been recorded in which a swordfish which had passed its beak through three inches of stout planking could withdraw without the loss of its sword. Mr. Buckland said that fish have no power of "backing," and expressed his belief that he could hold a swordfish by the beak; but then he admitted that the fish had considerable lateral power, and might so "wriggle its sword out of the hold." And so the insurance company will have to pay nearly £600 because an ill-tempered fish objected to be hooked and took its revenge by running full tilt against copper sheathing and oak planking.

The food of the swordfish is of a very mixed nature.

Doctor Fleming found the remains of sepias in its stomach, and also small fishes. Oppian stated that it eagerly devours the Hippuris (probably Coryphæna). A specimen taken off Saconnet July 22, 1875, had in its stomach the remains of small fish, perhaps Stromateus triacanthus, and jaws of a squid, perhaps Loligo pealin. Their food in the western Atlantic consists for the most part of the common schooling species of fishes. They feed on menhaden, mackerel, bonitoes, bluefish, and other species which swim in close schools. Their habits of feeding have often been described to me by old fishermen. They are said to rise beneath the school of small fish, striking to the right and left with their swords until they have killed a number, which they then proceed to devour. Menhaden have been seen floating at the surface which have been cut nearly in twain by a blow of a sword. Mr. John H. Thompson remarks that he has seen them apparently throw the fish in the air, catching them on the fall.

Capt. Benjamin Ashby says that they feed on mackerel, herring, whiting, and menhaden. He has found half a bucketful of small fish of these kind in the stomach of one swordfish. He has seen them in the act of feeding. They rise perpendicularly out of the water until the sword and two-thirds of the remainder of the body are exposed to view. He has seen a school of herring at the surface on Georges Banks as closely as they could be packed. A swordfish came up through the dense mass and fell flat on its side, striking many fish with the sides of its sword. He has at one time picked up as much as a bushel of herrings thus killed by a swordfish on Georges Banks.

But little is known regarding their time and place of breeding. They are said to deposit their eggs in large quantities on the coasts of Sicily, and European writers give their spawning-time occurring the latter part of spring and the beginning of summer. In the Mediterranean they occur of all sizes from four hundred pounds down, and the young are so plentiful as to become a common article of food.

M. Raymond, who brought to Cuvier a specimen of aistiophorn four inches long, taken in January, 1829, in the Atlantic, between the Cape of Good Hope and France, reported that there were good numbers of young sailfish in the place where this was taken.

Meunier, quoting Spollongain, states that the swordfish does not approach the coast of Sicily except in the season of reproduction; the males are then seen pursuing the females. It is a good time to capture them, for when the female has been taken the male lingers near and is easily approached. The fish are abundant in the Straits of Messina from the middle of April to the middle of September; early in the season they hug the Calabrian shore, approaching from the north; after the end of June they are most abundant on the Sicilian shore, approaching from the south.

From other circumstances, it seems certain that there are spawning-grounds in the seas near Sicily and Genoa, for from November to the 1st of March young ones are taken in the Straits of Messina, ranging in weight from half a pound to twelve pounds.

In the Mediterranean, as has been already stated, the young fish are found from November to March, and here from July to the middle of September the male fish are seen pursuing the female over the shoals, and at this time the males are easily taken. Old swordfish fishermen, Captain Ashby and Captain Kirby, assure me that on our coast, out of thousands of specimens they have taken, they have never seen one containing eggs. I have myself dissected several males, none of which were near breeding-time. In the European waters they are said often to be seen swimming in pairs, male and female. Many sentimental stories were current, especially among the old writers, concerning the conjugal affection and unselfish devotion of the swordfish, but they seem to have originated in the imaginative brain of the naturalist rather than in his perceptive faculties. It is said that when the female fish is taken the male seems devoid of fear, approaches the boat, and allows himself easily to be taken, but if this be true, it appears to be the case only in the height of the breeding season, and is easily understood. I cannot learn that two swordfish have ever been seen associated together in our waters, though I have made frequent and diligent inquiry.

There is no inherent improbability, however, in this story regarding the swordfish in Europe, for the same thing is stated by Professor Poey as the result upon the habits of Tetrapturus.

The only individual of which we have the exact measurements was taken off Saconnet, Rhode Island, July 23, 1874. This was seven feet seven inches long, weighing one hundred and thirteen pounds. Another, taken off No Man's Land, July 20, 1875, and cast in plaster for the collection of the National Museum, weighed one hundred and twenty pounds and measured about seven feet. Another, taken off Portland, August 15, 1878, was 3,999 millimeters long and weighed about six hundred pounds. Many of these fish doubtless attain the weight of four and five hundred pounds, and some perhaps grow to six hundred; but after this limit is reached, I am inclined to believe larger fish are exceptional. Newspapers are fond of recording the occurrence of giant fish, weighing one thousand pounds and upward, and old sailors will in good faith describe the enormous fish which they saw at sea, but could not capture; but one well-authenticated instance of accurate weighing is much more valuable. The largest one ever taken by Capt. Benjamin Ashby, for twenty years a swordfish fisherman, was killed on the shoals back of Edgartown, Massachusetts. When salted it weighed six hundred and thirty-nine pounds. Its live weight must have been as much as seven hundred and fifty or eight hundred. Its sword measured nearly six feet. This was an extraordinary fish among the three hundred or more taken by Captain Ashby in his long experience. He considers the average size to be about two hundred and fifty pounds dressed, or five hundred and twenty-five alive. Captain Martin, of Gloucester, estimated the average size at three to four hundred pounds. The largest known to Captain Michaux weighed six hundred and twenty-eight. The average about Block Island he considers to be two hundred pounds.

The size of the smallest swordfish taken on our eastern coast is a subject of much deeper interest, for it throws light on the time and place of breeding. There is some difference of testimony regarding the average size, but all fishermen with whom I have talked agree that very small ones do not find their way into our shore waters. Numerous very small specimens have, however, been already taken by the Fish Commission at sea, off our middle and southern coast.

Capt. John Rowe has seen one which did not weigh more than seventy-five pounds when taken out of the water.

Capt. R. H. Hurlbert killed near Block Island, in July, 1877, one which weighed fifty pounds and measured about two feet without its sword.

Captain Ashby's smallest weighed about twenty-five pounds when dressed; this he killed off No Man's Land. He tells me that a Bridgeport smack had one weighing sixteen pounds (or probably twenty-four when alive), and measuring eighteen inches without its sword.

In August, 1878, a small specimen of the mackerel-shark, Lamna cornubica, was captured at the mouth of Gloucester Harbor. In its nostril was sticking a sword, about three inches long, of a young swordfish. When this was pulled out the blood flowed freely, indicating that the wound was recent. The fish to which this sword belonged cannot have exceeded ten or twelve inches in length. Whether the small swordfish met with its misfortune in our waters, or whether the shark brought this trophy from beyond the sea, is an unsolved problem.

Lutken speaks of a very young individual taken in the Atlantic, latitude 32° 50' N., 74° 19' W. This must be about one hundred and fifty miles southeast of Cape Hatteras.

For many years from three to six hundred of these fish have been taken annually on the New England coast. It is not unusual for twenty-five or more to be seen in the course of a single day's cruising, and sometimes as many as this are visible from the masthead at one time. Captain Ashby saw twenty at one time, in August, 1889, between Georges Banks and the South Shoals. One Gloucester schooner, Midnight, Capt. Alfred Wixom, took fourteen in one day on Georges Banks in 1877.

Capt. John Rowe obtained twenty barrels, or four thousand pounds, of salt fish on one trip to Georges Banks; this amount represents twenty fish or more. Captain Ashby has killed one hundred and eight swordfish in one year; Capt. M. C. Tripp killed about ninety in 1874.

Such instances as these indicate in a general way the abundance of the swordfish. A vessel cruising within fifty miles of our coast, between Cape May and Cape Sable, during the months of June, July, August, and September, cannot fail, on a favorable day, to come in sight of several of them. Mr. Earll states that the fishermen of Portland never knew them more abundant than in 1879. This is probably due in part to the fact that the fishery there is of a very recent origin.

There is no evidence of any change in their abundance, either increase or decrease. Fishermen agree that they are as plentiful as ever, nor can any change be anticipated. The present mode does not destroy them in any considerable numbers, each individual fish being the object of special pursuit. The solitary habits of the species will always protect them from wholesale capture, so destructive to schooling fish. Even if this were not the case, the evidence proves that spawning swordfish do not frequent our waters. When a female shad is killed, thousands of possible young die also. The swordfish taken by our fishermen carry no such precious burden.

"The small swordfish is very good meat," remarked Josselyn, in writing of the fishes of England in the seventeenth century. Since Josselyn probably never saw a young swordfish, unless at some time he had visited the Mediterranean, it is fair to suppose that his information was derived from some Italian writer.

It is, however, a fact that the flesh of the swordfish, though somewhat oily, is a very acceptable article of food. Its texture is coarse; the thick, fleshy, muscular layers cause it to resemble that of the halibut in constituency. Its flavor is by many considered fine, and is not unlike that of the bluefish. Its color is gray. The meat of the young fish is highly prized on the Mediterranean, and is said to be perfectly white, compact, and of delicate flavor. Swordfish are usually cut up into steaks—thick slices across the body—and may be broiled or boiled.

The apparatus ordinarily employed for the capture of the swordfish is simple in the extreme. It is the harpoon with the detachable head. When the fish is struck, the head of the harpoon remains in the body of the fish, and carries with it a light rope which is either made fast or held by a man in a small boat, or is attached to some kind of a buoy, which is towed through the water by the struggling fish, and which marks its whereabouts after death.

The harpoon consists of a pole fifteen or sixteen feet in length, usually of hickory or some other hard wood, upon which the bark has been left, so that the harpooner may have a firmer hand-grip. This pole is from an inch and a half to two inches in diameter, and at one end is provided with an iron rod, or "shank," about two feet long and five-eighths of an inch in diameter. This "shank" is fastened to the pole by means of a conical or elongated, cuplike expansion at one end, which fits over the sharpened end of the pole, to which it is secured by screws or spikes. A light line extends from one end of the pole to the point where it joins the "shank" and in this line is tied a loop by which is made fast another short line which secures the pole to the vessel or boat, so that when it is thrown at the fish it cannot be lost.

Upon the end of the "shank" fits the head of the harpoon, known by the names swordfish-iron, lily-iron, and Indian dart. The form of this weapon has undergone much variation. The fundamental idea may very possibly have been derived from the Indian fish-dart, numerous specimens of which are in the National Museum, from various tribes of Indians of New England, British America, and the Pacific. However various the modifications may have been, the similarity of the different shapes is no less noteworthy from the fact that all are peculiarly American. In the enormous collection of fishery implements of all lands at the late exhibition at Berlin, nothing of the kind could be found. What is known to whalers as a toggle-harpoon is a modification of the lily-iron, but so greatly changed by the addition of a pivot by which the head of the harpoon is fastened to the shank that it can hardly be regarded as the same weapon. The lily-iron is, in principle, exactly what a whaleman would describe by the word "toggle." It consists of a two-pointed piece of metal, having in the center, at one side, a ring or socket the axis of which is parallel with the long diameter of the implement. In this is inserted the end of the pole-shank, and to it or near it is also attached the harpoon-line. When the iron has once been thrust point first through some solid substance, such as the side of a fish, and is released upon the other side by the withdrawal of the pole from the socket, it is free, and at once turns its long axis at right angle to the direction in which the harpoon-line is pulling, and this is absolutely prevented from withdrawal. The principle of the whale harpoon or toggle-iron is similar, except that the pole is not withdrawn, and the head, turning upon a pivot at its end, fastens the pole itself securely to the fish, the harpoon-line being attached to some part of the pole. The swordfish lily-iron head, as now ordinarily used, is about four inches in length, and consists of two lanceolate blades, each about an inch and a half long, connected by a central piece much thicker than they, in which, upon one side, and next to the flat side of the blade, is the socket for the insertion of the pole-shank. In this same central enlargement is forged an opening to which the harpoon-line is attached. The dart-head is usually made of steel; sometimes of iron, which is generally galvanized; sometimes of brass.

The entire weight of the harpoon—pole, shank, and head—should not exceed eighteen pounds.

The harpoon-line is from fifty to one hundred and fifty fathoms long, and is ordinarily what is known as "fifteen-thread line." At the end is sometimes fastened a buoy, and an ordinary mackerel-keg is generally used for this purpose.

In addition to the harpoon every swordfish fisherman carries a lance. This implement is precisely similar to a whaleman's lance, except that it is smaller, consisting of a lanceolate blade perhaps one inch wide and two inches long, upon the end of a shank of five-eighths-inch iron, perhaps two or three feet in length, fastened in the ordinary way upon a pole fifteen to eighteen feet in length.

The swordfish are always harpooned from the end of the bowsprit of a sailing-vessel. It is next to impossible to approach them in a small boat. All vessels regularly engaged in this fishery are supplied with a special apparatus called a "rest," or "pulpit," for the support of the harpooner as he stands on the bowsprit, and this is almost essential to success, although it is possible for an active man to harpoon a fish from this station without the aid of the ordinary framework. Not only the professional swordfish fisherman, but many mackerel-schooners and packets are supplied in this manner.

The swordfish never comes to the surface except in moderate, smooth weather. A vessel cruising in search of them proceeds to the fishing-ground, and cruises hither and thither wherever the abundance of small fish indicates that they ought to be found. Vessels which are met are hailed and asked whether any swordfish have been seen, and if tidings are thus obtained the ship's course is at once laid for the locality where they were last noticed. A man is always stationed at the masthead, where, with the keen eye which practice has given him, he can easily descry the telltale dorsal fins at a distance of two or three miles. When a fish has once been sighted, the watch "sings out," and the vessel is steered directly toward it. The skipper takes his place in the "pulpit" holding the pole in both hands by the small end, and directing the man at the wheel by voice and gesture how to steer. There is no difficulty in approaching the fish with a large vessel, although, as has already been remarked, they will not suffer a small boat to come near them. The vessel plows and swashes through the water, plunging its bowsprit into the waves without exciting their fears. Noises frighten them and drive them down. Although there would be no difficulty in bringing the end of a bowsprit directly over the fish, a skilful harpooner never waits for this. When the fish is from six to ten feet in front of the vessel it is struck. The harpoon is never thrown, the pole being too long. The strong arm of the harpooner punches the dart into the back of the fish, right at the side of the high dorsal fin, and the pole is withdrawn and fastened again to its place. When the dart has been fastened to the fish the line is allowed to run out as far as the fish will carry it, and is then passed in a small boat, which is towing at the stern. Two men jump into this, and pull in upon the line until the fish is brought in alongside; it is then killed with a whale-lance or a whale-spade, which is stuck into the gills.

The fish having been killed, it is lifted upon the deck by a purchase tackle of two double blocks rigged in the shrouds.

The pursuit of the swordfish is much more exciting than ordinary fishing, for it resembles the hunting of large animals upon the land and partakes more of the nature of the chase. There is no slow and careful baiting and patient waiting, and no disappointment caused by the accidental capture of worthless "bait-stealers." The game is seen and followed, and outwitted by wary tactics, and killed by strength of arm and skill. The swordfish is a powerful antagonist sometimes, and sends his pursuers' vessel into harbor leaking, and almost sinking, from injuries he has inflicted. I have known a vessel to be struck by wounded swordfish as many as twenty times in a season. There is even the spice of personal danger to savor the chase, for the men are occasionally wounded by the infuriated fish. One of Captain Ashby's crew was severely wounded by a swordfish which thrust his beak through the oak floor of a boat on which he was standing, and penetrated about two inches in his naked heel. The strange fascination draws men to this pursuit when they have once learned its charms. An old swordfish fisherman, who had followed the pursuit for twenty years, told me that when he was on the cruising-ground, he fished all night in his dreams, and that many a time he has rubbed the skin off his knuckles by striking them against the ceiling of his bunk when he raised his arms to thrust the harpoon into visionary monster swordfishes.

The Spear-fish or Bill-fish

The bill-fish or spear-fish, Tetrapturus indicus (with various related forms, which may or may not be specifically identical), occurs in the western Atlantic from the West Indies (latitude 10° to 20° N.) to southern England (latitude 40° N.); in the eastern Atlantic, from Gibraltar (latitude 45° N.) to the Cape of Good Hope (latitude 30° S.) in the Indian Ocean, the Malay Archipelago, New Zealand (latitude 40° S.), and on the west coast of Chile and Peru. In a general way, the range is between latitude 40° N. and latitude 40° S.

The species of Tetrapturus which we have been accustomed to call T. albidus, abundant about Cuba, is not very usual on the coast of southern New England. Several are taken every year by the swordfish fishermen. I have not known of their capture along the southern Atlantic coast of the United States. All I have known about were taken between Sandy Hook and the eastern part of Georges Banks.

The Mediterranean spear-fish, Tetrapturus balone, appears to be a landlocked form, never passing west of the Straits of Gibraltar.

The spear-fish in our waters is said by our fishermen to resemble the swordfish in its movements and manner of feeding. Professor Poey narrates that both the Cuban species swim at a depth of one hundred fathoms, and they journey in pairs, shaping their course toward the Gulf of Mexico, the females being full of eggs. Only adults are taken. It is not known whence they come, or where they breed, or how the young return. It is not even known whether the adult fish return by the same route. When the fish has swallowed the hook it rises to the surface, making prodigious leaps and plunges. At last it is dragged to the boat, secured with a boat-hook, and beaten to death before it is hauled on board. Such fishing is not without danger, for the spear-fish sometimes rushes upon the boat, drowning the fisherman, or wounding him with its terrible weapon. The fish becomes furious at the appearance of sharks, which are its natural enemies. They engage in violent combats, and when the spear-fish is attached to the fisherman's line it often receives frightful wounds from the adversaries.

The spear-fish strikes vessels in the same manner as the swordfish. I am indebted to Capt. William Spicer, of Noank, Connecticut, for this note:

Mr. William Taylor, of Mystic, a man seventy-six years old, who was in the smack Evergreen, Capt. John Appleman, tells me that they started from Mystic, October 3, 1832, on a fishing voyage to Key West, in company with the smack Morning Star, Captain Rowland. On the 12th were off Cape Hatteras, the winds blowing heavily from the northeast, and the smack under double-reefed sails. At ten o'clock in the evening they struck a woho, which shocked the vessel all over. The smack was leaking badly, and they made a signal to the Morning Star to keep close to them. The next morning they found the leak, and both smacks kept off Charleston. On arrival they took out the ballast, hove her out, and found that the sword had gone through the planking, timber, and ceiling. The plank was two inches thick, the timber five inches, and the ceiling one-and-a-half-inch white oak. The sword projected two inches through the ceiling, on the inside of the "after run." It struck by a butt on the outside, which caused the leak. They took out and replaced a piece of the plank, and proceeded on their voyage.

The Sailfish

The sailfish, Histiophorus gladius (with H. americanus and H. orientalis, questionable species, and H. pulchellus and H. immaculatus, young), occurs in the Red Sea, Indian Ocean, Malay Archipelago, and south at least as far as the Cape of Good Hope (latitude 35° S.); in the Atlantic on the coast of Brazil (latitude 30° S.) to the equator, and north to southern New England (latitude 42° N.); in the Pacific to southwestern Japan (latitude 30° to 10° N.). In a general way the range may be said to be in tropical and temperate seas, between latitude 30° S. and 40° N., and in the western parts of those seas.

The first allusion to this genus occurs in Piso's Historia Naturalis Brasiliæ printed in Amsterdam in 1648. In this book may be found an identical, though rough, figure of the American species, accompanied by a few lines of description, which, though good, when the fact that they were written in the seventeenth century is brought to mind, are of no value for critical comparison.

The name given to the Brazilian sailfish by Marcgrave, the talented young German who described the fish in the book referred to, and who afterward sacrificed his life in exploring the unknown fields of American zoology, is interesting, since it gives a clue to the derivation of the name "boohoo," by which this fish, and probably spear-fish, are known to English-speaking sailors in the tropical Atlantic.

Sailfish were observed in the East Indies by Renard and Valentijn, explorers of that region from 1680 to 1720, and by other Eastern voyagers. No species of the genus was, however, systematically described until 1786, when a stuffed specimen from the Indian Ocean, eight feet long, was taken to London, where it still remains in the collections of the British Museum. From this specimen M. Broussonet prepared a description, giving it the name Scomber gladius, rightly regarding it as a species allied to the mackerel.

From the time of Marcgrave until 1872 it does not appear that any zoologist had any opportunity to study a sailfish from America or even the Atlantic; yet in Gunther's Catalogue, the name H. americanus is discarded and the species of America is assumed to be identical with that of the Indian Ocean.

The materials in the National Museum consist of a skeleton and a painted plaster cast of the specimen taken near Newport, Rhode Island, in August, 1872, and given to Professor Baird by Mr. Samuel Powell, of Newport. No others were observed in our waters until March, 1878, when, according to Mr. Neyle

Habersham, of Savannah, Georgia, two were taken by a vessel between Savannah and Indian River, Florida, and were brought to Savannah, where they attracted much attention in the market. In 1873, according to Mr. E. G. Blackford, a specimen in a very mutilated condition was brought from Key West to New York City.

No observations have been made in this country, and recourse must be had to the statements of observers in the other hemisphere.

In the Life of Sir Stamford Raffles is printed a letter from Singapore, under date of November 30, 1822, with the following statement:

The only amusing discovery we have recently made is that of a sailing-fish, called by the natives "ikan layer," of about ten or twelve feet long, which hoists a mainsail, and often sails in the manner of a native boat, and with considerable swiftness. I have sent a set of the sails home, as they are beautifully cut and form a model for a fast-sailing boat. When a school of these are under sail together they are frequently mistaken for a school of native boats.

The fish referred to is in all likelihood Histiophorus gladius, a species very closely related to, if not identical with, our own.

The Cutlass-fish

The cutlass-fish, Trichiurus lepturus, unfortunately known in eastern Florida and at Pensacola as the swordfish; at New Orleans, in the St. John's River, and at Brunswick, Georgia, it is known as the "silver eel"; on the coast of Texas as "saber-fish," while in the Indian River region it is called the "skip-jack." No one of these names is particularly applicable, and, the latter being preoccupied, it would seem advantageous to use in this country the name "cutlass-fish," which is current for the same species in the British West Indies.

Its appearance is very remarkable on account of its long, compressed form and its glistening, silvery color. The name "scabbard-fish," which has been given to an allied species in Europe, would be very proper also for this species, for in general shape and appearance it looks very like the metallic scabbard of the sword. It attains the length of four or five feet, though ordinarily not exceeding twenty-five or thirty inches. This species is found in the tropical Atlantic, on the coast of Brazil, in the Gulf of California, the West Indies, the Gulf of Mexico, and north to Woods Hole, Massachusetts, where, during the past ten years, specimens have been occasionally taken. In 1845 one was found at Wellfleet, Massachusetts; and in the Essex Institute is a specimen which is said to have been found on the shores of the Norway Frith many years ago, and during the past decade it has become somewhat abundant in southern England. It does not, however, enter the Mediterranean. Some writers believed the allied species, Trichiurus haumela, found in the Indian Ocean and Archipelago and in various parts of the Pacific, to be specifically the same.

The cutlass-fish is abundant in the St. John's River, Florida, in the Indian River region, and in the Gulf of Mexico. Several instances were related to me in which these fish had thrown themselves from the water into rowboats, a feat which might be very easily performed by a lithe, active species like the Trichiurus. A small one fell into a boat crossing the mouth of the Arlington River, where the water is nearly fresh.

Many individuals of the same species are taken every year at the mouth of the St. John's River at Mayport. Stearn states that they are caught in the deep waters of the bays about Pensacola, swimming nearly at the surface, but chiefly with hooks and lines from the wharves. He has known them to strike at the oars of the boat and at the end of the ropes that trailed in the water. At Pensacola they reach a length of twenty to thirty inches, and are considered good food fish. Richard Hill states that in Jamaica this species is much esteemed, and is fished for assiduously in a "hole," as it is called—that is, a deep portion of the waters off Fort Augusta. This is the best fishing-place for the cutlass-fish, Trichiurus. The fishing takes place before day; all lines are pulled in as fast as they are thrown out, with the certainty that the cutlass has been hooked. As many as ninety boats have been counted on this fishing-ground at daybreak during the season.

CHAPTER X
THE GLADIATOR OF THE SEA

Three summers in Catalina waters I had tried persistently to capture my first broadbill swordfish; and so great were the chances against me that I tried really without hope. It was fisherman's pride, I imagined, rather than hope that drove me. At least I had a remarkably keen appreciation of the defeats in store for any man who aspired to experience with that marvel of the sea—Xiphius gladius, the broadbill swordsman.

On the first morning of my fourth summer, 1917, I was up at five. Fine, cool, fresh, soft dawn with a pale pink sunrise. Sea rippling with an easterly breeze. As the sun rose it grew bright and warm. We did not get started out on the water until eight o'clock. The east wind had whipped up a little chop that promised bad. But the wind gradually died down and the day became hot. Great thunderheads rose over the mainland, proclaiming heat on the desert. We saw scattered sheerwater ducks and a school of porpoises; also a number of splashes that I was sure were made by swordfish.

The first broadbill I sighted had a skinned tail, and evidently had been in a battle of some kind. We circled him three times with flying-fish bait and once with barracuda, and as he paid no attention to them we left him. This fish leaped half out on two occasions, once showing his beautiful proportions, his glistening silver white, and his dangerous-looking rapier.

The second one leaped twice before we neared him. And as we made a poor attempt at circling him, he saw the boat and would have none of our offers.

The third one was skimming along just under the surface, difficult to see. After one try at him we lost him.

They were not up on the surface that day, as they are when the best results are obtained. The east wind may have had something to do with that. These fish would average about three hundred pounds each. Captain Dan says the small ones are more wary, or not so hungry, for they do not strike readily.

I got sunburnt and a dizzy headache and almost seasick. Yet the day was pleasant. The first few days are always hard, until I get broken in.

Next morning the water and conditions were ideal. The first two swordfish we saw did not stay on the surface long enough to be worked. The third one stayed up, but turned away from the bait every time we got it near him. So we left him.

About noon I sighted a big splash a mile off shoreward, and we headed that way. Soon I sighted fins. The first time round we got the bait right and I felt the old thrill. He went down. I waited; but in vain.

He leaped half out, and some one snapped a picture. It looked like a fortunate opportunity grasped. We tried him again, with flying-fish and barracuda. But he would not take either. Yet he loafed around on the surface, showing his colors, quite near the boat. He leaped clear out once, but I saw only the splash. Then he came out sideways, a skittering sort of plunge, lazy and heavy. He was about a three-hundred pounder, white and blue and green, a rare specimen of fish. We tried him again and drew a bait right in front of him. No use! Then we charged him—ran him down. Even then he was not frightened, and came up astern. At last, discouraged at his indifference, we left him.

This day was ideal up to noon. Then the sun got very hot. My wrists were burnt, and neck and face. My eyes got tired searching the sea for fins. It was a great game, this swordfishing, and beat any other I ever tried, for patience and endurance. The last fish showed his cunning. They were all different, and a study of each would be fascinating and instructive.

Next morning was fine. There were several hours when the sea was smooth and we could have sighted a swordfish a long distance. We went eastward of the ship course almost over to Newport. At noon a westerly wind sprang up and the water grew rough. It took some hours to be out of it to the leeward of the island.

I saw a whale bend his back and sound and lift his flukes high in the air—one of the wonder sights of the ocean.

It was foggy all morning, and rather too cool. No fish of any kind showed on the surface. One of those inexplicably blank days that are inevitable in sea angling.

When we got to the dock we made a discovery. There was a kink in my leader about one inch above the hook. Nothing but the sword of old Xiphius gladius could have made that kink! Then I remembered a strange, quick, hard jerk that had taken my bait, and which I thought had been done by a shark. It was a swordfish striking the bait off!

Next day we left the dock at six fifteen, Dan and I alone. The day was lowering and windy—looked bad. We got out ahead of every one. Trolled out five miles, then up to the west end. We got among the Japs fishing for albacore.

About eleven I sighted a B. B. We dragged a bait near him and he went down with a flirt of his tail. My heart stood still. Dan and I both made sure it was a strike. But, no! He came up far astern, and then went down for good.

The sea got rough. The wind was chilling to the bone. Sheerwater ducks were everywhere, in flocks and singly. Saw one yellow patch of small bait fish about an inch long. This patch was forty yards across. No fish appeared to be working on it.

Dan sighted a big swordfish. We made for him. Dan put on an albacore. But it came off before I could let out the line. Then we tried a barracuda. I got a long line out and the hook pulled loose. This was unfortunate and aggravating. We had one barracuda left. Dan hooked it on hard.

"That'll never come off!" he exclaimed. We circled old Xiphius, and when about fifty yards distant he lifted himself clear out—a most terrifying and magnificent fish. He would have weighed four hundred. His colors shone—blazed—purple blue, pale green, iridescent copper, and flaming silver. Then he made a long, low lunge away from us. I bade him good-by, but let the barracuda drift back. We waited a long time while the line slowly bagged, drifting toward us. Suddenly I felt a quick, strong pull. It electrified me. I yelled to Dan. He said, excitedly, "Feed it to him!" but the line ceased to play out. I waited, slowly losing hope, with my pulses going back to normal. After we drifted for five minutes I wound in the line. The barracuda was gone and the leader had been rolled up. This astounded us. That swordfish had taken my bait. I felt his first pull. Then he had come toward the boat, crushing the bait off the hook, without making even a twitch on the slack line. It was heartbreaking. But we could not have done any different. Dan decided the fish had come after the teasers. This experience taught us exceeding respect for the broadbill.

Again we were off early in the morning. Wind outside and growing rough. Sun bright until off Isthmus, when we ran into fog. The Jap albacore-boats were farther west. Albacore not biting well. Sea grew rough. About eleven thirty the fog cleared and the sea became beautifully blue and white-crested.

I was up on the deck when a yell from below made me jump. I ran back. Some one was holding my rod, and on the instant that a huge swordfish got the bait had not the presence of mind to throw off the drag and let out line. We hurried to put on another flying-fish and I let out the line.

Soon Dan yelled, "There he is—behind your bait!"

I saw him—huge, brown, wide, weaving after my bait. Then he hit it with his sword. I imagined I could feel him cut it. Winding in, I found the bait cut off neatly back of the head. While Dan hurried with another bait I watched for the swordfish, and saw him back in the wake, rather deep. He was following us. It was an intensely exciting moment. I let the bait drift back. Almost at once I felt that peculiar rap at my bait, then another. Somehow I knew he had cut off another flying-fish. I reeled in. He had severed this bait in the middle. Frantically we baited again. I let out a long line, and we drifted. Hope was almost gone when there came a swift tug on my line, and then the reel whirred. I thumbed the pad lightly. Dan yelled for me to let him have it. I was all tingling with wonderful thrills. What a magnificent strike! He took line so fast it amazed me.

All at once, just as Dan yelled to hook him, the reel ceased to turn, the line slacked. I began to jerk hard and wind in, all breathless with excitement and frenzy of hope. Not for half a dozen pumps and windings did I feel him. Then heavy and strong came the weight. I jerked and reeled. But I did not get a powerful strike on that fish. Suddenly the line slacked and my heart contracted. He had shaken the hook. I reeled in. Bait gone! He had doubled on me and run as swiftly toward the boat as he had at first run from it.

The hook had not caught well. Probably he had just held the bait between his jaws. The disappointment was exceedingly bitter and poignant. My respect for Xiphius increased in proportion to my sense of lost opportunity. This great fish thinks! That was my conviction.

We sighted another that refused to take a bait and soon went down.

We had learned the last few days that broadbills will strike when not on the surface, just as Marlin swordfish do.

On our next day out we had smooth sea all morning, with great, slow-running swells, long and high, with deep hollows between. Vast, heaving bosom of the deep! It was majestic. Along the horizon ran dark, low, lumpy waves, moving fast. A thick fog, like a pall, hung over the sea all morning.

About eleven o'clock I sighted fins. We made a circle round him, and drew the bait almost right across his bill. He went down. Again that familiar waiting, poignant suspense!... He refused to strike.

Next one was a big fellow with pale fins. We made a perfect circle, and he went down as if to take the bait!... But he came up. We tried again. Same result. Then we put on an albacore and drew that, tail first, in front of him. Slowly he swam toward it, went down, and suddenly turned and shot away, leaving a big wake. He was badly scared by that albacore.

Next one we worked three times before he went down, and the last one gave us opportunity for only one circle before he sank.

They are shy, keen, and wise.

The morning following, as we headed out over a darkly rippling sea, some four miles off Long Point, where we had the thrilling strikes from the big swordfish, and which place we had fondly imagined was our happy hunting-ground—because it was near shore and off the usual fishing course out in the channel—we ran into Boschen fighting a fish.

This is a spectacle not given to many fishermen, and I saw my opportunity.

With my glass I watched Boschen fight the swordfish, and I concluded from the way he pulled that he was fast to the bottom of the ocean. We went on our way then, and that night when I got in I saw his wonderful swordfish, the world's record we all knew he would get some day. Four hundred and sixty-three pounds! And he had the luck to kill this great fish in short time. My friend Doctor Riggin, a scientist, dissected this fish, and found that Boschen's hook had torn into the heart. This strange feature explained the easy capture, and, though it might detract somewhat from Boschen's pride in the achievement, it certainly did not detract from the record.

That night, after coming in from the day's hunt for swordfish, Dan and I decided to get good bait. At five thirty we started for seal rocks. The sun was setting, and the red fog over the west end of the island was weird and beautiful. Long, slow swells were running, and they boomed inshore on the rocks. Seals were barking—a hoarse, raucous croak. I saw a lonely heron silhouetted against the red glow of the western horizon.

We fished—trolling slowly a few hundred yards offshore—and soon were fighting barracuda, which we needed so badly for swordfish bait.

They strike easily, and put up a jerky kind of battle. They are a long, slim fish, yellow and white in the water, a glistening pale bronze and silver when landed. I hooked a harder-fighting fish, which, when brought in, proved to be a white sea-bass, a very beautiful species with faint purplish color and mottled opal tints above the deep silver.

Next morning we left the bay at six thirty. It was the calmest day we had had in days. The sea was like a beveled mirror, oily, soft, and ethereal, with low swells barely moving. An hour and a half out we were alone on the sea, out of sight of land, with the sun faintly showing, and all around us, inclosing and mystical, a thin haze of fog.

Alone, alone, all alone on a wide, wide sea! This was wonderful, far beyond any pursuit of swordfish.

We sighted birds, gulls, and ducks floating like bits of colored cork, and pieces of kelp, and at length a broadbill. We circled him three times with barracuda, and again with a flying-fish. Apparently he had no interest in edibles. He scorned our lures. But we stayed with him until he sank for good.

Then we rode the sea for hours, searching for fins.

At ten forty we sighted another. Twice we drew a fresh fine barracuda in front of him, which he refused. It was so disappointing, in fact, really sickening.

Dan was disgusted. He said, "We can't get them to bite!"

And I said, "Let's try again!"

So we circled him once more. The sea was beautifully smooth, with the slow swells gently heaving. The swordfish rode them lazily and indifferently. His dorsal stood up straight and stiff, and the big sickle-shaped tail-fin wove to and fro behind. I gazed at them longingly, in despair, as unattainable. I knew of nothing in the fishing game as tantalizing and despairing as this sight.

We got rather near him this time, as he turned, facing us, and slowly swam in the direction of my bait. I could see the barracuda shining astern. Dan stopped the boat. I slowly let out line. The swordfish drifted back, and then sank.

I waited, intensely, but really without hope. And I watched my bait until it sank out of sight. Then followed what seemed a long wait. Probably it was really only a few moments. I had a sort of hopeless feeling. But I respected the fish all the more.

Then suddenly I felt a quiver of my line, as if an electric current had animated it. I was shocked keen and thrilling. My line whipped up and ran out.

"He's got it!" I called, tensely. That was a strong, stirring instant as with fascinated eyes I watched the line pass swiftly and steadily off the reel. I let him run a long way.

Then I sat down, jammed the rod in the socket, put on the drag, and began to strike. The second powerful sweep of the rod brought the line tight and I felt that heavy live weight. I struck at least a dozen times with all my might while the line was going off the reel. The swordfish was moving ponderously. Presently he came up with a great splash, showing his huge fins, and then the dark, slender, sweeping sword. He waved that sword, striking fiercely at the leader. Then he went down. It was only at this moment I realized I had again hooked a broadbill. Time, ten forty-five.

The fight was on.

For a while he circled the boat and it was impossible to move him a foot. He was about two hundred and fifty yards from us. Every once in a while he would come up. His sword would appear first, a most extraordinary sight as it pierced the water. We could hear the swish. Once he leaped half out. We missed this picture. I kept a steady, hard strain on him, pumping now and then, getting a little line in, which he always got back. The first hour passed swiftly with this surface fight alternating with his slow heavy work down. However, he did not sound.

About eleven forty-five he leaped clear out, and we snapped two pictures of him. It was a fierce effort to free the hook, a leap not beautiful and graceful, like that of the Marlin, but magnificent and dogged.

After this leap he changed his tactics. Repeatedly I was pulled forward and lifted from my seat by sudden violent jerks. They grew more frequent and harder. He came up and we saw how he did that. He was facing the boat and batting the leader with his sword. This was the most remarkable action I ever observed in a fighting fish. That sword was a weapon. I could hear it hit the leader. But he did most of this work under the surface. Every time he hit the leader it seemed likely to crack my neck. The rod bent, then the line slackened so I could feel no weight, the rod flew straight. I had an instant of palpitating dread, feeling he had freed himself—then harder came the irresistible, heavy drag again. This batting of the leader and consequent slacking of the line worried Dan, as it did me. Neither of us expected to hold the fish. As a performance it was wonderful. But to endure it was terrible. And he batted that leader at least three hundred times!

In fact, every moment or two he banged the leader several times for over an hour. It almost wore me out. If he had not changed those jerks again those jerks would have put a kink in my neck and back. But fortunately he came up on the surface to thresh about some more. Again he leaped clear, affording us another chance for a picture. Following that he took his first long run. It was about one hundred yards and as fast as a Marlin. Then he sounded. He stayed down for half an hour. When he came up somewhat he seemed to be less resistant, and we dragged him at slow speed for several miles. At the end of three hours I asked Dan for the harness, which he strapped to my shoulders. This afforded me relief for my arms and aching hands, but the straps cut into my back, and that hurt. The harness enabled me to lift and pull by a movement of shoulders. I worked steadily on him for an hour, five different times getting the two-hundred-foot mark on the line over my reel. When I tired Dan would throw in the clutch and drag him some more. Once he followed us without strain for a while; again we dragged him two or three miles. And most remarkable of all, there was a period of a few moments when he towed us. A wonderful test for a twenty-four-strand line! We made certain of this by throwing papers overboard and making allowance for the drift. At that time there was no wind. I had three and one-half hours of perfectly smooth water.

It was great to be out there on a lonely sea with that splendid fish. I was tiring, but did not fail to see the shimmering beauty of the sea, the playing of albacore near at hand, the flight of frightened flying-fish, the swooping down of gulls, the dim shapes of boats far off, and away above the cloud-bank of fog the mountains of California.

About two o'clock our indefatigable quarry began to belabor the leader again. He appeared even more vicious and stronger. That jerk, with its ragged, rough loosening of the line, making me feel the hook was tearing out, was the most trying action any fish ever worked on me. The physical effort necessary to hold him was enough, without that onslaught on my leader. Again there came a roar of water, a splash, and his huge dark-blue and copper-colored body surged on the surface. He wagged his head and the long black sword made a half-circle. The line was taut from boat to fish in spite of all I could do in lowering my rod. I had to hold it up far enough to get the spring. There was absolutely no way to keep him from getting slack. The dangerous time in fighting heavy, powerful fish is when they head toward the angler. Then the hook will pull out more easily than at any other time. He gave me a second long siege of these tactics until I was afraid I would give out. When he got through and sounded I had to have the back-rest replaced in the seat to rest my aching back.

Three o'clock came and passed. We dragged him awhile, and found him slower, steadier, easier to pull. That constant long strain must have been telling upon him. It was also telling upon me. As I tried to save some strength for the finish, I had not once tried my utmost at lifting him or pulling him near the boat. Along about four o'clock he swung round to the west in the sun glare and there he hung, broadside, about a hundred yards out, for an hour. We had to go along with him.

The sea began to ripple with a breeze, and at length white-caps appeared. In half an hour it was rough, not bad, but still making my work exceedingly hard. I had to lift the rod up to keep the seat from turning and to hold my footing on the slippery floor. The water dripping from the reel had wet me and all around me.

At five o'clock I could not stand the harness any longer, so had Dan remove it. That was a relief. I began to pump my fish as in the earlier hours of the fight. Eventually I got him out of that broadside position away from us and to the boat. He took some line, which I got back. I now began to have confidence in being able to hold him. He had ceased batting the leader. For a while he stayed astern, but gradually worked closer. This worried Dan. He was getting under the boat. Dan started faster ahead and still the swordfish kept just under us, perhaps fifty feet down. It was not long until Dan was running at full speed. But we could not lose the old gladiator! Then I bade Dan slow down, which he was reluctant to do. He feared the swordfish would ram us, and I had some qualms myself. At five thirty he dropped astern again and we breathed freer. At this time I decided to see if I could pull him close. I began to pump and reel, and inch by inch, almost, I gained line. I could not tell just how far away he was, because the marks had worn off my line. It was amazing and thrilling, therefore, to suddenly see the end of the double line appear. Dan yelled. So did I. Like a Trojan I worked till I got that double line over my reel. Then we all saw the fish. He was on his side, swimming with us—a huge, bird-shaped creature with a frightful bill. Dan called me to get the leader out of water and then hold. This took about all I had left of strength. The fish wavered from side to side, and Dan feared he would go under the boat. He ordered me to hold tight, and he put on more speed. This grew to be more than I could stand. It was desperately hard to keep the line from slipping. And I knew a little more of that would lose my fish. So I called Dan to take the leader. With his huge gaff in right hand, Dan reached for the leader with his left, grasped it, surged the fish up and made a lunge. There came a roar and a beating against the boat. Dan yelled for another gaff. It was handed to him and he plunged that into the fish.

Then I let down my rod and dove for the short rope to lasso the sweeping tail. Fortunately he kept quiet a moment in which I got the loop fast. It was then Xiphius gladius really woke up. He began a tremendous beating with his tail. Both gaff ropes began to loosen, and the rope on his tail flew out of my hands. Dan got it in time. But it was slipping. He yelled for me to make a hitch somewhere. I was pulled flat in the cockpit, but scrambled up, out on the stern, and held on to that rope grimly while I tried to fasten it. Just almost impossible! The water was deluging us. The swordfish banged the boat with sodden, heavy blows. But I got the rope fast. Then I went to Dan's assistance. The two of us pulled that tremendous tail up out of the water and made fast the rope. Then we knew we had him. But he surged and strained and lashed for a long while. And side blows of his sword scarred the boat. At last he sagged down quiet, and we headed for Avalon. Once more in smooth water, we loaded him astern. I found the hook just in the corner of his mouth, which fact accounted for the long battle.

Doctor Riggin, the University of Pennsylvania anatomist, and classmate of mine, dissected this fish for me. Two of the most remarkable features about Xiphius gladius were his heart and eye.

The heart was situated deep in just back of the gills. It was a big organ, exceedingly heavy, and the most muscular tissue I ever saw. In fact, so powerfully muscular was it that when cut the tissue contracted and could not be placed together again. The valves were likewise remarkably well developed and strong. This wonderful heart accounted for the wonderful vitality of the swordfish. The eyes of a swordfish likewise proved the wonder of nature. They were huge and prominent, a deep sea-blue set in pale crystal rims and black circles. A swordfish could revolve his eyes and turn them in their sockets so that they were absolutely protected in battle with his mates and rivals. The eye had a covering of bone, cup-shaped, and it was this bone that afforded protection. It was evident that when the eye was completely turned in the swordfish could not see at all. Probably this was for close battle. The muscles were very heavy and strong, one attached at the rim of the eye and the other farther back. The optic nerve was as large as the median nerve of a man's arm—that is to say, half the size of a lead-pencil. There were three coverings over the fluid that held the pupil. And these were as thick and tough as isinglass. Most remarkable of all was the ciliary muscle which held the capacity of contracting the lens for distant vision. A swordfish could see as far as the rays of light penetrated in whatever depth he swam. I have always suspected he had extraordinary eyesight, and this dissection of the eye proved it. No fear a swordfish will not see a bait! He can see the boat and the bait a long distance.

Doctor Riggin found no sperm in any of the male fish he dissected, which was proof that swordfish spawn before coming to Catalina waters. They are a warm-water fish, and probably head off the Japan current into some warm, intersecting branch that leads to spawning-banks.

This was happy knowledge for me, because it will be good to know that when old Xiphius gladius is driven from Catalina waters he will be roaming some other place of the Seven Seas, his great sickle fins shining dark against the blue.

CHAPTER XI

SEVEN MARLIN SWORDFISH IN ONE DAY

San Clemente lies forty miles south of Santa Catalina, out in the Pacific, open to wind and fog, scorched by sun, and beaten on every shore by contending tides. Seen from afar, the island seems a bleak, long, narrow strip of drab rock rising from a low west end to the dignity of a mountain near the east end. Seen close at hand, it is still barren, bleak, and drab; but it shows long golden slopes of wild oats; looming, gray, lichen-colored crags, where the eagles perch; and rugged deep cañons, cactus-covered on the south side and on the other indented by caves and caverns, and green with clumps of wild-lilac and wild-cherry and arbor-vitæ; and bare round domes where the wild goats stand silhouetted against the blue sky.

This island is volcanic in origin and structure, and its great caves have been made by blow-holes in hot lava. Erosion has weathered slope and wall and crag. For the most part these slopes and walls are exceedingly hard to climb. The goat trails are narrow and steep, the rocks sharp and ragged, the cactus thick and treacherous. Many years ago Mexicans placed goats on the island for the need of shipwrecked sailors, and these goats have traversed the wild oat slopes until they are like a network of trails. Every little space of grass has its crisscross of goat trails.

I rested high up on a slope, in the lee of a rugged rock, all rust-stained and gray-lichened, with a deep cactus-covered cañon to my left, the long, yellow, windy slope of wild oats to my right, and beneath me the Pacific, majestic and grand, where the great white rollers moved in graceful heaves along the blue. The shore-line, curved by rounded gravelly beach and jutted by rocky point, showed creeping white lines of foam, and then green water spotted by beds of golden kelp, reaching out into the deeps. Far across the lonely space rose creamy clouds, thunderheads looming over the desert on the mainland.

A big black raven soared by with dismal croak. The wind rustled the oats. There was no other sound but the sound of the sea—deep, low-toned, booming like thunder, long crash and continuous roar.

How wonderful to watch eagles in their native haunts! I saw a bald eagle sail by, and then two golden eagles winging heavy flight after him. There seemed to be contention or rivalry, for when the white-headed bird alighted the others swooped down upon him. They circled and flew in and out of the cañon, and one let out a shrill, piercing scream. They disappeared and I watched a lonely gull riding the swells. He at least was at home on the restless waters. Life is beautiful, particularly elemental life. Then far above I saw the white-tipped eagle and I thrilled to see the difference now in his flight. He was monarch of the air, king of the wind, lonely and grand in the blue. He soared, he floated, he sailed, and then, away across the skies he flew, swift as an arrow, to slow and circle again, and swoop up high and higher, wide-winged and free, ringed in the azure blue, and then like a thunderbolt he fell, to vanish beyond the crags.

Again I saw right before me a small brown hawk, poised motionless, resting on the wind, with quivering wings, and he hung there, looking down for his prey—some luckless lizard or rat. He seemed suspended on wires. There, down like a brown flash he was gone, and surely that swoop meant a desert tragedy.

I heard the bleat of a lamb or kid, and it pierced the melancholy roar of the sea.

If there is a rapture on the lonely shore, there was indeed rapture here high above it, blown upon by the sweet, soft winds. I heard the bleat close at hand. Turning, I saw a she-goat with little kid scarce a foot high. She crossed a patch of cactus. The kid essayed to follow here, but found the way too thorny. He bleated—a tiny, pin-pointed bleat—and his mother turned to answer encouragingly. He leaped over a cactus, attempted another, and, failing, fell on the sharp prickers. He bleated in distress and scrambled out of that hard and painful place. The mother came around, and presently, reunited, they went on, to disappear.

The island seemed consecrated to sun and sea. It lay out of the latitude of ships. Only a few Mexican sheep-herders lived there, up at the east end where less-rugged land allowed pasture for their flocks. A little rain falls during the winter months, and soon disappears from the porous cañon-beds. Water-holes were rare and springs rarer. The summit was flat, except for some rounded domes of mountains, and there the deadly cholla cactus grew—not in profusion, but enough to prove the dread of the Mexicans for this species of desert plant. It was a small bush, with cones like a pine cone in shape, growing in clusters, and over stems and cones were fine steel-pointed needles with invisible hooks at the ends.

A barren, lonely prospect, that flat plateau above, an empire of the sun, where heat veils rose and mirages haunted the eye. But at sunset fog rolled up from the outer channel, and if the sun blasted the life on the island, the fog saved it. So there was war between sun and fog, the one that was the lord of day, and the other the dew-laden savior of night.

South, on the windward side, opened a wide bay, Smugglers Cove by name, and it was infinitely more beautiful than its name. A great curve indented the league-long slope of island, at each end of which low, ragged lines of black rock jutted out into the sea. Around this immense bare amphitheater, which had no growth save scant cactus and patches of grass, could be seen long lines of shelves where the sea-levels had been in successive ages of the past.

Near the middle of the curve, on a bleached bank, stood a lonely little hut, facing the sea. Old and weather-beaten, out of place there, it held and fascinated the gaze. Below it a white shore-line curved away where the waves rolled in, sadly grand, to break and spread on the beach.

At the east end, where the jagged black rocks met the sea, I loved to watch a great swell rise out of the level blue, heave and come, slow-lifting as if from some infinite power, to grow and climb aloft till the blue turned green and sunlight showed through, and the long, smooth crest, where the seals rode, took on a sharp edge to send wisps of spray in the wind, and, rising sheer, the whole swell, solemn and ponderous and majestic, lifted its volume one beautiful instant, then curled its shining crest and rolled in and down with a thundering, booming roar, all the curves and contours gone in a green-white seething mass that climbed the reefs and dashed itself to ruin.

An extraordinary achievement and record fell to my brother R. C. It was too much good luck ever to come my way. Fame is a fickle goddess. R. C. had no ambition to make a great catch of swordfish. He angles for these big game of the sea more to furnish company for me than for any other reason. He likes best the golden, rocky streams where the bronze-back black-bass hide, or the swift, amber-colored brooks full of rainbow trout.

I must add that in my opinion, and Captain Danielson's also, R. C. is a superior angler, and all unconscious of it. He has not my intimate knowledge of big fish, but he did not seem to need that. He is powerful in the shoulders and arms, his hands are strong and hard from baseball and rowing, and he is practically tireless. He never rested while fighting a fish. We never saw him lean the rod on the gunwale. All of which accounts for his quick conquering of a Marlin swordfish. We have yet to see him work upon a broadbill or a big tuna; and that is something Captain Dan and I are anticipating with much pleasure and considerable doubt.

August 31st dawned fine and cool and pleasant, rather hazy, with warm sun and smooth sea.

The night before we had sat in front of our tents above the beach and watched the flying-fish come out in twos and threes and schools, all the way down the rugged coast. I told the captain then that swordfish were chasing them. But he was skeptical.

This morning I remembered, and I was watching. Just at the Glory Hole my brother yelled, "Strike!" I did not see the fish before he hit the bait. It is really remarkable how these swordfish can get to a bait on the surface without being seen. R. C. hooked the Marlin.

The first leap showed the fish to be small. He did not appear to be much of a jumper or fighter. He leaped six times, and then tried to swim out to sea. Slow, steady work of R. C.'s brought him up to the boat in fifteen minutes. But we did not gaff him. We estimated his weight at one hundred and thirty pounds. Captain Dan cut the leader close to the hook. I watched the fish swim lazily away, apparently unhurt, and sure to recover.

We got going again, and had scarce trolled a hundred yards when I saw something my companions missed. I stood up.

"Well, this starts out like your day," I remarked to my brother.

Then he saw a purple shape weaving back of his bait and that galvanized him into attention. It always thrilled me to see a swordfish back of the bait. This one took hold and ran off to the right. When hooked it took line with a rush, began to thresh half out, and presently sounded. We lost the direction. It came up far ahead of the boat and began to leap and run on the surface.

We followed while R. C. recovered the line. Then he held the fish well in hand; and in the short time of twelve minutes brought the leader to Dan's hand. The Marlin made a great splash as he was cut loose.

"Say, two swordfish in less than half an hour!" I expostulated. "Dan, this might be the day."

Captain Dan looked hopeful. We were always looking for that day which came once or twice each season.

"I'm tired," said my brother. "Now you catch a couple."

He talked about swordfish as carelessly as he used to talk about sunfish. But he was not in the least tired. I made him take up the rod again. I sensed events. The sea looked darkly rippling, inviting, as if to lure us on.

We had worked and drifted a little offshore. But that did not appear to put us out of the latitude of swordfish. Suddenly Captain Dan yelled, "Look out!" Then we all saw a blaze of purple back of R. C.'s bait. Dan threw out the clutch. But this Marlin was shy. He flashed back and forth. How swift! His motion was only a purple flash. He loomed up after the teasers. We had three of these flying-fish out as teasers, all close to the boat. I always wondered why the swordfish appear more attracted to the teasers than to our hooked baits only a few yards back. I made the mistake to pull the teasers away from this swordfish. Then he left us.

I was convinced, however, that this was to be R. C.'s day, and so, much to his amaze and annoyance, I put away my rod. No sooner had I quit fishing than a big black tail showed a few yards out from R. C.'s bait. Then a shining streak shot across under the water, went behind R. C.'s bait, passed it, came again. This time I saw him plainly. He was big and hungry, but shy. He rushed the bait. I saw him take it in his pointed jaws and swerve out of sight, leaving a boil on the surface. R. C. did not give him time to swallow the hook, but struck immediately. The fish ran off two hundred yards and then burst up on the surface. He was a jumper, and as he stayed in sight we all began to yell our admiration. He cleared the water forty-two times, all in a very few minutes. At the end of twenty-eight minutes R. C., with a red face and a bulging jaw, had the swordfish beaten and within reach of Captain Dan.

"He's a big one—over two hundred and fifty," asserted that worthy. "Mebbe you won't strike a bigger one."

"Cut him loose," I said, and my brother echoed my wish.

It was a great sight to see that splendid swordfish drift away from the boat—to watch him slowly discover that he was free.

"Ten o'clock! We'll hang up two records to-day!" boomed Captain Dan, as with big, swift hands he put on another bait for R. C.

"Do you fellows take me for a drag-horse?" inquired R. C., mildly. "I've caught enough swordfish for this year."

"Why, man, it's the day!" exclaimed Captain Dan, in amaze and fear.

"Humph!" replied my brother.

"But the chance for a record!" I added, weakly. "Only ten o'clock.... Three swordfish already.... Great chance for Dan, you know.... Beat the dickens out of these other fishermen."

"Aw, that's a lot of 'con'!" replied my brother.

Very eloquently then I elaborated on the fact that we were releasing the fish, inaugurating a sportsman-like example never before done there; that it really bid fair to be a wonderful day; that I was having a great chance to snap pictures of leaping fish; that it would be a favor to me for him to go the limit on this one occasion.

But R. C. showed no sign of wavering. He was right, of course, and I acknowledged that afterward to myself. On the instant, however, I racked my brain for some persuasive argument. Suddenly I had an inspiration.

"They think you're a dub fisherman," I declared, forcefully.

"They?" My brother glared darkly at me.

"Sure," I replied, hurriedly, with no intention of explaining that dubious they. "Now's your chance to fool them."

"Ahuh! All right, fetch on a flock of swordfish, and then some broadbills," remarked R. C., blandly. "Hurry, Dan! There's a fin right over there. Lead me to him! See."

Sure enough, R. C. pointed out a dark sickle fin on the surface. I marveled at the sight. It certainly is funny the luck some fishermen have! Captain Dan, beaming like a sunrise, swung the boat around toward the swordfish.

That Marlin rushed the teasers. I pulled all three away from him, while R. C. was reeling in his bait to get it close. Then the swordfish fell all over himself after it. He got it. He would have climbed aboard after it. The way R. C. hooked this swordfish showed that somebody had got his dander up and was out to do things. This pleased me immensely. It scared me a little, too, for R. C. showed no disposition to give line or be gentle to the swordfish. In fact, it was real fight now. And this particular fish appeared to have no show on earth—or rather in the water—and after fourteen leaps he was hauled up to the boat in such short order that if we had gaffed him, as we used to gaff Marlin, we would have had a desperate fight to hold him. But how easy to cut him free! He darted down like a blue streak. I had no fair sight of him to judge weight, but Captain Dan said he was good and heavy.

"Come on! Don't be so slow!" yelled R. C., with a roving eye over the deep.

Captain Dan was in his element. He saw victory perched upon the mast of the Leta D. He moved with a celerity that amazed me, when I remembered how exasperatingly slow he could be, fooling with kites. This was Captain Dan's game.

"The ocean's alive with swordfish!" he boomed. Only twice before had I heard him say that, and he was right each time. I gazed abroad over the beautiful sea, and, though I could not see any swordfish, somehow I believed him. It was difficult now, in this exciting zest of a record feat, to think of the nobler attributes of fishing. Strong, earnest, thrilling business it was indeed for Captain Dan.

We all expected to see a swordfish again. That was exactly what happened. We had not gone a dozen boat-lengths when up out of the blue depths lunged a lazy swordfish and attached himself to R. C.'s hook. He sort of half lolled out in lazy splashes four or five times. He looked huge. All of a sudden he started off, making the reel hum. That run developed swiftly. Dan backed the boat full speed. In vain! It was too late to turn. That swordfish run became the swiftest and hardest I ever saw. A four-hundred-yard run, all at once, was something new even for me. I yelled for R. C. to throw off the drag. He tried, but failed. I doubted afterward if that would have done any good. That swordfish was going away from there. He broke the line.

"Gee! What a run!" I burst out. "I'm sorry. I hate to break off hooks in fish."

"Put your hand on my reel," said R. C.

It was almost too hot to bear touching. R. C. began winding in the long slack line.

"Did you see that one?" he asked, grimly.

"Not plain. But what I did see looked big."

"Say, he was a whale!" R. C.'s flashing eyes showed he had warmed to the battle.

In just ten minutes another swordfish was chasing the teasers. It was my thrilling task to keep them away from him. Hard as I pulled, I failed to keep at least one of them from him. He took it with a "wop," his bill half out of the water, and as he turned with a splash R. C. had his bait right there. Smash! The swordfish sheered off, with the bait shining white in his bill. When hooked he broke water about fifty yards out and then gave an exhibition of high and lofty tumbling, water-smashing, and spray-flinging that delighted us. Then he took to long, greyhound leaps and we had to chase him. But he did not last long, with the inexorable R. C. bending back on that Murphy rod. After being cut free, this swordfish lay on the surface a few moments, acting as if he was out of breath. He weighed about one hundred and fifty, and was a particularly beautiful specimen. The hook showed in the corner of his mouth. He did not have a scratch on his graceful bronze and purple and silver body. I waved my hat at him and then he slowly sank.

"What next?" I demanded. "This can't keep up. Something is going to happen."

But my apprehension in no wise disturbed R. C. or Captain Dan.

They proceeded to bait up again, to put out the teasers, to begin to troll; and then almost at once a greedy swordfish appeared, absolutely fearless and determined. R. C. hooked him. The first leap showed the Marlin to be the smallest of the day so far. But what he lacked in weight he made up in activity. He was a great performer, and his forte appeared to be turning upside down in the air. He leaped clear twenty-two times. Then he settled down and tried to plug out to sea. Alas! that human steam-winch at the rod drew him right up to the boat, where he looked to weigh about one hundred and twenty-five pounds.

"Six!" I exclaimed, as we watched the freed fish swim away. "That's the record.... And all let go alive—unhurt.... Do you suppose any one will believe us?"

"It doesn't make any difference," remarked my brother. "We know. That's the best of the game—letting the fish go alive."

"Come on!" boomed Dan, with a big flying-fish in his hands. "You're not tired."

"Yes, I am tired," replied R. C.

"It's early yet," I put in. "We'll cinch the record for good. Grab the rod. I'll enjoy the work for you."

R. C. resigned himself, not without some remarks anent the insatiable nature of his host and boatman.

We were now off the east end of Clemente Island, that bleak and ragged corner where the sea, whether calm or stormy, contended eternally with the black rocks, and where the green and white movement of waves was never still. When almost two hundred yards off the yellow kelp-beds I saw a shadow darker than the blue water. It seemed to follow the boat, rather deep down and far back. But it moved. I was on my feet, thrilling.

"That's a swordfish!" I called.

"No," replied R. C.

"Some wavin' kelp, mebbe," added Dan, doubtfully.

"Slow up a little," I returned. "I see purple."

Captain Dan complied and we all watched. We all saw an enormous colorful body loom up, take the shape of a fish, come back of R. C.'s bait, hit it and take it.

"By George!" breathed R. C., tensely. His line slowly slipped out a little, then stopped.

"He's let go," said my brother.

"There's another one," cried Dan.

With that I saw what appeared to be another swordfish, deeper down, moving slowly. This one also looked huge to me. He was right under the teasers. It dawned upon me that he must have an eye on them, so I began to pull them in.

As they came in the purple shadow seemed to rise. It was a swordfish and he resembled a gunboat with purple outriggers. Slowly he came onward and upward, a wonderful sight.

"Wind your bait in!" I yelled to R. C.

Suddenly Dan became like a jumping-jack. "He's got your hook," he shouted to my brother. "He's had it all the time."

The swordfish swam now right under the stern of the boat so that I could look down upon him. He was deep down, but not too deep to look huge. Then I saw R. C.'s leader in his mouth. He had swallowed the flying-fish bait and had followed us for the teasers. The fact was stunning. R. C., who had been winding in, soon found out that his line went straight down. He felt the fish. Then with all his might he jerked to hook that swordfish.

Just then, for an instant my mind refused to work swiftly. It was locked round some sense of awful expectancy. I remembered my camera in my hands and pointed it where I expected something wonderful about to happen.

The water on the right, close to the stern, bulged and burst with a roar. Upward even with us, above us, shot a tremendously large, shiny fish, shaking and wagging, with heavy slap of gills.

Water deluged the boat, but missed me. I actually smelled that fish, he was so close. What must surely have been terror for me, had I actually seen and realized the peril, gave place to flashing thought of the one and great chance for a wonderful picture of a big swordfish close to the boat. That gripped me. While I changed the focus on my camera I missed seeing the next two jumps. But I heard the heavy sousing splashes and the yells of Dan and R. C., with the shrill screams of the ladies.

When I did look up to try to photograph the next leap of the swordfish I saw him, close at hand, monstrous and animated, in a surging, up-sweeping splash. I heard the hiss of the boiling foam. He lunged away, churning the water like a sudden whirl of a ferryboat wheel, and then he turned squarely at us. Even then Captain Dan's yell did not warn us. I felt rather than saw that he had put on full speed ahead. The swordfish dove toward us, went under, came up in a two-sheeted white splash, and rose high and higher, to fall with a cracking sound. Like a flash of light he shot up again, and began wagging his huge purple-barred body, lifting himself still higher, until all but his tail stood ponderously above the surface; and then, incredibly powerful, he wagged and lashed upright in a sea of hissing foam, mouth open wide, blood streaming down his wet sides and flying in red spray from his slapping gills—a wonderful and hair-raising spectacle. He stayed up only what seemed a moment. During this action and when he began again to leap and smash toward us, I snapped my camera three times upon him. But I missed seeing some of his greatest leaps because I had to look at the camera while operating it.

"Get back!" yelled Dan, hoarsely.

I was so excited I did not see the danger of the swordfish coming aboard. But Captain Dan did. He swept the girls back into the cabin doorway, and pushed Mrs. R. C. into a back corner of the cockpit. Strange it seemed to me how pale Dan was!

The swordfish made long, swift leaps right at the boat. On the last he hit us on the stern, but too low to come aboard. Six feet closer to us would have landed that huge, maddened swordfish right in the cockpit! But he thumped back, and the roar of his mighty tail on the water so close suddenly appalled me. I seemed to grasp how near he had come aboard at the same instant that I associated the power of his tail with a havoc he would have executed in the boat. It flashed over me that he would weigh far over three hundred.

When he thumped back the water rose in a sounding splash, deluging us and leaving six inches in the cockpit. He sheered off astern, sliding over the water in two streaks of white running spray, and then up he rose again in a magnificent wild leap. He appeared maddened with pain and fright and instinct to preserve his life.

Again the fish turned right at us. This instant was the most terrifying. Not a word from R. C.! But out of the tail of my eye I saw him crouch, ready to leap. He grimly held on to his rod, but there had not been a tight line on it since he struck the fish.

Yelling warningly, Captain Dan threw the wheel hard over. But that seemed of no use. We could not lose the swordfish.

He made two dives into the air, and the next one missed us by a yard, and showed his great, glistening, striped body, thick as a barrel, and curved with terrible speed and power, right alongside the cockpit. He passed us, and as the boat answered to the wheel and turned, almost at right angles, the swordfish sheered too, and he hit us a sounding thud somewhere foreward. Then he went under or around the bow and began to take line off the reel for the first time. I gave him up. The line caught all along the side of the boat. But it did not break, and kept whizzing off the reel. I heard the heavy splash of another jump. When we had turned clear round, what was our amaze and terror to see the swordfish, seemingly more tigerish than ever, thresh and tear and leap at us again. He was flinging bloody spray and wigwagging his huge body, so that there was a deep, rough splashing furrow in the sea behind him. I had never known any other fish so fast, so powerful, so wild with fury, so instinct with tremendous energy and life. Dan again threw all his weight on the wheel. The helm answered, the boat swung, and the swordfish missed hitting us square. But he glanced along the port side, like a toboggan down-hill, and he seemed to ricochet over the water. His tail made deep, solid thumps. Then about a hundred feet astern he turned in his own length, making a maelstrom of green splash and white spray, out of which he rose three-quarters of his huge body, purple-blazed, tiger-striped, spear-pointed, and, with the sea boiling white around him, he spun around, creating an indescribable picture of untamed ferocity and wild life and incomparable beauty. Then down he splashed with a sullen roar, leaving a red foam on the white.

That appeared the end of his pyrotechnics. It had been only a few moments. He began to swim off slowly and heavily. We followed. After a few tense moments it became evident that his terrible surface work had weakened him, probably bursting his gills, from which his life-blood escaped.

We all breathed freer then. Captain Dan left the wheel, mopping his pale, wet face. He gazed at me to see if I had realized our peril. With the excitement over, I began to realize. I felt a little shaky then. The ladies were all talking at once, still glowing with excitement. Easy to see they had not appreciated the danger! But Captain Dan and I knew that if the swordfish had come aboard—which he certainly would have done had he ever slipped his head over the gunwale—there would have been a tragedy on the Leta D.

"I never knew just how easy it could happen," said Dan. "No one ever before hooked a big fish right under the boat."

"With that weight, that tail, right after being hooked, he would have killed some of us and wrecked the boat!" I exclaimed, aghast.

"Well, I had him figured to come into the boat and I was ready to jump overboard," added my brother.

"We won't cut him loose," said Dan. "That's some fish. But he acts like he isn't goin' to last long."

Still, it took two hours longer of persistent, final effort on the part of R. C. to bring this swordfish to gaff. We could not lift the fish up on the stern and we had to tow him over to Mr. Jump's boat and there haul him aboard by block and tackle. At Avalon he weighed three hundred and twenty-eight pounds.

R. C. had caught the biggest Marlin in 1916—three hundred and four pounds, and this three-hundred-and-twenty-eight-pound fish was the largest for 1918. Besides, there was the remarkable achievement and record of seven swordfish in one day, with six of them freed to live and roam the sea again. But R. C. was not impressed. He looked at his hands and said:

"You and Dan put a job up on me.... Never again!"

CHAPTER XII

RANDOM NOTES

AVALON, July 1, 1918.

Cool, foggy morning; calm sea up until one o'clock, then a west wind that roughened the water white. No strikes. Did not see a fish. Trolled with kite up to the Isthmus and back. When the sun came out its warmth was very pleasant. The slopes seemed good to look at—so steep and yellow-gray with green spots, and long slides running down to the shore. The tips of the hills were lost in the fog. It was lonely on the sea, and I began again to feel the splendor and comfort of the open spaces, the free winds, the canopy of gray and blue, the tidings from afar.

July 3d.

Foggy morning; pale line of silver on eastern horizon; swell, but no wind. Warm. After a couple of hours fog disintegrated. Saw a big Marlin swordfish. Worked him three times, then charged him. No use!

Gradually rising wind. Ran up off Long Point and back. At 3:30 was tired. We saw a school of tuna on the surface. Flew the kite over them. One big fellow came clear out on his side and got the hook. He made one long run, then came in rather easily. Time, fifteen minutes. He was badly hooked. Seventy-eight pounds.

We trolled then until late afternoon. I saw some splashes far out. Tuna! We ran up. Found patches of anchovies. I had a strike. Tuna hooked himself and got off. We tried again. I had another come clear out in a smashing charge. He ran off heavy and fast. It took fifty minutes of very hard work to get him in. He weaved back of the boat for half an hour and gave me a severe battle. He was hooked in the corner of the mouth and was a game, fine fish. Seventy-three and one-half pounds.

July 6th.

Started out early. Calm, cool, foggy morning; rather dark. Sea smooth, swelling, heaving. Mysterious, like a shadowed opal. Long mounds of water waved noiselessly, wonderfully, ethereally from the distance, and the air was hazy, veiled, and dim. A lonely, silent vastness.

We saw several schools of tuna, but got no strikes. Worked a Marlin swordfish, but he would not notice the bait.

It was a long, hard day on the sea.

July 10th.

We got off at 6:30 before the other boats. Smooth water. Little breeze. Saw a school of tuna above Long Point. Put up the kite. The school went down. But R. C. got a little strike. Did not hook fish.

Then we sighted a big school working east. We followed it, running into a light wind. Kite blew O. K. and R. C. got one fish (seventy-one pounds), then another (forty-eight pounds). They put up fair fights.

Then I tried light tackle. All the time the school traveled east, going down and coming up. The first fish that charged my bait came clear out after it. He got it and rushed away. I had the light drag on, and I did not thumb the pad hard, but the tuna broke the line. We tried again. Had another thrilling strike. The fish threw the hook. We had to pull in the kite, put up another one—get it out, and all the time keep the school in sight. The tuna traveled fast. The third try on light tackle resulted in another fine strike, and another tuna that broke the line.

Then R. C. tried the heavy tackle again, and lost a fish.

When my turn came I was soon fast to a hard-fighting fish, but he did not stay with me long. This discouraged me greatly.

Then R. C. took his rod once more. It was thrilling to run down on the school and skip a flying-fish before the leaders as they rolled along, fins out, silver sides showing, raising little swells and leaving a dark, winkling, dimpling wake behind them. When the bait got just right a larger tuna charged furiously, throwing up a great splash. He hit the bait, and threw the hook before R. C. could strike hard.

We had nine bites out of this school. Followed it fifteen miles. Twice we were worried by other boats, but for the rest of the time had the school alone.

July 11th.

Morning was cold, foggy, raw. East wind. Disagreeable. Trolled out about six miles and all around. Finally ran in off east end, where I caught a yellow-fin. The sun came up, but the east wind persisted. No fish. Came in early.

July 12th.

Went out early. Clear morning. Cool. Rippling sea. Fog rolled down like a pale-gray wall. Misty, veiled, vague, strange, opaque, silent, wet, cold, heavy! It enveloped us. Then we went out of the bank into a great circle, clear and bright, with heaving, smooth sea, surrounded by fog.

After an hour or two the fog rose and drifted away.

We trolled nine hours. Three little fish struck at the bait, but did not get the hook.

August 6th.

To-day I went out alone with Dan. Wonderful sea. Very long, wide, deep, heaving swells, beautiful and exhilarating to watch. No wind. Not very foggy. Sunshine now and then. I watched the sea—marveled at its grace, softness, dimpled dark beauty, its vast, imponderable racing, its restless heaving, its eternal motion. I learned from it. I found loneliness, peace.

Saw a great school of porpoises coming. Ran toward them. About five hundred all crashing in and out of the great swells, making a spectacle of rare sea action and color and beauty. They surrounded the bow of the boat, and then pandemonium broke loose. They turned to play with us, racing, diving, leaping, shooting—all for our delight. I stood right up on the bow and could see deep. It was an unforgetable experience.

August 7th.

Long run to-day, over eighty miles. East to Point Vincent, west to end of Catalina, then all around. Fine sea and weather. Just right for kite. Saw many ducks and a great number of big sharks. The ducks were traveling west, the sharks east. We saw no tuna.

Coming back the wind sprang up and we had a following sea. It was fine to watch the green-and-white rollers breaking behind us.

The tuna appear to be working farther and farther off the east end. Marlin swordfish have showed up off the east end. Three caught yesterday and one to-day. I have not yet seen a broadbill, and fear none are coming this year.

August 8th.

Went off east end. Had a Marlin strike. The fish missed the hook. A shark took the bait. When it was pulled in to the gaff Captain Dan caught the leader, drew the shark up, and it savagely bit the boat. Then it gave a flop and snapped Captain Dan's hand.

I was frightened. The captain yelled for me to hit the shark with a club. I did not lose a second. The shark let go. We killed it, and found Dan's hand badly lacerated. My swiftness of action saved Dan's hand.

CHAPTER XII

BIG TUNA

It took me five seasons at Catalina to catch a big tuna, and the event was so thrilling that I had to write to my fisherman friends about it. The result of my effusions seem rather dubious. Robert H. Davis, editor of Munsey's, replies in this wise: "If you went out with a mosquito-net to catch a mess of minnows your story would read like Roman gladiators seining the Tigris for whales." Now, I am at a loss to know how to take that compliment. Davis goes on to say more, and he also quotes me: "You say 'the hard, diving fight of a tuna liberates the brute instinct in a man.' Well, Zane, it also liberates the qualities of a liar!" Davis does not love the sweet, soft scent that breathes from off the sea. Once on the Jersey coast I went tuna-fishing with him. He was not happy on the boat. But once he came up out of the cabin with a jaunty feather in his hat. I admired it. I said:

"Bob, I'll have to get something like that for my hat."

"Zane," he replied, piercingly, "what you need for your hat is a head!"

My friend Joe Bray, who publishes books in Chicago, also reacts peculiarly to my fish stories. He writes me a satiric, doubting letter—then shuts up his office and rushes for some river or lake. Will Dilg, the famous fly-caster, upon receipt of my communication, wrote me a nine-page prose-poem epic about the only fish in the world—black-bass. Professor Kellogg always falls ill and takes a vacation, during which he writes me that I have not mental capacity to appreciate my luck.

These fellows will illustrate how my friends receive angling news from me. I ought to have sense enough to keep my stories for publication. I strongly suspect that their strange reaction to my friendly feeling is because I have caught more and larger black-bass than they ever saw. Some day I will go back to the swift streams and deep lakes, where the bronze-backs live, and fish with my friends, and then they will realize that I never lie about the sport and beauty and wonder of the great outdoors.

Every season for the five years that I have been visiting Avalon there has been a run of tuna. But the average weight was from sixty to ninety-five pounds. Until this season only a very few big tuna had been taken. The prestige of the Tuna Club, the bragging of the old members, the gossip of the boatmen—all tend to make a fisherman feel small until he has landed a big one. Come to think of it, considering the years of the Tuna Club fame, not so very many anglers have captured a blue-button tuna. I vowed I did not care in particular about it, but whenever we ran across a school of tuna I acted like a boy.

A good many tuna fell to my rod during these seasons. During the present season, to be exact, I caught twenty-two. This is no large number for two months' fishing. Boschen caught about one hundred; Jump, eighty-four; Hooper, sixty. Among these tuna I fought were three that stand out strikingly. One seventy-three-pounder took fifty minutes of hard fighting to subdue; a ninety-one-pounder took one hour fifty; and the third, after two hours and fifty minutes, got away. It seems, and was proved later, that the number fifty figured every time I hooked one of the long, slim, hard-fighting male tuna.

Beginning late in June, for six weeks tuna were caught almost every day, some days a large number being taken. But big ones were scarce. Then one of the Tuna Club anglers began to bring in tuna that weighed well over one hundred pounds. This fact inspired all the anglers. He would slip out early in the morning and return late at night. Nobody knew where his boatman was finding these fish. More than one boatman tried to follow him, but in vain. Quite by accident it was discovered that he ran up on the north side of the island, clear round the west end. When he was discovered on the west side he at once steered toward Clemente Island, evidently hoping to mislead his followers. This might have succeeded but for the fact that both Bandini and Adams hooked big tuna before they had gone a mile. Then the jig was up. That night Adams came in with a one-hundred-and-twenty-and a one-hundred-and-thirty-six-pound tuna, and Bandini brought the record for this season—one hundred and forty-nine pounds.

Next day we were all out there on the west side, a few miles offshore. The ocean appeared to be full of blackfish. They are huge, black marine creatures, similar to a porpoise in movement, but many times larger, and they have round, blunt noses that look like battering-rams. Some seemed as big as gunboats, and when they heaved up on the swells we could see the white stripes below the black. I was inclined to the belief that this species was the orca, a whale-killing fish. Boatmen and deep-sea men report these blackfish to be dangerous and had better be left alone. They certainly looked ugly. We believed they were chasing tuna.

The channel that day contained more whales than I ever saw before at one time. We counted six pairs in sight. I saw as many as four of the funnel-like whale spouts of water on the horizon at once. It was very interesting to watch these monsters of the deep. Once when we were all on top of the boat we ran almost right upon two whales. The first spouted about fifty feet away. The sea seemed to open up, a terrible roar issued forth, then came a cloud of spray and rush of water. Then we saw another whale just rising a few yards ahead. My hair stood up stiff. Captain Dan yelled, leaped down to reverse the engine. The whale saw us and swerved. Dan's action and the quickness of the whale prevented a collision. As it was, I looked down in the clear water and saw the huge, gleaming, gray body of the whale as he passed. That was another sight to record in the book of memory. The great flukes of his tail moved with surprising swiftness and the water bulged on the surface. Then we ran close to the neighborhood of a school of whales, evidently feeding. They would come up and blow, and then sound. To see a whale sound and then raise his great, broad, shining flukes in the air, high above the water, is in my opinion the most beautiful spectacle to be encountered upon the ocean. Up to this day, during five seasons, I had seen three whales sound with tails in the air. And upon this occasion I had the exceeding good fortune to see seven. I tried to photograph one. We followed a big bull. When he came up to blow we saw a yellow moving space on the water, then a round, gray, glistening surface, then a rugged snout. Puff! His blow was a roar. He rolled on, downward a little; the water surged white and green. When he came up to sound he humped his huge back. It was shiny, leathery, wonderfully supple. It bent higher and higher in an arch. Then this great curve seemed to slide swiftly out of sight and his wonderful tail, flat as a floor and wide as a house, emerged to swing aloft. The water ran off it in sheets. Then it waved higher, and with slow, graceful, ponderous motion sank into the sea. That sight more than anything impressed me with the immensity of the ocean, with its mystery of life, with the unattainable secrets of the deep.

The tuna appeared to be scattered, and none were on the surface. I had one strike that plowed up the sea, showing the difference between the strike of a big tuna and that of a little one. He broke my line on the first rush. Then I hooked another and managed to stop him. I had a grueling battle with him, and at the end of two hours and fifty minutes he broke my hook. This was a disappointment far beyond reason, but I could not help it.

Next day was windy. The one following we could not find the fish, and the third day we all concluded they had gone for 1918. I think the fame of tuna, the uncertainty of their appearance, the difficulty of capturing a big one, are what excite the ambition of anglers. Long effort to that end, and consequent thinking and planning and feeling, bring about a condition of mind that will be made clear as this story progresses.

But Captain Danielson did not give up. The fifth day we ran off the west side with several other boats, and roamed the sea in search of fins. No anchovies on the surface, no sheerwater ducks, no sharks, nothing to indicate tuna. About one o'clock Captain Dan sheered southwest and we ran sixteen miles toward Clemente Island.

It was a perfect day, warm, hazy, with light fog, smooth, heaving, opalescent sea. There was no wind. At two thirty not one of the other boats was in sight. At two forty Captain Dan sighted a large, dark, rippling patch on the water. We ran over closer.

"School of tuna!" exclaimed the captain, with excitement. "Big fish! Oh, for some wind now to fly the kite!"

"There's another school," said my brother, R. C., and he pointed to a second darkly gleaming spot on the smooth sea.

"I've spotted one, too!" I shouted.

"The ocean's alive with tuna—big tuna!" boomed Captain Dan. "Here we are alone, blue-button fish everywhere—and no wind."

"We'll watch the fish and wait for wind," I said.

This situation may not present anything remarkable to most fishermen. But we who knew the game realized at once that this was an experience of a lifetime. We counted ten schools of tuna near at hand, and there were so many farther on that they seemed to cover the sea.

"Boys," said Captain Dan, "here's the tuna we heard were at Anacapa Island last week. The Japs netted hundreds of tons. They're working southeast, right in the middle of the channel, and haven't been inshore at all. It's ninety miles to Anacapa. Some traveling!... That school close to us is the biggest school I ever saw and I believe they're the biggest fish."

"Run closer to them," I said to him.

We ran over within fifty feet of the edge of the school, stopped the boat, and all climbed up on top of the deck.

Then we beheld a spectacle calculated to thrill the most phlegmatic fisherman. It simply enraptured me, and I think I am still too close to it to describe it well. The dark-blue water, heaving in great, low, lazy swells, showed a roughened spot of perhaps two acres in extent. The sun, shining over our shoulders, caught silvery-green gleams of fish, flashing wide and changing to blue. Long, round, bronze backs deep under the surface, caught the sunlight. Blue fins and tails, sharp and curved, like sabers, cleared the water. Here a huge tuna would turn on his side, gleaming broad and bright, and there another would roll on the surface, breaking water like a tarpon with a slow, heavy souse.

"Look at the leaders," said Captain Dan. "I'll bet they're three-hundred-pound fish."

I saw then that the school, lazy as they seemed, were slowly following the leaders, rolling and riding the swells. These leaders threw up surges and ridges on the surface. They plowed the water.

"What'd happen if we skipped a flying-fish across the water in front of those leaders?" I asked Captain Dan.

He threw up his hands. "You'd see a German torpedo explode."

"Say! tuna are no relation to Huns!" put in my brother.

It took only a few moments for the school to drift by us. Then we ran over to another school, with the same experience. In this way we visited several of these near-by schools, all of which were composed of large tuna. Captain Dan, however, said he believed the first two schools, evidently leaders of this vast sea of tuna, contained the largest fish. For half an hour we fooled around, watching the schools and praying for wind to fly the kite. Captain Dan finally trolled our baits through one school, which sank without rewarding us with a strike.

At this juncture I saw a tiny speck of a boat way out on the horizon. Captain Dan said it was Shorty's boat with Adams. I suggested that, as we had to wait for wind to fly the kite, we run in and attract Shorty's attention. I certainly wanted some one else to see those magnificent schools of tuna. Forthwith we ran in several miles until we attracted the attention of the boatman Captain Dan had taken to be Shorty. But it turned out to be somebody else, and my good intentions also turned out to my misfortune.

Then we ran back toward the schools of tuna. On the way my brother hooked a Marlin swordfish that leaped thirty-five times and got away. After all those leaps he deserved to shake the hook. We found the tuna milling and lolling around, slowly drifting and heading toward the southeast. We also found a very light breeze had begun to come out of the west. Captain Dan wanted to try to get the kite up, but I objected on the score that if we could fly it at all it would only be to drag a bait behind the boat. That would necessitate running through the schools of tuna, and as I believed this would put them down, I wanted to wait for enough wind to drag a bait at right angles with the boat. This is the proper procedure, because it enables an angler to place his bait over a school of tuna at a hundred yards or more from the boat. It certainly is the most beautiful and thrilling way to get a strike.

So we waited. The boatman whose attention we had attracted had now come up and was approaching the schools of tuna some distance below us. He put out a kite that just barely flew off the water and it followed directly in the wake of his boat. We watched this with disgust, but considerable interest, and we were amazed to see one of the anglers in that boat get a strike and hook a fish.

That put us all in a blaze of excitement. Still we thought the strike they got might just have been lucky. In running down farther, so we could come back against the light breeze, we ran pretty close to the school out of which the strike had been gotten. Captain Dan stood up to take a good look.

"They're hundred-pounders, all right," he said. "But they're not as big as the tuna in those two leading schools. I'm glad those ginks in that boat are tied up with a tuna for a spell."

I took a look at the fisherman who was fighting the tuna. Certainly I did not begrudge him one, but somehow, so strange are the feelings of a fisherman that I was mightily pleased to see that he was a novice at the game, was having his troubles, and would no doubt be a long, long time landing his tuna. My blood ran cold at the thought of other anglers appearing on the scene, and anxiously I scanned the horizon. No boat in sight! If I had only known then what sad experience taught me that afternoon I would have been tickled to pieces to see all the great fishermen of Avalon tackle this school of big tuna.

Captain Dan got a kite up a little better than I had hoped for. It was not good, but it was worth trying. My bait, even on a turn of the boat, skipped along just at the edge of the wake of the boat. And the wake of a boat will almost always put a school of tuna down.

We headed for the second school. My thrilling expectancy was tinged and spoiled with doubt. I skipped my bait in imitation of a flying-fish leaping and splashing along. We reached the outer edge of the school. Slowly the little boils smoothed out. Slowly the big fins sank. So did my heart. We passed the school. They all sank. And then when Captain Dan swore and I gave up there came a great splash back of my bait. I yelled and my comrades echoed me. The tuna missed. I skipped the bait. A sousing splash— and another tuna had my bait. My line sagged. I jerked hard. But too late! The tuna threw the hook before it got a hold.

"They're hungry!" exclaimed Dan. "Hurry—reel the kite in. We'll get another bait on quick.... Look! that school is coming up again! They're not shy of boats. Boys, there's something doing."

Captain Dan's excitement augmented my own. I sensed an unusual experience that had never before befallen me.

The school of largest fish was farther to the west. The breeze lulled. We could not fly the kite except with the motion and direction of the boat. It was exasperating. When we got close the kite flopped down into the water. Captain Dan used language. We ran back, picked up the kite. It was soaked, of course, and would not fly. While Dan got out a new kite, a large silk one which we had not tried yet, we ran down to the eastward of the second school. To our surprise and delight this untried kite flew well without almost any wind.

We got in position and headed for the school. I was using a big hook half embedded near the tail of the flying-fish and the leader ran through the bait. It worked beautifully. A little jerk of my rod sent the bait skittering over the water, for all the world like a live flying-fish. I knew now that I would get another strike. Just as we reached a point almost opposite the school of tuna they headed across our bow, so that it seemed inevitable we must either run them down or run too close. My spirit sank to zero. Something presaged bad luck. I sensed disaster. I fought the feeling, but it persisted. Captain Dan swore. My brother shouted warnings from over us where he sat on top. But we ran right into the leaders. The school sank. I was sick and furious.

"Jump your bait! It's not too late," called Dan.

I did so. Smash! The water seemed to curl white and smoke. A tuna had my bait. I jerked. I felt him. He threw the hook. Half the bait remained upon it. Smash! A great boil and splash! Another tuna had that. I tried to jerk. But both kite and tuna pulling made my effort feeble. This one also threw out the hook. It came out with a small piece of mangled red flying-fish still hanging to it. Instinctively I jumped that remains of my bait over the surface. Smash! The third tuna cleaned the hook.

Captain Dan waxed eloquent and profane.

My brother said, "What do you know about that?"

As for myself, I was stunned one second and dazzled the next. Three strikes on one bait! It seemed disaster still clogged my mind, but what had already happened was new and wonderful. Half a mile below us I saw the angler still fighting the tuna he had hooked. I wanted him to get it, but I hoped he would be all afternoon on the job.

"Hurry, Cap!" was all I said.

Ordinarily Dan is the swiftest of boatmen. To-day he was slower than molasses and all he did went wrong. What he said about the luck was more than melancholy. I had no way to gauge my own feelings because I had never had such an experience before. Nor had I ever heard or read of any one having it.

We got a bait on and the kite out just in time to reach the first and larger school. I was so excited that I did not see we were heading right into it. My intent gaze was riveted upon my bait as it skimmed the surface. The swells were long, low, smooth mounds. My bait went out of sight behind one. It was then I saw water fly high and I felt a tug. I jerked so hard I nearly fell over. My bait shot over the top of the swell. Then that swell opened and burst—a bronze back appeared. He missed the hook. Another tuna, also missing, leaped into the air—a fish of one hundred and fifty pounds, glittering green and silver and blue, jaws open, fins stiff, tail quivering, clear and clean-cut above the surface. Again we all yelled. Actually before he fell there was another smash and another tuna had my bait. This one I hooked. His rush was irresistible. I released the drag on the reel. It whirled and whizzed. The line threw a fine spray into my face. Then the tip of my rod flew up with a jerk, the line slacked. We all knew what that meant. I reeled in. The line had broken above the few feet of double line which we always used next the leader. More than ever disaster loomed over me. The feeling was unshakable now.

Nevertheless, I realized that wonderful good fortune attended us in the fact that the school of big tuna had scarcely any noticeable fear of the boat; they would not stay down, and they were ravenous.

On our next run down upon them I had a smashing strike. The tuna threw the hook. Another got the bait and I hooked him. He sounded. The line broke. We tried again. No sooner had we reached the school when the water boiled and foamed at my bait. Before I could move that tuna cleaned the hook. Our next attempt gained another sousing strike. But he was so swift and I was so slow that I could not fasten to him.

"He went away from here," my brother said, with what he meant for comedy. But it was not funny.

Captain Dan then put on a double hook, embedding it so one hook stood clear of the bait. We tested my line with the scales and it broke at fifty-three pounds, which meant it was a good strong line. The breeze lulled and fanned at intervals. It seemed, however, we did not need any breeze. We had edged our school of big tuna away from the other schools, and it was milling on the surface, lazily and indifferently. But what latent speed and power lay hidden in that mass of lolling tuna.

R. C. from his perch above yelled: "Look out! You're going to drag your bait in front of the leaders this time!"

That had not happened yet. I glowed in spite of the fact that I was steeped in gloom. We were indeed heading most favorably for the leaders. Captain Dan groaned. "Never seen the like of this!" he added. These leaders were several yards apart, as could be told by the blunt-nosed ridges of water they shoved ahead of them. That was another moment added to the memorable moments of my fishing years. It was strained suspense. Hope would not die, but disaster loomed like a shadow.

Before I was ready, before we expected anything, before we got near these leaders, a brilliant, hissing, white splash burst out of the sea, and a tuna of magnificent proportions shot broadside along and above the surface, sending the spray aloft, and he hit that bait with incredible swiftness, raising a twenty-foot-square, furious splash as he hooked himself. I sat spellbound. I heard my line whistling off the reel. But I saw only that swift-descending kite. So swiftly did the tuna sound that the kite shot down as if it had been dropping lead. My line broke and my rod almost leaped out of my hands.

We were all silent a moment. The school of tuna showed again, puttering and fiddling around, with great blue-and-green flashes caught by the sun.

"That one weighed about two hundred and fifty," was all Captain Dan said.

R. C. remarked facetiously, evidently to cheer me, "Jakey, you picks de shots out of that plue jay an' we makes ready for anudder one!"

"Say, do you imagine you can make me laugh!" I asked, in tragic scorn.

"Well, if you could have seen yourself when that tuna struck you'd have laughed," replied he.

While Dan steered the boat R. C. got out on the bow and gaffed the kite. I watched the tuna tails standing like half-simitars out of the smooth, colored water. The sun was setting in a golden haze spotted by pink clouds. The wind, if anything, was softer than ever; in fact, we could not feel it unless we headed the boat into it. The fellow below us was drifting off farther, still plugging at his tuna.

Captain Dan put the wet kite on the deck to dry and got out another silk one. It soared aloft so easily that I imagined our luck was changing. Vain fisherman's delusion! Nothing could do that. There were thousands of tons—actually thousands of tons of tuna in that three-mile stretch of ruffled water, but I could not catch one. It was a settled conviction. I was reminded of what Enos, the Portuguese boatman, complained to an angler he had out, "You mos' unluck' fisherman I ever see!"

We tried a shorter kite-line and a shorter length of my line, and we ran down upon that mess of tuna once more. It was strange—and foolish—how we stuck to that school of biggest fish. This time Dan headed right into the thick of them. Out of the corners of my eyes I seemed to see tuna settling down all around. Suddenly my brother yelled.

Zam! That was a huge loud splash back of my bait. The tuna missed. R. C. yelled again. Captain Dan followed suit:

"He's after it!... Oh, he's the biggest yet!"

Then I saw a huge tuna wallowing in a surge round my bait. He heaved up, round and big as a barrel, flashing a wide bar of blue-green, and he got the hook. If he had been strangely slow he was now unbelievably swift. His size gave me panic. I never moved, and he hooked himself. Straight down he shot and the line broke.

My brother's sympathy now was as sincere as Captain Dan's misery. I asked R. C. to take the rod and see if he could do better.

"Not much!" he replied. "When you get one, then I'll try. Stay with 'em, now!"

Not improbably I would have stayed out until the tuna quit if that had taken all night. Three more times we put up the kite—three more flying-fish we wired on the double hooks—three more runs we made through that tantalizing school of tuna that grew huger and swifter and more impossible—three more smashing wide breaks of water on the strike—and quicker than a flash three more broken lines!

I imagined I was resigned. My words to my silent comrades were even cheerful.

"Come on. Try again. Where there's life there's hope. It's an exceedingly rare experience—anyway. After all, nothing depends upon my catching one of these tuna. It doesn't matter."

All of which attested to the singular state of my mind.

Another kite, another leader and double hook, another bait had to be arranged. This took time. My impatience, my nervousness were hard to restrain. Captain Dan was pale and grim. I do not know how I looked. Only R. C. no longer looked at me.

As we put out the bait we made the discovery that the other anglers, no doubt having ended their fight, were running down upon our particular school of tuna. This was in line with our luck. Other schools of tuna were in sight, but these fellows had to head for ours. It galled me when I thought how sportsman-like I had been to attract their attention. We aimed to head them off and reach the school first. As we were the closest all augured well for our success. But gloom invested whatever hopes I had.

We beat the other boat. We had just gotten our boat opposite the school of tuna when Dan yelled: "Look out for that bunch of kelp! Jump your bait over it!"

Then I spied the mass of floating seaweed. I knew absolutely that my hook was going to snag it. But I tried to be careful, quick, accurate. I jumped my bait. It fell short. The hook caught fast in the kelp. In the last piece! The kite fluttered like a bird with broken wings and dropped. Captain Dan reversed the boat. Then he burst out. Now Dan was a big man and he had a stentorian voice, deep like booming thunder. No man ever swore as Dan swore then. It was terrible. It was justified. But it was funny, and despite all this agony of disappointment, despite the other boat heading into the tuna and putting them down, I laughed till I cried.

The fishermen in that other boat hooked a fish and broke it off. We saw from the excitement on board that they had realized the enormous size of these tuna. We hurried to get ready again. It was only needful to drag a bait anywhere near that school. And we alternated with the other boat. I saw those fishermen get four more strikes and lose the four fish immediately. I had even worse luck. In fact, disaster grew and grew. But there is no need for me to multiply these instances. The last three tunas I hooked broke the double line on the first run. This when I had on only a slight drag!

The other boat puddled around in our school and finally put it down for good, and, as the other schools had disappeared, we started for home.

This was the most remarkable and unfortunate day I ever had on the sea, where many strange fishing experiences have been mine. Captain Dan had never heard of the like in eighteen years as boatman. No such large-sized tuna, not to mention numbers, had visited Catalina for many years. I had thirteen strikes, not counting more than one strike to a bait. Seven fish broke the single line and three the double line, practically, I might say, before they had run far enough to cause any great strain. And the parting of the double line, where, if a break had occurred, it would have come on the single, convinced us that all these lines were cut. Cut by other tuna! In this huge school of hungry fish, whenever one ran for or with a bait, all the others dove pellmell after him. The line, of course, made a white streak in the water. Perhaps the tuna bit it off. Perhaps they crowded it off. However they did it, the fact was that they cut the line. Probably it would have been impossible to catch one of those large tuna on the Tuna Club tackle. I hated to think of breaking off hooks in fish, but, after it was too late, I remembered with many a thrill the size and beauty and tremendous striking energy of those tuna, the wide, white, foamy, furious boils on the surface, the lunges when hooked, and the runs swift as bullets.

That experience would never come to me again. It was like watching for the rare transformations of nature that must be waited for and which come so seldom.

But, such is the persistence of mankind in general and the doggedness of fishermen in particular, Captain Dan and I kept on roaming the seas in search of tuna. Nothing more was seen or heard of the great drifting schools. They had gone down the channel toward Mexico, down with the mysterious currents of the sea, fulfilling their mission in life. However, different anglers reported good-sized tuna off Seal Rocks and Silver Cañon. Several fish were hooked. Mr. Reed brought in a one-hundred-and-forty-one-pound tuna that took five hours to land. It made a dogged, desperate resistance and was almost unbeatable. Mr. Reed is a heavy, powerful man, and he said this tuna gave him the hardest task he ever attempted. I wondered what I would have done with one of those two-or three-hundred-pounders. There is a difference between Pacific and Atlantic tuna. The latter are seacows compared to these blue pluggers of the West. I have hooked several very large tuna along the Seabright coast, and, though these fish got away, they did not give me the battle I have had with small tuna of the Pacific. Mr. Wortheim, fishing with my old boatman, Horse-mackerel Sam, landed a two-hundred-and-sixty-two-pound Atlantic tuna in less than two hours. Sam said the fish made a loggy, rolling, easy fight. Crowninshield, also fishing with Sam, caught one weighing three hundred pounds in rather short order. This sort of feat cannot be done out here in the Pacific. The deep water here may have something to do with it, but the tuna are different, if not in species, then in disposition.

My lucky day came after no tuna had been reported for a week. Captain Dan and I ran out off Silver Cañon just on a last forlorn hope. The sea was rippling white and blue, with a good breeze. No whales showed. We left Avalon about one o'clock, ran out five miles, and began to fish. Our methods had undergone some change. We used a big kite out on three hundred yards of line; we tied this line on my leader, and we tightened the drag on the reel so that it took a nine-pound pull to start the line off. This seemed a fatal procedure, but I was willing to try anything. My hope of getting a strike was exceedingly slim. Instead of a flying-fish for bait we used a good-sized smelt, and we used hooks big and strong and sharp as needles.

We had not been out half an hour when Dan left the wheel and jumped up on the gunwale to look at something.

"What do you see?" I asked, eagerly.

He was silent a moment. I dare say he did not want to make any mistakes. Then he jumped back to the wheel.

"School of tuna!" he boomed.

I stood up and looked in the direction indicated, but I could not see them. Dan said only the movement on the water could be seen. Good long swells were running, rather high, and presently I did see tuna showing darkly bronze in the blue water. They vanished. We had to turn the boat somewhat, and it began to appear that we would have difficulty in putting the bait into the school. So it turned out. We were in the wrong quarter to use the wind. I saw the school of tuna go by, perhaps two hundred feet from the boat. They were traveling fast, somewhat under the surface, and were separated from one another. They were big tuna, but nothing near the size of those that had wrecked my tackle and hopes. Captain Dan said they were hungry, hunting fish. To me they appeared game, swift, and illusive.

We lost sight of them. With the boat turned fairly into the west wind the kite soared, pulling hard, and my bait skipped down the slopes of the swells and up over the crests just like a live, leaping little fish. It was my opinion that the tuna were running inshore. Dan said they were headed west. We saw nothing of them. Again the old familiar disappointment knocked at my heart, with added bitterness of past defeat. Dan scanned the sea like a shipwrecked mariner watching for a sail.

"I see them!... There!" he called. "They're sure traveling fast."

That stimulated me with a shock. I looked and looked, but I could not see the darkened water. Moments passed, during which I stood up, watching my bait as it slipped over the waves. I knew Dan would tell me when to begin to jump it. The suspense grew to be intense.

"We'll catch up with them," said Dan, excitedly. "Everything's right now. Kite high, pulling hard—bait working fine. You're sure of a strike.... When you see one get the bait hook him quick and hard."

The ambition of years, the long patience, the endless efforts, the numberless disappointments, and that never-to-be-forgotten day among the giant tuna—these flashed up at Captain Dan's words of certainty, and, together with the thrilling proximity of the tuna we were chasing, they roused in me emotion utterly beyond proportion or reason. This had happened to me before, notably in swordfishing, but never had I felt such thrills, such tingling nerves, such oppression on my chest, such a wild, eager rapture. It would have been impossible, notwithstanding my emotional temperament, if the leading up to this moment had not included so much long-sustained feeling.

"Jump your bait!" called Dan, with a ring in his voice. "In two jumps you'll be in the tail-enders."

I jerked my rod. The bait gracefully leaped over a swell—shot along the surface, and ended with a splash. Again I jerked. As the bait rose into the air a huge angry splash burst just under it, and a broad-backed tuna lunged and turned clear over, his tail smacking the water.

"Jump it!" yelled Dan.

Before I could move, a circling smash of white surrounded my bait. I heard it. With all my might I jerked. Strong and heavy came the weight of the tuna. I had hooked him. With one solid thumping splash he sounded. Here was test for line and test for me. I could not resist one turn of the thumb-wheel, to ease the drag. He went down with the same old incomparable speed. I saw the kite descending. Dan threw out the clutch—ran to my side. The reel screamed. Every tense second, as the line whizzed off, I expected it to break. There was no joy, no sport in that painful watching. He ran off two hundred feet, then, marvelous to see, he slowed up. The kite was still high, pulling hard. What with kite and drag and friction of line in the water, that tuna had great strain upon him. He ran off a little more, slower this time, then stopped. The kite began to flutter.

I fell into the chair, jammed the rod-butt into the socket, and began to pump and wind.

"Doc, you're hooked on and you've stopped him!" boomed Dan. His face beamed. "Look at your legs!"

It became manifest then that my knees were wabbling, my feet puttering around, my whole lower limbs shaking as if I had the palsy. I had lost control of my lower muscles. It was funny; it was ridiculous. It showed just what was my state of excitement.

The kite fluttered down to the water. The kite-line had not broken off, and this must add severely to the strain on the fish. Not only had I stopped the tuna, but soon I had him coming up, slowly yet rather easily. He was directly under the boat. When I had all save about one hundred feet of line wound in the tuna anchored himself and would not budge for fifteen minutes. Then again rather easily he was raised fifty more feet. He acted like any small, hard-fighting fish.

"I've hooked a little one," I began. "That big fellow missed the bait, and a small one grabbed it."

Dan would not say so, but he feared just that. What miserable black luck! Almost I threw the rod and reel overboard. Some sense, however, prevented me from such an absurdity. And as I worked the tuna closer and closer I grew absolutely sick with disappointment. The only thing to do was to haul this little fish in and go hunt up the school. So I pumped and pulled. That half-hour seemed endless and bad business altogether. Anger possessed me and I began to work harder. At this juncture Shorty's boat appeared close to us. Shorty and Adams waved me congratulations, and then made motions to Dan to get the direction of the school of tuna. That night both Shorty and Adams told me that I was working very hard on the fish, too hard to save any strength for a long battle.

Captain Dan watched the slow, steady bends of my rod as the tuna plugged, and at last he said, "Doc, it's a big fish!"

Strange to relate, this did not electrify me. I did not believe it. But at the end of that half-hour the tuna came clear to the surface, about one hundred feet from us, and there he rode the swells. Doubt folded his sable wings! Bronze and blue and green and silver flashes illumined the swells. I plainly saw that not only was the tuna big, but he was one of the long, slim, hard-fighting species.

Presently he sounded, and I began to work. I was fresh, eager, strong, and I meant to whip him quickly. Working on a big tuna is no joke. It is a man's job. A tuna fights on his side, with head down, and he never stops. If the angler rests the tuna will not only rest, too, but he will take more and more line. The method is a long, slow lift or pump of rod—then lower the rod quickly and wind the reel. When the tuna is raised so high he will refuse to come any higher, and then there is a deadlock. There lives no fisherman but what there lives a tuna that can take the conceit and the fight out of him.

For an hour I worked. I sweat and panted and burned in the hot sun; and I enjoyed it. The sea was beautiful. A strong, salty fragrance, wet and sweet, floated on the breeze. Catalina showed clear and bright, with its colored cliffs and yellow slides and dark ravines. Clemente Island rose a dark, long, barren, lonely land to the southeast. The clouds in the west were like trade-wind clouds, white, regular, with level base-line.

At the end of the second hour I was tiring. There came a subtle change of spirit and mood. I had never let up for a minute. Captain Dan praised me, vowed I had never fought either broadbill or roundbill swordfish so consistently hard, but he cautioned me to save myself.

"That's a big tuna," he said, as he watched my rod.

Most of the time we drifted. Some of the time Dan ran the boat to keep even with the tuna, so he could not get too far under the stern and cut the line. At intervals the fish appeared to let up and at others he plugged harder. This I discovered was merely that he fought the hardest when I worked the hardest. Once we gained enough on him to cut the tangle of kite-line that had caught some fifty feet above my leader. This afforded cause for less anxiety.

"I'm afraid of sharks," said Dan.

Sharks are the bane of tuna fishermen. More tuna are cut off by sharks than are ever landed by anglers. This made me redouble my efforts, and in half an hour more I was dripping wet, burning hot, aching all over, and so spent I had to rest. Every time I dropped the rod on the gunwale the tuna took line—zee—zee—zee—foot by foot and yard by yard. My hands were cramped; my thumbs red and swollen, almost raw. I asked Dan for the harness, but he was loath to put it on because he was afraid I would break the fish off. So I worked on and on, with spurts of fury and periods of lagging.

At the end of three hours I was in bad condition. I had saved a little strength for the finish, but I was in danger of using that up before the crucial moment arrived. Dan had to put the harness on me. I knew afterward that it saved the day. By the aid of the harness, putting my shoulders into the lift, I got the double line over the reel, only to lose it. Every time the tuna was pulled near the boat he sheered off, and it did not appear possible for me to prevent it. He got into a habit of coming to the surface about thirty feet out, and hanging there, in plain sight, as if he was cabled to the rocks of the ocean. Watching him only augmented my trouble. It had ceased long ago to be fun or sport or game. It was now a fight and it began to be torture. My hands were all blisters, my thumbs raw. The respect I had for that tuna was great.

He plugged down mostly, but latterly he began to run off to each side, to come to the surface, showing his broad green-silver side, and then he weaved to and fro behind the boat, trying to get under it. Captain Dan would have to run ahead to keep away from him. To hold what gain I had on the tuna was at these periods almost unendurable. Where before I had sweat, burned, throbbed, and ached, I now began to see red, to grow dizzy, to suffer cramps and nausea and exceeding pain.

Three hours and a half showed the tuna slower, heavier, higher, easier. He had taken us fifteen miles from where we had hooked him. He was weakening, but I thought I was worse off than he was. Dan changed the harness. It seemed to make more effort possible.

The floor under my feet was wet and slippery from the salt water dripping off my reel. I could not get any footing. The bend of that rod downward, the ceaseless tug, tug, tug, the fear of sharks, the paradoxical loss of desire now to land the tuna, the change in my feeling of elation and thrill to wonder, disgust, and utter weariness of spirit and body—all these warned me that I was at the end of my tether, and if anything could be done it must be quickly.

Relaxing, I took a short rest. Then nerving myself to be indifferent to the pain, and yielding altogether to the brutal instinct this tuna-fighting rouses in a fisherman, I lay back with might and main. Eight times I had gotten the double line over the reel. On the ninth I shut down, clamped with my thumbs, and froze there. The wire leader sung like a telephone wire in the cold. I could scarcely see. My arms cracked. I felt an immense strain that must break me in an instant.

Captain Dan reached the leader. Slowly he heaved. The strain upon me was released. I let go the reel, threw off the drag, and stood up. There the tuna was, the bronze-and-blue-backed devil, gaping, wide-eyed, shining and silvery as he rolled, a big tuna if there ever was one, and he was conquered.

When Dan lunged with the gaff the tuna made a tremendous splash that deluged us. Then Dan yelled for another gaff. I was quick to get it. Next it was for me to throw a lasso over that threshing tail. When I accomplished this the tuna was ours. We hauled him up on the stern, heaving, thumping, throwing water and blood; and even vanquished he was magnificent. Three hours and fifty minutes! The number fifty stayed with me. As I fell back in a chair, all in, I could not see for my life why any fisherman would want to catch more than one large tuna.

CHAPTER XIV

AVALON, THE BEAUTIFUL

If you are a fisherman, and aspire to the study or conquest of the big game of the sea, go to Catalina Island once before it is too late.

The summer of 1917 will never be forgotten by those fishermen who were fortunate enough to be at Avalon. Early in June, even in May, there were indications that the first record season in many years might be expected. Barracuda and white sea-bass showed up in great schools; the ocean appeared to be full of albacore; yellowtail began to strike all along the island shores and even in the bay of Avalon; almost every day in July sight of broadbill swordfish was reported, sometimes as many as ten in a day; in August the blue-fin tuna surged in, school after school, in vast numbers; and in September returned the Marlin, or roundbill swordfish that royal-purple swashbuckler of the Pacific.

This extraordinary run of fish appeared like old times to the boatmen and natives who could look back over many Catalina years. The cause, of course, was a favorable season when the sardines and anchovies came to the island in incalculable numbers. Acres and acres of these little bait fish drifted helplessly to and fro, back and forth with the tides, from Seal Rocks to the west end. These schools were not broken up until the advent of the voracious tuna; and when they arrived the ocean soon seemed littered with small, amber-colored patches, each of which was a densely packed mass of sardines or anchovies, drifting with the current. It has not yet been established that swordfish feed on these schools, but the swordfish were there in abundance, at any rate; and it was reasonable to suppose that some of the fish they feed on were in pursuit of the anchovies.

Albacore feeding on the surface raise a thin, low, white line of water or multitudes of slight, broken splashes. Tuna raise a white wall, tumbling and spouting along the horizon; and it is a sight not soon to be forgotten by a fisherman. Near at hand a big school of feeding tuna is a thrilling spectacle. They move swiftly, breaking water as they smash after the little fish, and the roar can be heard quite a distance. The wall of white water seems full of millions of tiny, glinting fish, leaping frantically from the savage tuna. And when the sunlight shines golden through this wall of white spray, and the great bronze and silver and blue tuna gleam for an instant, the effect is singularly exciting and beautiful.

All through August and much of September these schools of tuna, thousands of them, ranted up and down the coast of Catalina, thinning out the amber patches of anchovies, and affording the most magnificent sport to anglers.

These tuna may return next year and then again they may not return for ten years. Some time again they will swing round the circle or drift with the currents, in that mysterious and inscrutable nature of the ocean. And if a fisherman can only pick out the year or have the obsession to go back season after season he will some day see these wonderful schools again.

But as for the other fish—swordfish, white sea-bass, yellowtail, and albacore—their doom has been spelled, and soon they will be no more. That is why I say to fishermen if they want to learn something about these incomparable fish they must go soon to Catalina before it is too late.

The Japs, the Austrians, the round-haul nets, the canneries and the fertilizer-plants—that is to say, foreigners and markets, greed and war, have cast their dark shadow over beautiful Avalon. The intelligent, far-seeing boatmen all see it. My boatman, Captain Danielson, spoke gloomily of the not distant time when his occupation would be gone. And as for the anglers who fish at Catalina, some of them see it and many of them do not. The standard raised at Avalon has been to haul in as many of the biggest fish in the least possible time. One famous fisherman brought in thirteen tuna—nine hundred and eighty-six pounds of tuna—that he caught in one day! This is unbelievable, yet it is true. Another brought in eleven tuna in one day. These fishermen are representative of the coterie who fish for records. All of them are big, powerful men, and when they hook a fish they will not give him a foot of line if they can help it. They horse him in, and if they can horse him in before he wakes up to real combat they are the better pleased. All of which is to say that the true motive (or pleasure, if it can be such) is the instinct to kill. I have observed this in many fishermen. Any one who imagines that man has advanced much beyond the savage stage has only carefully to observe fishermen.

I have demonstrated the practicability of letting Marlin swordfish go after they were beaten, but almost all of the boatmen will not do it. The greater number of swordfish weigh under two hundred pounds, and when exhausted and pulled up to the boat they can be freed by cutting the wire leader close to the hook. Probably all these fish would live. A fisherman will have his fun seeing and photographing the wonderful leaps, and conquering the fish, and when all this is over it would be sportsman-like to let him go. Marlin are not food fish, and they are thrown to the sharks. During 1918, however, many were sold as food fish. It seems a pity to treat this royal, fighting, wonderful, purple-colored fish in this way. But the boatmen will not free them. My boatman claimed that his reputation depended upon the swordfish he caught; and that in Avalon no one would believe fish were caught unless brought to the dock. It was his bread and butter. His reputation brought him new fishermen, and so he could not afford to lose it. Nevertheless, he was persuaded to do it in 1918. The fault, then, does not lie with the boatman.

The Japs are the greatest market fishermen in the world. And some five hundred boats put out of San Pedro every day, to scour the ocean for "the chicken of the sea," as albacore are advertised to the millions of people who are always hungry. It must be said that the Japs mostly fish square. They use a hook, and a barbless hook at that. Usually four Japs constitute the crew of one of these fast eighty-horse-power motor-boats. They roam the sea with sharp eyes ever alert for that thin white line on the horizon, the feeding albacore. Their method of fishing is unique and picturesque. When they sight albacore they run up on the school and slow down.

In the stern of the boat stands a huge tank, usually painted red. I have become used to seeing dots of red all over the ocean. This tank is kept full of fresh sea-water by a pump connected with the engine, and it is used to keep live bait—no other than the little anchovies. One Jap, using a little net, dips up live bait and throws them overboard to the albacore. Another Jap beats on the water with long bamboo poles, making splashes. The other two Japs have short, stiff poles with a wire attached and the barbless hook at the end. They put on a live bait and toss it over. Instantly they jerk hard, and two big white albacore, from fifteen to thirty pounds, come wiggling up on to the stern of the boat. Down goes the pole and whack! goes a club. It is all done with swift mechanical precision. It used to amaze me and fill me with sadness. If the Japs could hold the school of albacore they would very soon load the boat. But usually a school of albacore cannot be held long.

You cannot fish in the channel any more without encountering these Jap boats. Once at one time in 1917 I saw one hundred and thirty-two boats. Most of them were fishing! They ran to and fro over the ocean, chasing every white splash, and they make an angler's pleasure taste bitter.

Fortunately the Japs had let the tuna alone, for the simple and good reason that they had not found a way to catch the wise blue-fins. But they will find a way! Yet they drove the schools down, and that was almost as bad. As far as swordfish are concerned, it is easy to see what will happen, now that the albacore have become scarce. Broadbill swordfish are the finest food fish in the sea. They can be easily harpooned by these skilful Japs. And so eventually they will be killed and driven away. This misfortune may not come at once, but it will come.

In this connection it is interesting to note that I tried to photograph one of the Austrian crews in action. But Captain Dan would not let me get near enough to take a picture. There is bad blood between Avalon boatmen and these foreign market fishermen. Shots had been exchanged more than once. Captain Dan kept a rifle on board. This news sort of stirred me. And I said: "Run close to that bunch, Cap. Maybe they'll take a peg at me!" But he refused to comply, and I lost a chance to serve my country!

The Japs, however, are square fishermen, mostly, and I rather admire those albacore-chasers, who at least give the fish a chance. Some of them use nets, and against them and the Austrian round-haul netters I am exceedingly bitter. These round-haul nets, some of them, must be a mile long, and they sink two hundred feet in the water. What chance has a school of fish against that? They surround a school and there is no escape.

Clemente Island, the sister island to Catalina, was once a paradise for fish, especially the beautiful, gamy yellowtail. But there are no more fish there, except Marlin swordfish in August and September. The great, boiling schools of yellowtail are gone. Clemente Island has no three-mile law protecting it, as has Catalina. But that Catalina law has become a farce. It is violated often in broad daylight, and probably all night long. One Austrian round-haul netter took seven tons of white sea-bass in one haul. Seven tons! Did you ever look at a white sea-bass? He is the most beautiful of bass—slender, graceful, thoroughbred, exquisitely colored like a paling opal, and a fighter if there ever was one.

What becomes of these seven tons of white sea-bass and all the other tons and tons of yellowtail and albacore? That is a question. It needs to be answered. During the year 1917 one heard many things. The fish-canneries were working day and night, and every can of fish—the whole output had been bought by the government for the soldiers. Very good. We are a nation at war. Our soldiers must be properly fed and so must our allies. If it takes all the fish in the sea and all the meat on the land, we must and will win this war.

But real patriotism is one thing and misstatement is another. If there were not so much deceit and greed in connection with this war it would be easier to stomach.

As a matter of cold fact, that round-haul netter's seven tons of beautiful white sea-bass did not go into cans for our good soldiers or for our fighting allies. Those seven tons of splendid white sea-bass went into the fertilizer-plant, where many and many a ton had gone before!

It is not hard to comprehend. When they work for the fertilizer-plants they do not need ice—they do not need to hurry to the port to save spoiling—they can stay out till the boat is packed full. So often a greater part of the magnificent schools of white sea-bass, albacore, and yellowtail—splendid food fish— go into the fertilizer-plants to make a few foreign-born hogs rich. Hundreds of aliens, many of them hostile to the United States, are making big money, which is sent abroad.

I believe that the great kelp-beds round Catalina are the spawning-grounds of these fish in question. And not only a spawning-ground, but, what is more important, a feeding-ground. And now the kelp-beds are being exploited. The government needs potash. Formerly our supply of potash came from Germany. But, now that we are not on amiable terms with those nice gentle Germans, we cannot get any potash. Hence the great, huge kelp-cutters that you hear cut only the tops of the kelp-beds. Six feet they say, and it all grows up again quickly. But in my opinion the once vast, heaving, wonderful beds of kelp along the Clemente and Catalina shores have been cut too deeply. They will die.

Some of my predictions made in 1917 were verified in 1918.

A few scattered schools of albacore appeared in the channel in July. But these were soon caught or chased away by the market boats. Albacore-fishing was poor in other localities up and down the coast. Many of the Jap fishermen sold their boats and sought other industry. It was a fact, and a great pleasure, that an angler could go out for tuna without encountering a single market boat on the sea. Maybe the albacore did not come this year; maybe they were mostly all caught; maybe they were growing shyer of boats; at any event, they were scarce, and the reason seems easy to see.

It was significant that the broadbill swordfish did not return to Avalon in 1918, as in former years. I saw only one in two months roaming the ocean. A few were seen. Not one was caught during my stay on the island. Many boatmen and anglers believe that the broadbills follow the albacore. It seems safe to predict that when the albacore cease to come to Catalina there will not be any fishing for the great flat-sworded Xiphias.

The worst that came to pass in 1918, from an angler's viewpoint, was that the market fishermen found a way to net the blue-fin tuna, both large and small. All I could learn was that the nets were lengthened and deepened. The Japs got into the great schools of large tuna which appeared off Anacapa Island and netted tons and tons of hundred-pound tuna. These schools drifted on down the middle of the Clemente Channel, and I was the lucky fellow who happened to get among them for one memorable day.

Take it all in all, my gloomy prophecies of other years were substantiated in 1918, especially in regard to the devastated kelp-beds; but there have been a few silver rifts in the black cloud, and it seems well to end this book with mention of brighter things.

All fish brought into Avalon in 1918 were sold for food.

We inaugurated the releasing of small Marlin swordfish.

There was a great increase in the interest taken in the use of light tackle.

We owe the latter stride toward conservation and sportsmanship to Mr. James Jump, and to Lone Angler, and to President Coxe of the Tuna Club. I had not been entirely in sympathy with their feats of taking Marlin swordfish and tuna on light tackle. My objections to the use of too light tackle have been cited before in this book. Many fish break away on the nine-thread. I know this because I tried it out. Fifteen of those small tuna, one after another, broke my line on the first rush. But I believe that was my lack of skill with handling of rod and boat.

As for Marlin, I have always known that I could take some of these roundbill swordfish on light tackle. But likewise there have been some that could not have been taken so, and these are the swordfish I have fished for.

Nevertheless, I certainly do not want to detract from Jump's achievements, as I will show. They have been remarkable. And they have attracted wide attention to the possibilities of light tackle. Thus Mr. Jump has done conservative angling an estimable good, as well as placed himself in a class alone.

The use of light tackle by experts for big game fish of the sea has come to be an established practice in American angling. A few years ago, when sport with light tackle was exceptional, it required courage to flaunt its use in the faces of fishermen of experience and established reputation. Long Key, now the most noted fishing resort on the Atlantic coast, was not many years back a place for hand-lines and huge rods and tackle, and boat-loads of fish for one man. It has become a resort for gentlemen anglers, and its sportsmen's club claims such experts and fine exponents of angling as Heilner, Lester, Cassiard, Crowninshield, Conill, the Schutts, and others, who can safely be trusted to advance the standard. Fishermen are like sheep—they follow the boldest leaders. And no one wants to be despised by the elect. Long Key, with its isolation, yet easy accession, its beauty and charm, its loneliness and quiet, its big game fish, will become the Mecca of high-class light tackle anglers, who will in time answer for the ethics and sportsmanship of the Atlantic seaboard.

On the Pacific side the light tackle advocates have had a different row to hoe. With nothing but keen, fair, honest, and splendid zealousness Mr. James Jump has pioneered this sport almost single-handed against the heavy tackle record-holder who until recently dominated the Tuna Club and the boatmen and the fishing at Avalon. To my shame and regret I confess that it took me three years to recognize Jump's bigness as an angler and his tenacity as a fighter. But I shall make amends. It seems when I fished I was steeped in dreams of the sea and the beauty of the lonely islands. I am not in Jump's class as a fisherman, nor in Lone Angler's, either. They stand by themselves. But I can write about them, and so inspire others.

Jump set out in 1914 to catch swordfish on light tackle, and incidentally tuna under one hundred pounds. He was ridiculed, scorned, scoffed at, made a butt of by this particular heavy tackle angler, and cordially hated for his ambitions. Most anglers and boatmen repudiated his claims and looked askance at him. Personally I believed Jump might catch some swordfish or tuna on light tackle, but only one out of many, and that one not the fighting kind. I was wrong. It was Lone Angler who first drew my attention to Jump's achievements and possibilities. President Coxe was alive to them also, and he has rebuilt and rejuvenated the Tuna Club on the splendid standard set by its founder, Dr. Charles Frederick Holder, and with infinite patience and tact and labor, and love of fine angling and good fellowship, he has put down that small but mighty clique who threatened the ruin of sport at fair Avalon. This has not been public news, but it ought to be and shall be public news.

The malignant attack recently made upon Mr. Jump's catches of Marlin swordfish on light tackle was uncalled for and utterly false. It was an obvious and jealous attempt to belittle, discredit, and dishonor one of the finest gentlemen sportsmen who ever worked for the good of the game. I know and I will swear that Jump's capture of the three-hundred-and-fourteen-pound Marlin on light tackle in twenty-eight minutes was absolutely as honest as it was skilful, as sportsman-like as it was wonderful. A number of well-known sportsmen watched him take this Marlin. Yet his enemies slandered him, accused him of using ropes and Heaven knows what else! It was vile and it failed.

Jump has performed the apparently impossible. Marlin swordfish hooked on light tackle can be handled by an exceedingly skilful angler. They make an indescribably spectacular, wonderful fight, on the surface all the time, and can be taken as quickly as on heavy tackle. Obviously, then, this becomes true of tarpon and sailfish and small tuna. What a world to conquer lies before the fine-spirited angler! A few fish on light outfits magnifying all the excitement and thrills of many fish on heavy outfits! There are no arguments against this, for men who have time and money.

We pioneers of light tackle are out of the woods now. There was a pride in a fight against odds—a pride of silence, and a fight of example and expressed standards and splendid achievements. But now we have followers, disciples who have learned, who have profited, who have climbed to the heights, and we are no longer alone. Hence we can scatter the news to the four winds and ask for the comradeship of kindred spirits, of men who love the sea and the stream and the gameness of a fish. The Open Sesame to our clan is just that love, and an ambition to achieve higher things. Who fishes just to kill? At Long Key last winter I met two self-styled sportsmen. They were eager to convert me to what they claimed was the dry-fly class angling of the sea. And it was to jab harpoons and spears into porpoises and manatee and sawfish, and be dragged about in their boat. The height of their achievements that winter had been the harpooning of several sawfish, each of which gave birth to a little one while being fought on the harpoon! Ye gods! It would never do to record my utterances.

But I record this fact only in the hope of opening the eyes of anglers. I have no ax to grind for myself. I have gone through the game, over to the fair side, and I want anglers to know.

We are a nation of fishermen and riflemen. Who says the Americans cannot shoot or fight? What made that great bunch of Yankee boys turn back the Hun hordes? It was the quick eye, the steady nerve, the unquenchable spirit of the American boy—his heritage from his hunter forefathers. We are great fishermen's sons also, and we can save the fish that are being depleted in our waters.

Let every angler who loves to fish think what it would mean to him to find the fish were gone. The mackerel are gone, the bluefish are going, the menhaden are gone, every year the amberjack and kingfish grow smaller and fewer. We must find ways and means to save our game fish of the sea; and one of the finest and most sportsman-like ways is to use light tackle.

Wiborn, the Lone Angler, is also in a class by himself. To my mind Wiborn is the ideal angler of the sea. I have aspired to his method, but realize it is impossible for me. He goes out alone. Hence the name Lone Angler. He operates his motor-launch, rigs his tackle and bait and teasers, flies his kite, finds the fish, fights the one he hooks, and gaffs and hauls it aboard or releases it, all by himself. Any one who has had the slightest experience in Pacific angling can appreciate this hazardous, complicated, and laborsome job of the Lone Angler. Any one who ever fought a big tuna or swordfish can imagine where he would have been without a boatman. After some of my fights with fish Captain Danielson has been as tired as I was. His job had been as hard as mine. But Wiborn goes out day by day alone, and he has brought in big tuna and swordfish. Not many! He is too fine a sportsman to bring in many fish.

And herein is the point I want to drive home in my tribute to Lone Angler. No one can say how many fish he catches. He never tells. Always he has a fine, wonderful, beautiful day on the water. It matters not to him, the bringing home of fish to exhibit. This roused my admiration, and also my suspicion. I got to believing that Lone Angler caught many more fish than he ever brought home.

So I spied upon him. Whenever chance afforded I watched him through my powerful binoculars. He was always busy. His swift boat roamed the seas. Always he appeared a white dot on the blue horizon, like the flash of a gull. I have watched his kite flutter down; I have seen his boat stop and stand still; I have seen sheeted splashes of water near him; and more than once I have seen him leaning back with bent rod, working and pumping hard. But when he came into Avalon on these specific occasions, he brought no tuna, no swordfish—nothing but a cheerful, enigmatic smile and a hopeful question as to the good luck of his friends.

"But I saw you hauling away on a fish," I ventured to say, once.

"Oh, that was an old shark," he replied, laughing.

Well, it might have been, but I had my doubts. And at the close of 1918 I believed, though I could not prove, that Lone Angler let the most of his fish go free. Hail to Lone Angler! If a man must roam the salt sea in search of health and peace, and in a manly, red-blooded exercise—here is the ideal. I have not seen its equal. I envy him—his mechanical skill, his fearlessness of distance and fog and wind, his dexterity with kite and rod and wheel, but especially I envy him the lonesome rides upon a lonesome sea—

Alone, all alone on a wide, wide sea.

The long, heaving swells, the windy lanes, the flight of the sheerwater and the uplifted flukes of the whale, the white wall of tuna on the horizon, the leap of the dolphin, the sweet, soft scent that breathes from off the sea, the beauty and mystery and color and movement of the deep—these are Lone Angler's alone, and he is as rich as if he had found the sands of the Pacific to be pearls, the waters nectar, and the rocks pure gold.

Happily, neither war nor business nor fish-hogs can ruin the wonderful climate of Catalina Island. Nature does not cater to evil conditions. The sun and the fog, the great, calm Pacific, the warm Japanese current, the pleasant winds—these all have their tasks, and they perform them faithfully, to the happiness of those who linger at Catalina.

Avalon, the beautiful! Somehow even the fire that destroyed half of Avalon did not greatly mar its beauty. At a distance the bay and the grove of eucalyptus-trees, the green-and-gold slopes, look as they always looked. Avalon has a singular charm outside of its sport of fishing. It is the most delightful and comfortable place I ever visited. The nights are cool. You sleep under blankets even when over in Los Angeles people are suffocating with the heat. At dawn the hills are obscured in fog and sometimes this fog is chilly. But early or late in the morning it breaks up and rolls away. The sun shines. It is the kind of sunshine that dazzles the eye, elevates the spirit, and warms the back. And out there rolls the vast blue Pacific—calm, slowly heaving, beautiful, and mysterious.

During the summer months Avalon is gay, colorful, happy, and mirthful with its crowds of tourists and summer visitors. The one broad street runs along the beach and I venture to say no other street in America can compare with it for lazy, idle, comfortable, pleasant, and picturesque effects. It is difficult to determine just where the beach begins and the street ends, because of the strollers in bathing-suits. Many a time, after a long fishing-day on the water, as I was walking up the middle of the street, I have been stunned to a gasp by the startling apparition of Venus or Hebe or Little Egypt or Annette Kellermann parading nonchalantly to and fro. It seems reasonable and fair to give notice that broadbill swordfish are not the only dangers to encounter at Avalon. I wish they had a policeman there.

But the spirit of Avalon, like the climate, is something to love. It is free, careless, mirthful, wholesome, restful, and serene. The resort is democratic and indifferent and aloof. Yet there is always mirth, music, and laughter. Many and many a night have I awakened, anywhere from ten to one, to listen to the low lap of the waves on the beach, the soft tones of an Hawaiian ukulele, the weird cry of a nocturnal sea-gull, the bark of a sea-lion, or the faint, haunting laugh of some happy girl, going by late, perhaps with her lover.

Avalon is so clean and sweet. It is the only place I have been, except Long Key, where the omnipresent, hateful, and stinking automobile does not obtrude upon real content. Think of air not reeking with gasolene and a street safe to cross at any time! Safe, I mean, of course, from being run down by some joy-rider. You are liable to encounter one of the Loreleis or Aphrodites at any hour from five till sunset. You must risk chance of that.

So, in conclusion, let me repeat that if you are a fisherman of any degree, and if you aspire to some wonderful experiences with the great and vanishing game fish of the Pacific, and if you would love to associate with these adventures some dazzling white hot days, and unforgetable cool nights where your eyelids get glued with sleep, and the fragrant salt breath of the sea, its music and motion and color and mystery and beauty—then go to Avalon before it is too late.

ZANE GREY – A SHORT BIOGRAPHY

Pearl Zane Grey was born January 31st, 1872, in Zanesville, Ohio.

He was the fourth of five children born to Alice "Allie" Josephine Zane, whose English Quaker immigrant ancestor Robert Zane came to the North American colonies in 1673, and her husband, Lewis M. Gray, a dentist. His family changed the spelling of their last name to "Grey" after his birth. Later Grey dropped Pearl and used Zane as his first name.

Grey grew up in Zanesville, a city founded by his maternal great-grandfather Ebenezer Zane, an American Revolutionary War patriot, and from an early age, he was intrigued by history as well as developing passions for fishing, baseball, and writing, all of which would stimulate his later success.

Growing up he engaged in violent brawls, despite his father punishing him with severe beatings. His relationship with his father was often tense and prone to physical punishment. Grey was nurtured by a loving mother and, in an effort to find a more meaningful father figure, struck up a friendship with an old man called Muddy Miser, a man with an unconventional life, and who encouraged the young boy's passions of fishing and writing.

His father told him to steer clear but such was Grey's nature that he spent much of the next few years at Miser's side.

Grey was an avid reader of adventure stories, consuming dime store novels by the dozen. By age fifteen he had written his first story; Jim of the Cave. His father tore it to shreds and then beat him.

His father's disastrous investment in 1889 caused the family to up sticks and move to Columbus, Ohio. There Lewis Grey re-established his dental practice and, after teaching his son to perform basic extractions, sent the boy out to perform them at house calls. Eventually the State Board heard about it and stopped him.

Grey's brother, Romer, added to the family income by driving a delivery truck and Grey himself did part time work as a movie usher.

Both boys were keen fisherman and baseball players playing summer baseball for the Columbus Capitols, with aspirations of playing in the major leagues. Eventually, Grey was spotted by a baseball scout and received offers from colleges. Romer also attracted scouts' attention and went on to have a professional baseball career.

Grey enrolled at the University of Pennsylvania on a baseball scholarship and studied dentistry. Naturally arriving on a scholarship really meant you had to be able to play. He rose to the occasion by playing against the Riverton club, pitching five scoreless innings and producing a double in the tenth which tied down the win. The Ivy League was highly competitive and an excellent training ground for future pro baseball players. Grey was a solid hitter and an excellent pitcher who relied on a sharply dropping curve ball.

Sadly for him in 1894 the rules were changed and the distance from the pitcher's mound to the plate was lengthened by ten feet (primarily to reduce the effects of Cy Young's pitching). Grey's pitching also suffered. He was now re-positioned to the outfield and the short, wiry baseball player continued as a campus hero, this time on the strength of his batting.

Sports scholarship kids can be average scholars. Grey certainly was. He preferred to spend his time outside class not trying to raise his grades but playing baseball, swimming, and writing, especially poetry.

At university he was shy and teetotal, more of a loner than a party animal. Grey struggled with the idea of becoming a writer or baseball player for his career, but unhappily resolved that dentistry was the practical choice. Although introverted Grey had a string of girlfriends, even having to settle a paternity suit whilst still at university, paid for by his father. In 1896 his studies over, he graduated and was ready for the world.

Grey's career in baseball was to be only for the minor leagues and so he set up his dental practice in New York as Dr. Zane Grey in 1896. Though a dentist his real ambition now was to be a writer and New York had lots of publishers. Evenings were set aside for writing to offset the tedium of his dental practice. Although a naturally gifted writer he struggled financially and emotionally, his work stiff and grammatically weak.

Whenever possible, he played baseball with the Orange Athletic Club in New Jersey, a team of former collegiate players that was one of the best amateur teams in the country. He played with several teams, including the Newark, New Jersey Colts in 1898 and also the Orange Athletic Club for a few years. His brother Romer Carl "Reddy" Grey (known as "R.C." in the family) did better and played professionally in the minor leagues with also a single major league game in 1903 for the Pittsburgh Pirates.

Grey often went camping with his R.C. in Lackawaxen, Pennsylvania, where they fished in the upper Delaware River. When canoeing in 1900, Grey met seventeen-year-old Lina Roth, better known as "Dolly". Dolly came from a family of physicians and was studying to be a schoolteacher.

His first magazine article, "A Day on the Delaware," a human-interest story about a Grey brothers' fishing expedition, was published in the May 1902 issue of Recreation magazine. Grey was elated and offered reprints to patients in his waiting room. In writing, Grey found temporary escape from the bleak outlook of his life and his demons. "Realism is death to me. I cannot stand life as it is." By this time, he had given up baseball.

Grey read Owen Wister's great Western novel The Virginian. In studying its style and structure in detail, he determined to write a full-length work. Betty Zane was the result. He sent it to Harpers in 1903. It was rejected and he lapsed into despair. The novel dramatized the heroism of an ancestor who had saved Fort Henry.

However, even though his writing was still some way from 'best-seller' quality it was now, in 1905, after a long, intense and passionate courtship dotted with many quarrels that Grey and Dolly married.

Although fit and athletic Grey was to suffer depression, anger, and mood swings, most of his life. As he said; "A hyena lying in ambush—that is my black spell! I conquered one mood only to fall prey to the next... I wandered about like a lost soul or a man who was conscious of imminent death."

It was only part of his make up. A string of girlfriends were never really put behind him. He always wanted to revisit. Grey was very careful to be honest and open with Dolly; "But I love to be free. I cannot change my spots. The ordinary man is satisfied with a moderate income, a home, wife, children, and all that.... But I am a million miles from being that kind of man and no amount of trying will ever do any good... I shall never lose the spirit of my interest in women".

After they married Dolly gave up her teaching career. They moved to a farmhouse at Lackawaxen, Pennsylvania, where Grey's mother and sister joined them. He had given up his dental practice in pursuit of life as a writer. His new wife's inheritance providing the financial cushion for the career change.

While Dolly managed Grey's career and raised their three children Grey would often spent months away from the family. He fished, wrote, and spent time with his girlfriends. Dolly knew of his behavior but seemed to feel it was his handicap rather than a choice. For his part Grey valued her management of his career and their family, and her solid emotional support.

In addition to her considerable editorial skills, she had good business sense and handled all his contract negotiations with publishers, agents, and movie studios. All his income was split fifty-fifty with her; from her "share", she covered the family expenses.

After attending a lecture in New York in 1907 Grey arranged for a mountain lion hunting trip to the North Rim of the Grand Canyon. He brought along a camera to document the trip.

It was now he also began the taking of copious notes; scenery, activities and dialogue. Grey learned about the scale and sense of adventure that he had. Treacherous river crossings, unpredictable beasts, bone-chilling cold, searing heat, parching thirst, bad water, irascible tempers, and heroic cooperation all became real to him and helped give him the confidence to write convincingly about the American West, its characters, and its landscape.

He wrote, "Surely, of all the gifts that have come to me from contact with the West, this one of sheer love of wildness, beauty, color, grandeur, has been the greatest, the most significant for my work."

Upon returning home in 1909, Grey wrote a new novel, The Last of the Plainsmen, describing the adventures of Buffalo Jones. Harper's editor Ripley Hitchcock rejected it, the fourth work in a row. He told Grey, "I do not see anything in this to convince me you can write either narrative or fiction."

Grey wrote dejectedly, "I don't know which way to turn. I cannot decide what to write next. That which I desire to write does not seem to be what the editors want... I am full of stories and zeal and fire... yet I am inhibited by doubt, by fear that my feeling for life is false".

The book was later published by Outing magazine, which provided Grey some satisfaction. Grey next wrote a series of magazine articles and juvenile novels.

With the birth of his first child pending, Grey felt compelled to complete his next novel and his first Western, The Heritage of the Desert. He wrote it in four months in 1910. Grey again took his work to Hitchcock; this time Harper published his work, an historical romance in which Mormon characters were of central importance. Here was Grey's over arching themes; Manifest Destiny, the conquest of the Old West, and men wrestling with elemental conditions. It was the breakthrough. It quickly became a bestseller.

Two years later Grey produced his best-known book, Riders of the Purple Sage (1912), his all-time best-seller. Hitchcock rejected it, but Grey took his manuscript directly to the vice president of Harper, who accepted it. With its publication Zane Grey became a household name, after that Harper eagerly received all his manuscripts. They also began to pair his novels with work from some of the best illustrators around including N. C. Wyeth, Frank Schoonover, Douglas Duer, Herbert W. Dunton, W. H. D. Koerner, and Charles Russell.

With the help of Dolly's proofreading and copy editing, Grey gradually improved his writing. He was certainly prolific and with better told narratives sales increased. He often expressed great gratitude for the efforts and sacrifices made by his wife and stated that despite his unorthodox behavior she was the only love of his life.

Grey co-founded the "Porpoise Club" with his friend, Robert H. Davis of Munsey's Magazine, to popularize the sport of hunting of dolphins and porpoises. Their first catch was off Seabright, New Jersey on September 21, 1912, where they harpooned and reeled in a bottlenose dolphin.

Grey started his association with Hollywood when William Fox bought the rights to Riders of the Purple Sage for $2,500 in 1916. His writing career would now rise in sync with that of the movie industry. It was voracious for good commercial material and here was a best-selling writer who could deliver story after story.

The Greys moved to California in 1918 to be both nearer the fishing grounds that Grey was so keen on but also to be nearer Hollywood and the lucrative source of income it was now offering. His first two books had been adapted and Grey had formed his own motion picture company. This allowed him to control production values and keep their faith to his books. After seven films he sold his company to Jesse Lasky, a co-founder of Paramount Pictures. Paramount made a number of movies based on Grey's writings and hired him as advisor. Many of his films were shot at locations described in his books.

In 1920 Grey and his family settled in Altadena and purchased a mansion on East Mariposa Street, locally known as "Millionaire's Row".

Grey had the time and money to engage in his first and greatest passion: fishing. From 1918 until 1932, he was a regular contributor to Outdoor Life magazine. As one of its first celebrity writers, he began to popularize big-game fishing. Several times he went deep-sea fishing in Florida to relax and to write in solitude. Although he commented that "the sea, from which all life springs, has been equally with the desert my teacher and religion," Although he never wrote about the sea directly, the closest he came was writing about fishing, he felt the sea soothed his moods, reduced his depressions, and gained him the opportunity to harvest deeper thoughts: "The lure of the sea is some strange magic that makes men love what they fear. The solitude of the desert is more intimate than that of the sea. Death on the shifting barren sands seems less insupportable to the imagination than death out on the boundless ocean, in the awful, windy emptiness. Man's bones yearn for dust".

Until his death Grey would now divide up his year between months traveling and fishing and the rest for writing novels and articles.

Unlike writers who could write every day, Grey would have fallow periods and then creative bursts in which he could write 100,000 words in a single month.

From 1923 to 1930, he would spend some weeks a year at his cabin on the Mogollon Rim, in Central Arizona.

His novel The Vanishing American (1925), first serialized in 1922, prompted a heated debate. People recognized its Navajo hero as patterned after Jim Thorpe, a great Native American athlete. Grey portrayed the struggle of the Navajo to preserve their identity and culture against corrupting influences of the white government and of missionaries. This viewpoint enraged religious groups. Grey contended, "I have studied the Navaho Indians for twelve years. I know their wrongs. The missionaries sent out there are almost everyone mean, vicious, weak, immoral, useless men." To have the book published, Grey agreed to some structural changes. At this point in his career his books were at their most majestic with his mature talent writing on major themes, character types, and settings.

During the crash and subsequent depression of the 1930s, the publishing industry was hard work. Sales fell off. Serializations were harder to sell. Grey was lucky. He had avoided investing in the Stock Market, he was still writing – and popular and continued to earn royalty income. This also coincided with the time that nearly half of the film adaptations of his novels were made.

From 1925 to his death in 1939, Grey traveled further and more frequently away from his family. He became interested in exploring unspoiled lands, particularly the islands of South Pacific, New Zealand and Australia. He thought Arizona was beginning to be overrun by tourists and speculators. Near the end of his life, Grey looked into the future and wrote: "The so-called civilization of man and his works shall perish from the earth, while the shifting sands, the red looming walls, the purple sage, and the towering monuments, the vast brooding range show no perceptible change".

He first visited New Zealand in 1926 and caught several large fish, including a mako shark. Grey wrote many articles in international sporting magazines highlighting the uniqueness of New Zealand fishing, which has produced many world records. Grey himself held numerous world records and invented the teaser, a hookless bait that is still used today to attract fish.

Grey would return a further three times to New Zealand and become a frequent visitor to Tahiti. He fished the surrounding waters for several months at a time. He claimed that these were the most difficult waters he had ever fished, but it was here he reputedly reeled in the first marlin ever caught over 1,000 pounds.

Despite his widespread popular and commercial appeal Grey was constantly being savaged by established critics. The charge was always that his depictions of the West were too fanciful, too violent, and not faithful to the moral realities of the frontier. They thought his characters unrealistic and much larger-than-life. One cruelly wrote that "the substance of any two Zane Grey books could be written upon the back of a postage stamp."

Grey based his work in his own varied first-hand experience, supported by careful note taking, and considerable research. And they sold. Despite this the reviews sometimes caused black moods of depression.

Grey had built a getaway home in Santa Catalina Island, California, which now serves as the Zane Grey Pueblo Hotel. He served as president of Catalina's exclusive fishing club, the Tuna Club of Avalon.

Zane Grey died of heart failure on October 23rd, 1939, at his home in Altadena, California. He was interred at the Lackawaxen and Union Cemetery, Lackawaxen, Pennsylvania.

Looking back over his career it is easy to see why Grey became one of the first millionaire authors. His veracity and emotional intensity connected with millions of readers worldwide and inspired many Western writers who followed him.

Zane Grey was a major force in shaping the myths of the Old West. He was the author of more than 90 books, some published posthumously and/or based on serials originally published in magazines.

Grey wrote not only Westerns, but two hunting books, six children's books, three baseball books, and eight fishing books. Many of them became bestsellers. It is estimated that he wrote over nine million words in his career. From 1917 to 1926, Grey was in the top ten best-seller list nine times, which required sales of over 100,000 copies each time.

Even after his death, Harper had a stockpile of manuscripts and published a new title each year up to 1963 and, as former books were reprinted as paperbacks, his sales rocketed.

His success translated from books and movies across to two radio series and TV; The Zane Grey Show, which ran on the Mutual Broadcasting System for five months in the 1940s, and the "Zane Grey Western Theatre", which had a five-year run of 145 episodes.

ZANE GREY – A CONCISE BIBLIOGRAPHY

Betty Zane (1903) Historical

Spirit of the Border (1906) Historical (Sequel to Betty Zane)
The Last of the Plainsmen (1907) Western
The Last Trail (1906) Historical   (Sequel to Spirit of the Border)
The Short Stop (1906) Baseball
The Heritage of the Desert (1910) Western
The Young Forester (1910) Western
The Young Pitcher (1911) Baseball
The Young Lion Hunter (1911) Western
Riders of the Purple Sage (1912) Western
Ken Ward in the Jungle (1912) Western
Desert Gold (1913) Western
The Light of Western Stars (1914) Western
The Rustlers of Pecos County (1914) Western
The Lone Star Ranger (1915) Western
The Rainbow Trail (1915) Western (Sequel to Riders of the Purple Sage)
The Border Legion (1916) Western
Wildfire (1917) Western
The UP Trail (1918) Western
The Desert of Wheat (1919) Western
Tales of Fishes (1919) Fishing
The Man of the Forest (1920) Western
The Redheaded Outfield & Other Baseball Stories (1920) Baseball
The Mysterious Rider (1921) Western
To the Last Man (1921) Western
The Day of the Beast (1922) Fiction
Tales of Lonely Trails (1922) Adventure
Wanderer of the Wasteland (1923) Western
Tappan's Burro (1923) Western
The Call of the Canyon (1924) Western
Roping Lions in the Grand Canyon (1924) Adventure
Tales of Southern Rivers (1924) Fishing
The Thundering Herd (1925) Western
The Vanishing American (1925) Western
Tales of Fishing Virgin Seas (1925) Fishing
Under the Tonto Rim (1926) Western
Tales of the Angler's Eldorado, New Zealand (1926) Fishing
Forlorn River (1927) Western
Tales of Swordfish and Tuna (1927) Fishing
Nevada Western (1928) (Sequel to Forlorn River)
Wild Horse Mesa (1928) Western
Don, the Story of a Lion Dog (1928) Western
Avalanche (1928) Western
Tales of Fresh Water Fishing (1928) Fishing
Fighting Caravans (1929) Western
Stairs of Sand (1929) Western
The Wolf Tracker (1930) Western
The Shepherd of Guadaloupe (1930) Western
Sunset Pass (1931) Western

Tales of Tahitian Waters (1931) Fishing
Book of Camps and Trails (1931) Adventure (Partial re-print of Tales of Lonely Trails)
Arizona Ames (1932) Western
Robbers' Roost (1932) Western
The Drift Fence (1933) Western
The Hash Knife Outfit (1933) Western (Sequel to The Drift Fence)
The Code of the West (1934) Western
Thunder Mountain (1935) Western
The Trail Driver (1935) Western
The Lost Wagon Train (1936) Western
West of the Pecos (1937) Western
An American Angler in Australia (1937) Fishing
Raiders of Spanish Peaks (1938) Western
Western Union (1939) Western
Knights of the Range (1939) Western
Thirty Thousand on the Hoof (1940) Western
Twin Sombreros (1940) Western (Sequel to Knights of the Range)
Majesty's Rancho (1942) Western (Sequel to Light of Western Stars)
Omnibus (1943) Western
Stairs of Sand (1943) Western (Sequel to Wanderer of the Wasteland)
The Wilderness Trek (1944) Western
Shadow on the Trail (1946) Western
Valley of Wild Horses (1947) Western
Rogue River Feud (1948) Fishing /Western
The Deer Stalker (1949) Western
The Maverick Queen (1950) Western
The Dude Ranger (1951) Western
Captives of the Desert (1952) Western
Adventures in Fishing (1952) Fishing
Wyoming (1953) Western
Lost Pueblo (1954) Western
Black Mesa (1955) Western
Stranger from the Tonto (1956) Western
The Fugitive Trail (1957) Western
Arizona Clan (1958) Western
Horse Heaven Hill (1959) Western
The Ranger & Other Stories (1960) Western
Blue Feather & Other Stories (1961) Western
Boulder Dam (1963) Historical

Films

Between 1911 and 1996, 112 films were adapted from the novels and stories of Zane Grey. In addition, three television series included episodes adapted from his work, including Dick Powell's Zane Grey Theatre (1956–58). As well as the year of release we have also given where possible its source.

Fighting Blood (1911 short) novel
Graft (1915) story
The Border Legion (1918) novel
Riders of the Purple Sage (1918) novel
The Rainbow Trail (1918) story
The Light of the Western Stars (1918) novel
The Lone Star Ranger (1919) novel
The Last of the Duanes (1919) story
Desert Gold (1919)
Riders of the Dawn (1920) novel The Desert of Wheat
Days of Daring (1920 short) novel In the Days of Thundering Herd
The U.P. Trail (1920) novel
Man of the Forest (1921) novel
The Mysterious Rider (1921) novel
The Last Trail (1921) novel
When Romance Rides (1922) novel Wildfire
Golden Dreams (1922) story
To the Last Man (1923) novel
The Lone Star Ranger (1923) novel
The Call of the Canyon (1923) story
Heritage of the Desert (1924) novel
Wanderer of the Wasteland (1924) novel
The Border Legion (1924) novel
The Last of the Duanes (1924) story
The Thundering Herd (1925) novel
Riders of the Purple Sage (1925) novel
Code of the West (1925) novel
The Rainbow Trail (1925) story
The Light of Western Stars (1925) novel
Wild Horse Mesa (1925) novel
The Vanishing American (1925) novel
Desert Gold (1926) novel
Born to the West (1926) story
Forlorn River (1926) novel
Man of the Forest (1926) novel
The Last Trail (1927) novel
The Mysterious Rider (1927) novel
Drums of the Desert (1927) novel Captives of the Desert
Lightning (1927) story
Nevada (1927) novel
Open Range (1927) novel Valley of Wild Horses
Under the Tonto Rim (1928) novel
The Vanishing Pioneer (1928) novel Golden Dreams
The Water Hole (1928) story
Avalanche (1928) novel
Sunset Pass (1929) novel
Stairs of Sand (1929) novel
The Lone Star Ranger (1930) novel

The Light of Western Stars (1930) novel
The Border Legion (1930) novel
The Last of the Duanes (1930) novel
El último de los Vargas (1930) novel
Fighting Caravans (1931) novel Wagon Wheels
Riders of the Purple Sage (1931) novel
The Rainbow Trail (1932) story
Heritage of the Desert (1932) story
The Golden West (1932) story
Wild Horse Mesa (1932) novel
End of the Trail (1932) story
Robbers' Roost (1932) novel
The Woman Accused (1933) story Liberty Magazine
Smoke Lightning (1933) novel Canyon Walls
The Thundering Herd (1933) story
Under the Tonto Rim (1933) novel The Bee Hunter
Sunset Pass (1933) novel
Life in the Raw (1933) novel
The Last Trail (1933) novel
Man of the Forest (1933) novel
To the Last Man (1933) story
The Last Round-Up (1934) novel The Border Legion
Wagon Wheels (1934) novel Fighting Caravans
The Dude Ranger (1934) story
West of the Pecos (1934) novel
Home on the Range (1935) novel Code of the West
Rocky Mountain Mystery (1935) novel Golden Dreams
Wanderer of the Wasteland (1935) novel
Thunder Mountain (1935) novel
Nevada (1935) novel
Drift Fence (1936) novel
Desert Gold (1936) novel
The Arizona Raiders (1936) novel Raiders of Spanish Peaks
King of the Royal Mounted (1936) story
End of the Trail (1936) novel Outlaws of Palouse
Arizona Mahoney (1936) novel Stairs of Sand
Rangle River (1936) novel
Forlorn River (1937) novel
Roll Along, Cowboy (1937) novel The Dude Ranger
Thunder Trail (1937) story "Arizona Ames"
Born to the West (1937) novel
The Mysterious Rider (1938) characters
Heritage of the Desert (1939) novel
The Light of Western Stars (1940) novel
Knights of the Range (1940) story
The Border Legion (1940) novel
Western Union (1941) novel
Last of the Duanes (1941) story

Riders of the Purple Sage (1941) novel
Lone Star Ranger (1942) novel
Nevada (1944) novel
Wanderer of the Wasteland (1945) novel
West of the Pecos (1945) novel
Sunset Pass (1946) novel
Code of the West (1947) novel
Thunder Mountain (1947) novel
Gunfighters (1947) novel Twin Sombreros
Under the Tonto Rim (1947) novel
Wild Horse Mesa (1947) novel
Red Canyon (1949) novel Wildfire
Robbers' Roost (1955) story
The Vanishing American (1955) novel
Chevron Hall of Stars (1956, TV) story "The Lone Hand"
Schlitz Playhouse of Stars (1956 TV) story "A Tale of Wells Fargo"
The Maverick Queen (1956) novel
Dick Powell's Zane Grey Theatre (1956–58 TV) stories for 6 episodes
Riders of the Purple Sage (1996) novel

Made in United States
North Haven, CT
15 July 2022

21430118R00070